THE LAST MULBERRY TREE

Christina Kellaris Tranter

ISBN: 978-1-5272-8760-0

First published 2021

CHAPTER 1

1935

A short distance inland from the rugged coastline of northern Cyprus stood an elevated village with far-reaching views across the changing turquoise waters of the Mediterranean Sea. With a population of just a few hundred people, it had for centuries relied on self-sufficiency and the barest minimum. Anna's family were proud to live in that tranquil location, perched on the landscape and facing out to sea like a lighthouse.

"I'll race you up the mountain," said eight-year-old Anna, playfully poking her sister with an olive branch. With a beaming smile, six-year-old Kate ran after her sister, knowing she could never catch up. With heavy boots and thick tights, the girls ran along overgrown paths where wildflowers grew in abundance, their dots of colour peeking between pebbles like jewels. They jumped over rocks and shrubs as they clambered up the mountain, racing like exuberant wild cats for the last fish supper.

"Beat you!" panted Anna, laughing. With cheeks rosy as pink laurel they reached their favourite rocks and stretched out their arms like parachutes, waiting for the wind to blow them away. At last, they were free from their mother's over-protection.

"I love this smell," Anna delighted, swallowing and inhaling the wind as it kissed her face. "It reminds me of when we pick oranges and lemons in the field."

But Kate wasn't listening. The rocks had become their sacred tabernacle and Kate had begun to unearth their artefacts from beneath stones that protected them from the mountain goats that ate everything in sight. "Ahhh… they're still here," delighted Kate, carefully removing their treasures of twigs, dried flowers and fabric scraps from Eleni's dress shop just as a mountain goat changed its course.

The girls sat for hours playing with their secret bounty, enthralled with the freedom to do as they please.

"One day I'm going to make beautiful dresses and hats, and they're going to be even more beautiful than Eleni's," said Kate assertively, as she bound twigs with straw and sealed them with mud from a nearby pothole.

But Anna wasn't listening either. Absorbed by the radiance of shimmering opalescent blues of the sea, Anna felt the blinding brightness of a clear spring sky. She sat consumed with inspiration, fashioning her own works of art, with no one to question or judge her behaviour.

"This is the only place God can't hear us," said Anna convincingly; and true to form, Kate believed every word. "We should call these rocks Koukles, after our dolls," exclaimed Anna, laughing.

Chapter 1 – 1935

But as the bright light dimmed and the wind smacked instead of kissed her face, Anna knew it was time to take her little sister home.

The next day was Sunday which meant church for most of the village, a serious ecclesiastical event for their mother, Christina.

"I'm ready!" cheered their ten-year-old brother Vasili, proudly circling his mother in the courtyard and shooing chickens into the run.

"Of course you are, my sweet boy," Christina said, gently brushing his thick dark curls with her thin dry fingers. "If only your sisters were as organized. Get a move on, girls, it's like this every Sunday morning," she hollered across the courtyard.

Within a few minutes the family were trekking up the dusty, winding road sandwiched between traditional buildings, with the occasional scattering of modern buildings in contrast to the oldest mud huts. The village was a picturesque collage, a worn-out patchwork quilt from a collection of fabrics, each with its own story to tell.

Walking to church, Vasili always made his mother laugh and Christina looked forward to the ritual. Vasili would tell her stories of becoming a Hollywood film star where he had everything worked out. He would always be the star of a funny film and all the women would follow him around like a magnet because he was so rich, famous and of course... handsome!

"And I'll change my name to something new like Tony Curtis did, and send you rolls of money wrapped in vine leaves," he would say, laughing with his mother.

"Don't be silly," she would reply, barely able to get the words out for laughter. "Americans don't have grapevines."

Christina's eyes would sparkle as she listened to his banter, proud of her confident son who could do no wrong. Being a proud, religious woman meant emotions were an indulgence and she was not one to show her feelings like other mothers.

Higher up the village, the church stood proud on a level ridge, waiting patiently for its parishioners, just as it had done for centuries. With a backdrop of mountains to the south, the antiquated church had been there longer than any elder could remember and some swore it was the secret meeting place of Aphrodite and her lover, Ares. Now, it was the dilapidated remains of its former glory but the village believed its legendary origin kept it from collapsing into the sea. Three arched windows facing the mountains, where Aphrodite once gazed in wait for her lover, were now Anna's watchtower. Inside, faded frescoes from years gone by adorned the walls between the arches like perfectly framed renaissance paintings, such as could only be seen in great art museums of the world.

"Straighten your scarves," insisted Christina, as the girls walked prudently to light candles.

The sisters then sat quietly, trying not to giggle and fidget. An occasional glance through the middle window revealed their rock trio in the distance.

Chapter 1 – 1935

After the sermon, Christina looked around for her mother. She found her outside, leaning against a pillar, preoccupied with the day's conversation. Dressed in black and bent over her walking stick, she was one of a handful of old ladies defending their usual place.

"I hear it's exactly ten years since the British took over our island!" she shrieked.

"We're a crown colony, old woman! They're protecting us," dismissed the local council worker, appalled at the woman and everyone who believed her.

"No, they're using us, you young upstart! Don't you have eyes or are you simple?" She began waving her fists at him. "They tried to trade us to Greece so Greece would fight for them in the war. I don't call that protection, young man, now go away and take your foolish ideas with you. And they have guns!"

"Well of course they do, they're soldiers!" The man rolled his eyes.

"Yiayia, stop!" whispered Anna to her grandmother.

Yiayia Stavrou shrugged her shoulders and walked away from her granddaughter.

"Don't tell me what to do, young lady! These youngsters think they know what's best for us! They know nothing of our struggles."

As the conversation became more heated and before their mother pointed out whose grandfather had just passed away, and whose son had just moved to Athens, and whose daughter just got engaged, Anna and Kate found it a perfect time to make their escape down the long winding path to the beach, knowing that if their father Christophoro saw them from the coffee shop, he wouldn't care. And sure enough, they could see him through the grapevine, towering above his friends as he read his newspaper in Happy Harri's coffee shop.

The sisters reached the seashore, out of breath but ready to let their hair down. Their brother and his friends were already there searching for crabs, starfish and baby octopus.

"Vasili, why doesn't dad go to church?" asked Kate as the clan investigated a microcosm of life in the rock pools.

"He doesn't like gossiping old women," growled Vasili with his fingers carefully clasping a crab, ready to chase Anna or anyone else he could tease.

The following day, Anna woke a little later than usual.

"Kate, hurry up, or we'll be late for school!" Anna yelled, pouring through the contents of her school bag. "Stop brushing your hair and get your shoes on!"

"Why are you always in a hurry to get to that horrible teacher?" complained Kate.

"I'm not… I just want to find out what happens in our story," smiled Anna, ushering her sister away from the mirror.

The three siblings rushed across the dusty courtyard, past clucking chickens and 'Big Red', their cockerel, then ran all the way to their modern two-room school, situated a stone's throw from the beach. The school stood on the grandest street in the village, the only tarmacked road, lined with coconut palms and olive trees that continuously attracted foraging creatures to feast on a blend of fallen black and red berries.

The siblings entered through the large, black iron gates and were immediately surrounded by a frenzy of animated children.

"Why does Mr. Leos have such hairy eyebrows? Is he always frowning?" Kate asked her sister as they walked up the concrete steps to their classroom.

"I don't know, but I don't want to get too close," whispered Anna as they took their seats. "He smells bad."

Mr. Leos entered and stood self-assured in front of his class. His bald head was already misted with sweat, wispy hair protruded from his ears.

"Sit," he demanded without looking at his students. He sat abruptly and took papers from his worn leather briefcase, frowning as though the weight of the world were on his shoulders. His navy cotton suit, worn almost threadbare, was bleached from years of hanging in the sun to dry. He took off his jacket and hung it on the back of his chair, revealing armpit stains on a dull white shirt.

"Six-year-olds, take out book one and read the first chapter. Seven- and eight-year-olds, turn to page twelve of your maths books," he demanded.

As the children settled into their Monday routine, Mr. Leos conducted his morning inspection, the dreaded walk between desks. In a flash, he erupted into his usual morning fury.

"How many times, Menelao?" he screeched at the seven-year-old boy. "How many times have I told you to come to school with clean fingernails?"

"But my dad…"

"Don't interrupt me, boy!" he barked at sobbing Menelao.

Every Monday morning, Menelao tried to explain his hands were permanently stained from working in his father's tanning workshop, and every Monday morning he was reprimanded for having dirty fingernails. With the ritual over, Mr. Leos turned to the chalkboard and listed the day's activities.

"What does item one say?" he shouted, swiftly turning to his deadly silent class. Anna raised her hand immediately. Mr. Leos saw her clearly but ignored her, turning instead to Menelao. The class watched as the boy tried to overcome his stutter.

"You don't know, do you?" laughed Mr. Leos. "You're an idiot, Menelao! You'll never amount to anything unless you learn to read."

The day continued with Mr. Leos's wrath aimed at the most vulnerable, and by two o'clock, the siblings met at the gates to go home.

"Do you want to see the baby starfish today?" Kate asked her sister with a wicked grin, while Vasili dashed off with his friends.

"No, we need to get home and help father sort the olives," Anna grumbled, concerned at her sister's lack of commitment.

Chapter 1 – 1935

"Oh, come on Anna... Please? Just for a few minutes, they're so pretty." Kate stared into her sister's eyes like a lost puppy.

Anna sighed. "Well, just for a few minutes," she said officiously.

The girls were rushing towards the beach, giggling and wondering how their teacher could smell so bad, when they caught sight of Menelao running home. Poor boy, thought Anna. How is he going to cope when he goes next door to Mr Onassis' class and how was she going to survive his verbal and physical abuse?

CHAPTER 2

1938

As Anna's last days of school approached, she sat listening to her teacher's instructions.

"Eleven-year-old girls, your mothers will teach you to cook and clean if you don't already know. You should be ashamed of yourselves if you don't!" bellowed Mr. Onassis as he paced back and forth, hands clenched behind his back. His neat black trousers, pressed to perfection, maintained a crisp front crease as sharp as his tongue. "You're women now, you should all know how to do these things!" he said irritably, perching his overweight rear on a small wooden chair. "Ooooh, we have a girl who thinks she knows better than me," he mocked, having seen Anna roll her eyes at Kate. "And what would you prefer to do instead…hmmm?" He mocked as the children sniggered. "Speak up, girl… What's keeping you from sharing your secret?" He tilted his head and stared at her with eyes like a bulldog.

Anna blushed; her green eyes flashed with embarrassment and a rosy glow appeared on her porcelain skin.

"Well… er, I would one day love to study in England

sir." Her voice trembled as she stared at his shiny, flared, sweaty nostrils.

"England… You? You'd get lost and end up in Turkey!" He laughed, encouraging the class to do the same. The children roared with laughter, an incident so rare and raucous that Mr. Leos from next door came in to see what the commotion was about. Anna sat quietly as the class gawked, laughed, pointed and made faces at her.

"Settle down now, Friday's your last day, so make sure you finish all your assignments. Boys going on to secondary school, make sure you read the recommended books. The rest of you will stay peasants all your lives." He smirked, staring at two boys sitting at the back, whispering. Then with one swift motion, he swung his arm full circle, and threw a piece of chalk as hard as he possibly could.

"Yooooou! What did I just say?" he yelled at the top of his voice, pointing to Luca.

"Er, we… we need to read, sir," said Luca apprehensively, hoping to avoid a smack on the head or twisted ear.

Anna cringed in silence, trying to focus on the afternoon's literature, especially after her own plight. She was looking forward to reading the last few chapters of Charles Dickens.

After lunch, Mr. Onassis returned late with a stench of whisky, cigarettes and perspiration.

"Take out your English Literature books. Anna, you think you're clever, don't you? Start reading where we left off." He sat in his chair with his eyes transfixed on a pile of papers.

Anna gently stroked the translated version of *Great Expectations* and turned the once glossy front cover. Read by numerous students in their last term of school, it had a curious, faintly fishy smell, yet it was peculiarly soothing. She read out loud, savouring every word, desperate to find out who Pip's heir was, and what happened to Estella and Miss Havisham. The story unfolded in a revelation of excitement and courage that captivated her.

As her last day of school approached, Anna was heartbroken. The notion of being deprived of a feast of fascinating and riveting writing was a dismal concept. So, on the last day, when nobody was looking, she surreptitiously snuck her copy of *Great Expectations* into her bag.

A week later, from her bed she could hear her mother complaining from the kitchen.

"Vasili's already collected the vegetables from the bottom field and cleaned the stable this morning. What have you done today?"

Anna was embarrassed and frightened. Overnight cramps had resulted in blood-stained sheets she couldn't explain. Worried and ashamed, Anna didn't know what to tell her mother. So when Kate left for school, Anna slid out of bed, trying to hide her blood-stained clothes, then staggered into the kitchen where her mother had her hands deep in washing up, and was shooing escaped chickens with her foot.

"I… I think I'm dying, mother," she sobbed, clenching her stomach. "I… I think I have cancer!"

Chapter 2 – 1938

"Ahhh… OK, umm…" muttered Christina at the talk she needed to have. "You're not dying, girl." She laughed. Slowly, she locked the kitchen door and sat her daughter down. She then took a pan of water and lit one of the two gas burners. "You will get this every month for about a week, but you must be prepared," she whispered, showing her daughter rags she'd have to use and wash out every month. "And you need to hide them away from the rest of the laundry. We can't have men seeing them on the washing line!"

"Will it stop soon?" begged Anna, surprised at her mother's kindness.

"No, my dear," replied Christina, laughing hysterically. "It's going to last until you're about fifty."

"Whaaat!"

"And you can't enter God's house while you're menstruating. It's an abomination, its dirty!" her mother warned, resorting back to her old self.

"But I don't un…"

"God is pure! Do not question his wisdom!" Christina stood proud.

Anna didn't dare question her mother or God. Well, at least this means I have one Sunday off every month, she thought, looking on the bright side.

Anna spent that summer learning how to sew, preserve fruit, pickle vegetables, make bread and cheese, and many other skills passed on by yiayia Stavrou.

"I want to show you how to mend sheets," said her grandmother, taking her sewing box from under her bed. Anna and her best friend Aliki spent the morning carefully cutting cotton sheets down the middle.

"Be careful, girls," screamed yiayia Stavrou. "The middle is the most worn part; you mustn't tear it." She took the sharp, raspy scissors from Aliki's hand and showed her how it was done. "One clean cut, all the way down the middle." Yiayia Stavrou turned the two panels inside out, leaving the worn parts on the outside, then laid them on the ground. "Now, we sew down the middle and the sheet will last many more years," she said proudly.

"But now the outer edges are worn, Madam Stavrou," said Aliki, more interested in sewing crafts than her best friend.

"Ah… clever girl. Anna, stop staring at that mountain!" demanded Yiayia, without taking her eyes off the sheet. "Now we strengthen the new ends with embroidery." She was delighted to show off her intricate embroidery skills.

"This embroidery is beautiful, Madam Stavrou, thank you for showing me. My mother said you're the best in the village at fine needlework."

"Well, thank you," the old lady responded, trying to be modest. "It's a shame my daydreaming granddaughter doesn't appreciate it as much as you!"

When, later that afternoon, the best friends left with sheets neatly folded in their arms, Aliki sensed Anna's withdrawn frame of mind.

Chapter 2 – 1938

"What's wrong, Anna?"

"I don't know. I… I'm just bored with all this stuff." She flicked the sheets under her arm. "I want to get better at English. I want to read more Charles Dickens and learn poetry."

"But you know more English than most of us!" Aliki looked down at her handiwork. "Why don't you ask your father to buy you books? You're lucky, he listens to you. My father just tells me what to do and when to do it. And you're so pretty, Anna! You'll probably marry Grigori or Aristo," she whispered bashfully. "I prefer Aristo, he has a beautiful smile, and he can kick a ball such a long way, he might become a football player one day." Aliki stared into space.

When the girls reached Anna's house, they hung on to the gate, watching out for Old Red.

"It's not fair that they only let boys go on to secondary school!" Anna whined.

"Anna, what are you saying? You'll never get a husband if you talk like that… Look, Old Red's gone to bother the chickens, you can run across the courtyard – hurry!" Aliki kissed her friend on the cheek and laughed as Anna weaved amidst the mayhem in a demented dance.

For the next six years, Anna kept hearing talk of the war in Europe. Sundays after the sermon were filled with arguments about volunteers signing up to fight alongside the British. She was tired of the scuffles and disagreements, preferring instead to stay in the background.

"I don't know why so many of our boys are volunteering for this war. It's not even our war!" Christina complained as she poured water into the long stone sink. "Just because Winston Churchill paid us a visit, it doesn't change anything. The idiot promised to help us... We'll provide you with food, he said. Damn liar! You'll have to work hard to stand out if you want to find a husband, so many of our boys are disappearing Anna."

As Anna listened to her mother she could see her destiny unfolding right before her eyes. Her path was to perfect her homemaking skills and become a woman in a young girl's body. She focused so hard on trying to please her mother and her community, that she felt she was drowning in depths of the mundane, the ordinary and the unremarkable.

"When will you start taking life seriously, girl? I've told you, just a small handful of wet soot. We need enough to clean everything!" moaned her mother. "I saw your needlework yesterday, it's getting better, but it's still not good enough. You want to make your husband proud one day soon, don't you? This family has a reputation to maintain, our women have been the best at embroidery for generations, we can't break that chain. I won't let it happen because you're a daydreamer, Anna!"

Anna watched her mother take small handfuls of soot from an empty butter tin she kept next to the sink. How can she get so excited over soot? Anna despaired. She watched her mother's small coarse hands rub frantically against glasses and saucepans that were once graced with handles.

Then she stacked them neatly to one side of the shallow granite sink. In that moment it all felt like a lifetime of bondage and constriction for Anna.

She glared at her mother's small stature, astounded as to where her strength came from. She had never seen her mother laugh a hearty laugh, the type that would erupt into a show of her identity. Neither had she seen her mother kiss any of her children. But it didn't matter, for her mother was well respected in the community.

"Finished!" she declared, rolling her black muslin sleeves down. At thirty-five, her mother was as content as she needed to be: no more and no less. She didn't wake up every morning wanting to scream. She woke up knowing exactly what needed to be done that day and would move heaven and earth to complete her tasks. But if Anna was to survive the overflowing questions that gnawed at her daily, she would have to find a way to stop the continuous flurry of discontent, circling her thoughts like a headless chicken.

Her mother tightened her head scarf and wrapped it close around her neck, revealing pierced ears that never wore earrings and skin on the verge of losing its luminosity.

Anna looked curious. What did she mean by 'want to make your husband proud one day soon?' What was her mother plotting?

She needed to clear her head, so later that windy day in early spring, she snuck away to 'Koukles' on her own, listening to the gentle melody of cicadas, donkeys and honeybees. As she approached her rocks, she noticed a young strawberry tree had grown in front of the large cedar pine, partially blocking her view of the horizon. She closed her eyes and with a huge intake of breath, inhaled the beautiful, clean smell like she'd done so many times before.

"I wonder what seventeen-year-old girls do in England?" she thought, opening a notebook she had made from discarded packaging, brown paper and string from Eleni's shop. It was an idyllic time to gather perfect thoughts in her imperfect world of drudgery and oppression.

She spent the afternoon trying to remember translated words, writing them over and over again to improve her penmanship and add them in sentences. As she flicked through the clumsy pages, Anna read and re-read her poems, endlessly editing and perfecting them. She imagined herself on stage, exaggerating hand and body gestures as if she were in a performance of *Great Expectations*, playing the part of a cold Estella.

"Father, I want to study English in England and one day become a famous writer," she said out loud but her foolish thoughts swiftly changed to guilt, knowing thousands of people had died during the war, and there she was, with the audacity to want something for herself again.

She sat for a while longer, enjoying the view and the solitude. Then, as the wind tossed her light brown wavy hair into disarray, and her full lips began to dry, she knew it was time to go home.

Anna started clambering down the steep mountain in her heavy shoes so she could finish her chores before her father noticed she was gone. Her brown, calf-length cotton dress covered her thick tights and collected dust along the way. Prickly pear cactus protruded from between friable rocks, catching at the hem of her dress.

It was a short and effortless walk back home, yet still Anna was absorbed in unruly thoughts. She walked slowly, incapable of ignoring the bursts of pink bougainvillea and dots of orange and yellow from citrus trees breaking the palette of green like a Henri Rousseau painting she once saw on the cover of a magazine in the village shop. A profound and eerie silence fell as she approached her house. The streets were empty, for it was late afternoon and hotter than usual for that time of year. Anna glanced over to her neighbour's house. Azra was watching Anna struggling to open her squeaky gate as usual.

"Yassou," said Azra, with a shy smile as Anna entered her courtyard to the sound of chickens clucking.

"Yassou, ti kanis?" asked Anna.

Her father had said it was OK to speak to Azra because despite their problems, both Turkish and Greek Cypriots were neighbours and had been living in harmony since their arrival during the Ottoman empire.

"Azra's harmless," he often said when the subject arose, though Christina revealed her own thoughts with a clear expression of disdain.

"That woman is a spy! You mark my words; the truth will come out one day," she would repeat. "How else can she feed so many children and be that happy? Selling honey isn't enough to feed a family. She'll not buy my loyalty with pots of second-rate honey!"

Azra was a young widow with six children. No one knew where her husband was, or if he was still alive yet somehow she found a way to feed her children, stay courteous and retain her Turkish heritage in a village full of Greek Cypriots. Christina refused to speak to her.

Azra wasn't much older than Anna, hence Anna felt empathy towards her, hoping she wouldn't one day end up in the same situation; trapped in a house with no water, no light, and very little food. Anna had high aspirations for her own life.

Anna smiled at her neighbour as she entered her own family's courtyard. She could see at a glance the eggs had been collected, the goat had been milked, and her mother had the day's vegetables washed and prepared on the stone sink ready for the evening meal, although she was nowhere in sight. Anna wasn't sure what chores her father wanted her to do, so she went to find him in the only place he was likely to be, but before she left the house, she inspected under her bed. Her secret, washed-out butter tin hadn't been tampered with. Her notes still intact, she placed her booklet safely inside.

She felt uncomfortable going to the coffee shop looking for her father, for she always suspected he was discussing a suitor for her. As she approached the small square, she could see, smell and hear the coffee shop nestled comfortably in the middle of the village. Its splintered wooden door with fleeting evidence of paint had become legendary in the village. Customers could often be seen trying to balance their tables and chairs on the rough cobbles to prevent spilled drinks, a ritual that often took place while Happy Harri had his back turned. Men would sit under the vines for hours at a time, listening to native warblers singing their songs in the background while they discussed politics, land and family disputes.

Please God, don't let him embarrass me today! she thought, adjusting her headscarf. She walked past the decrepit building onto the square where Harri was adjusting the door so it didn't fall on his customers. Anna could hear his usual gloomy sentiments.

"One day when it's too late, you'll all take sympathy on a disabled old man!"

She could see her father, Christophoro, laughing with his friends, sitting under the cascading vine supported by a precarious pergola. The smell of tobacco infiltrated the chairs, the napkins, the tables, and everything nearby.

Christophoro's face and conversation abruptly changed as he saw his daughter approaching.

"So…err...yes…they need to round up those extremist scoundrels, so they don't terrorize innocent people!" His voice wasn't convincing. With a mixture of folly and confusion, his friends turned to Anna. "Ah, Anna, I've only just got here, come and join us."

She stared at the numerous empty tea glasses and smouldering ashtray brimming with cigarette butts. Despite his quirks and rigorous scruples, he was her mentor, her teacher and her rock. Anna was reminded of her conversation with Aliki. 'Anna you're lucky, you can get almost anything out of your father when you flash those bright green eyes of yours.'

If only I could talk to him about the one thing I really want in my life, she deliberated as she walked between the tables, aware of two clean shaven young men staring at her, wearing foolish grins they couldn't disguise.

"Anna, sit down over here," her father demanded with a sense of pride and authority. Anna sat next to him, and as far away from preying eyes as possible. She was no longer in the mood to discuss chores, for as she saw it, her father had given her the afternoon off. At times when he was angry, his bright blue eyes pierced with an uncompromising energy that always scared her. Known in the village for his modesty, hard work and respect for tradition and religion, he had become somewhat of a legend when it came to his creative and entrepreneurial skills. He'd mastered the art of making mulberry wine and his own brand of zivania could strip paint and make your eyes water. When times were really hard, Anna's mother would force him to sell it.

"Keep your hands off my belongings, woman!" he would yell.

Christina wasn't afraid of her husband. Even at 4ft 10in, she would snatch the bottles off her giant of a husband and do what she had to.

Chapter 2 – 1938

Christophoro ordered a glass of mint and aniseed tea for Anna. She sat and rearranged her muslin headscarf, wiping the sweat from her neck, before taking her first cooling sip.

"Do you know how much tax I had to pay last year?" Harri mumbled, as he wiped the broken Formica counter-top. "Well... it was… it was too much. I work harder than all of you! And the bastards take all my money."

Christophoro and his friends laughed quietly in their cool, shady corner. They were used to Harri ranting about his hard life, how he hated the British more than Hitler, and how his grown-up children no longer cared because they had found new lives in America. If it wasn't for his disability, Christophoro was convinced someone would have punched him by now, but everyone was aware of his tragic accident and made exceptions for him. Harri hobbled towards them with his walking stick.

"He's going to hit you with his stick!" Christophoro's friend whispered, but Harri walked past them and waved his stick in the air, trying to scare the warblers from his vines.

"Pesky birds…" He jiggled the walking stick between pergola slats. "Every year I cut these vines back, and every year they grow back stronger and faster, just to make my life a misery!"

"You're lucky it's not the migrating season," said one of the grinning young men who worked at the British base, without taking his eyes off Anna. "Then you would really be in trouble with bird droppings."

Christophoro and his entourage knew what was coming next and huddled together, unable to contain their hysteria.

"Do you know how much pain I'm in, and how much work I do in this square, so you all have somewhere to sit?" The speech turned into one of Harri's epic rants as he continued to complain about his bad back, bad leg, bad hip, weak heart and the local council's lack of commitment to the community.

An hour later, Christophoro and Anna left and walked home, taking advantage of the cool evening breeze. Anna loved evenings like this, where she could have her father to herself and he was in good spirits with his red-hot temper at bay.

"Is it true what they say about Harri's accident?" Anna asked softly. "That he was chasing rabbits in the field that day and his father didn't see him in the hay?"

"Yes, it's true," her father answered and sighed. "They say that if he wasn't so small for his age, his father might have seen him and he might have been spared, but God had other plans that day. His father swung the scythe hard and fast; it was harvest and they'd been out working for hours without food or water, they were exhausted." Christophoro's voice mellowed with what he was about to share with his daughter. "The scythe sliced Harri's left thigh clean away from the bone. His cries could be heard as far away as the schoolhouse." Christophoro displayed his kind, empathetic voice that Anna loved so much. "When he came back from the hospital, he was a different person. That's why we tolerate him and why no one's thrown a punch at him when he starts complaining."

They continued to walk home in silence with a gaudy view of army base rooftops in the distance. Situated at the edge of the village, they could just about make out rolls of barbed wire on the perimeter fence while the Union Jack thrashed its weight in the wind. Once a month, the village was disturbed by an early morning trumpet call, commanding the regiment into the yard for routine training. Anna would get out of bed, boil water for her tea and just as the sound of heavy boots reverberate the mint leaves released streaks and flushes of green, filling the kitchen with their refreshing aroma.

Anna felt safe walking by her father's side and observed the mix of pines, large and small, growing steadfast between cottages like the illustrations in her first reading book. Hungry hens pecked at the pink carob blossom laying on the ground. Anna empathized with their hunger. For she, along with the rest of the island, had been feeling the effects of a food shortage for many months.

Then suddenly, her father divulged some shocking news.

"Anna, your mother and I have decided to send Vasili to England. We don't have enough food here and there are terrorist gangs everywhere trying to recruit young men. They're becoming violent and no one knows who to trust anymore. Vasili can make a better life for himself in England." Her father's words suggested some kind of permanence.

Anna was horrified: that was her dream! Vasili hadn't even wanted to go. He had told her just days earlier that he was ready to join the army. She had watched him many times, standing upright and admiring his reflection as he held a broomstick against his side. How could life be so unfair? But she tightened her lips and remained quiet, for it was her father's wish.

CHAPTER 3
1945

As the autumn of 1945 approached, burnished golden leaves fell to the ground like confetti. Spiralling from branches and flaunting hues of red on a carpet of ochre, they secured the next generation of saplings by protecting and feeding them for future generations.

"Hurry up girls, we need to get to church before someone antagonizes yiayia Stavrou!" Christina shouted at her daughters.

"Hurry up Anna, you're not eighteen till next week, stop trying to look pretty!" Kate was first to get ready for a change.

"I'm not!" said Anna, embarrassed by her sister's comment.

The three women rushed to church. It felt strange walking without Vasili and despite her efforts to hide it, Christina desperately missed her only son.

During the long church liturgy, Anna looked at her mother's headscarf and counted the rare times she'd seen her hair flowing freely. Her long braids were wrapped twice around her head and hidden beneath a scarf, never to be seen outside the house. Her hair was washed once a week, combed, braided and set in place.

With the liturgy well underway, Anna could see the hard work bestowed by the three eccentric sisters who regularly washed the church floor. Having a reputation for being 'mad', they often appeared in the streets on a Saturday afternoon, chanting from the bible to instil fear on all sinners. Although they were harmless enough, Anna found them annoying and interfering.

Anna and Kate stood in the pew listening to the service in ancient Greek, both wishing they were somewhere else. Anna looked graciously at her sister's profile and wondered how she could resemble their father so much yet be so very different to him. It made her smile. She remembered how shocked she was on Kate's fifteenth birthday, the year before.

"I want to marry George the fishmonger," Kate suddenly blurted, full of conviction, as if she'd rehearsed it a million times but couldn't get it right, so she shut her eyes and hoped for the best.

"But Kate, father doesn't approve of George," Anna remembered saying, watching her sister's raven eyes filling with tears. Their families had hated each other since George's mother pushed Christina into a prickly pear cactus for saying she was a bad Orthodox Christian. "Besides, he never went to school! Do you really think you'll get father's blessing?"

That was almost a year ago, and now, Anna could see her sister praying hard. She looked down at the mass of light green marble that adorned the floor. She loved the beautiful, translucent emerald colour of the marble, found nowhere else in the village, and every Sunday she marvelled at its beauty. Some days when the sun was not so hot, and the three mad sisters were behind in their cleaning routine, the marble was still wet, and its colour enhanced to a vibrant green like a jewel sparkling in the sunshine. It boasted its beauty for a short time, matching the brightness of Anna's eyes and she would stare until the power of the sun made it vanish like a bold thief in the middle of morning prayer.

After church, the girls were free from chores for a whole afternoon, but Anna was worried and suspicious about Kate's behaviour. She had to find out what her sister was up to. Meanwhile, Christina helped her ageing mother outside and prepared herself for her mother's erratic and unpredictable conduct. It was the highlight of yiayia Stavrou's week.

"My father's coming home from the war next week," broadcasted cousin Stella, with delight.

"Why was he there in the first place?" asked Menelao's father, reeking of the tree bark and acid he used to dye animal hide. "He's a fool! That war wasn't our war... We have our own problems right here! Is he a spy for the British?" he demanded, getting closer and more intimidating.

"Leave her be!" cried Stella's mother with a voice as shrill as her sister Stavrou's. She was ready to defend her husband at any cost. "It wouldn't have hurt your family to show courage and volunteer to stop that monster invading

Europe!" she shouted, airing bad blood between the feuding families.

Menelao's father left in his tractor, mumbling and cursing at her, and all the conscripts who volunteered. "It'd serve them right if they never came back at all. Anyway, it's going to be over soon!" he yelled as his tractor roared and spat diesel fumes at the congregation.

Anna and Kate kept quiet. They'd been hearing about war every Sunday for years, but humbled by the stories as they were, they just didn't know enough to join in the discussions, so once again, they quietly slipped away to the beach.

With almost everyone preoccupied outside the church or at home preparing food, the beach was empty. The girls walked judiciously on the slippery rocks in their best shoes, careful not to taint them with sea water like they did when they were younger, and their mother scolded them for going home with a display of salty lacework on their feet. The girls stared at the calm, clear water in a rockpool, studying little creatures swimming, floating and sitting just below the surface, basking in the ebb and flow of gentle waves.

"Do you remember when you thought sea urchins were big olives?" asked Anna, smiling.

"Well, I was only five!" Kate laughed.

Surrounded by treacherous rocks, they continued to step gingerly, while Anna searched for a favourable moment to talk her sister. Unable to hold back her thoughts, she suddenly blurted, "I know you're up to something. You've been seeing George in secret, haven't you?"

Chapter 3 – 1945

Kate couldn't look at her sister. "Well... Yes," she said in her soft, childlike voice as she leant down to remove seaweed from her path. "He's asked me to... to go to England and marry him. His cousin is already there and can give us a place to live." She held her head high in an attempt to justify her statement. The voice was not characteristic of Kate and her sister knew it was coming from a difficult place.

Anna was silent for a while, wondering what to say to her younger sister. She was shocked, for she hadn't realized it was so serious.

"Don't say anything! If you were offered a place at university in England, you would go in a heartbeat, wouldn't you?" said Kate, abruptly.

"This is very different, and you know it! Are you seriously thinking about it? What about Mum and Dad, and..." But before she could finish her long list of reasons why her sister shouldn't go, Kate stormed off, angry and in tears. Anna wasn't sure what to do next. She sat on a rock, watching a squid rein in a tiny shrimp towards its beak, then break it down before feasting. Frothy bubbles hissed with the tide that gently tossed the squid against the rocks before it was buried under a handful of sand. Anna took a deep breath, closed her eyes and smelled the freshness of the sea. It was the place where dreams could begin, and fears could be faced. A place with no distance or time; only the realm beyond to provide clear thoughts and find solutions. She opened her eyes and glanced out to sea, deciding to return home in case a storm came in.

Slowly she walked, wondering what to do. It was an impossible situation to be in. On the one hand, her brother had already gone to England and his letters suggested he was very happy there, but on the other, although Kate was now sixteen and ready for marriage, their father just didn't approve of George. Anna remembered a conversation between her father and cousin Yanni, just a few days ago, about Jews escaping from the terrible conditions in their temporary camps. "Karaolos is very close," Yanni told her father. "We don't know if these Jews are violent, or what they're capable of."

Her father had said something about them being frightened. "Can you blame them for not trusting politicians, man? I wouldn't trust them either after all the horrors they were subjected to." Anna didn't understand what they were talking about. How could a new country be formed while people waited? If there was any truth in it, should she urge her father to let her go to England with the others?

Anna didn't know how to advise her younger sister. Maybe England really was the best opportunity for her. Anna strolled past the schoolhouse and looked through the tall iron gates into her old classroom. She had very few fond memories of those days. Despite learning about the Mycenaean Dynasty, the beginning of currency and the Bubonic plague in Athens, a few facts that fed her curiosity, how could she forget the ridicule and humiliation from Mr. Onassis towards all girls?

In the last seven years, she'd only acquired one more

book, donated by Grigori as he prepared for secondary school in Nicosia.

"Anna, Grigori likes you, that's why he gave you that book," she remembered Aliki whispering in her ear.

"Don't be silly, he doesn't want or need it anymore!" said Anna, dismissing her friend's claims as her cheeks began to burn.

The Taming of the Shrew sat next to *Great Expectations* in Anna's dowry chest and only came out at night when Anna tried to advance her knowledge. Her English was limited but her washed-out butter tin continued to grow with notes, phrases and poems.

When Anna got home it was beginning to get dark. Exhausted from the day's events, she went straight to the room she shared with Kate and found her fast asleep on her bed. Her head turned to one side; Anna could see her sister's long hair stuck to her face from salty tears. Anna took a deep breath, sat on her own bed, and quietly continued with her secret literary quest.

Finally, she had some alone time. She reached under her bed, grabbed the tin and pulled out her home-made dictionary. Spending all its life curled inside the tin like a cat in a cosy blanket, it refused to flatten with ease. Anna took off her heavy work boots, lifted her mattress and flattened it underneath for a few minutes. She tiptoed quietly towards to her dowry chest and paused for a second, listening for sounds of movement nearby. With the coast clear, Anna lifted the layers of beautiful hand-embroidered linens given to her by aunts, cousins and yiayia Stavrou, and unearthed her two books. At the very bottom was a copy of *Vogue* from 1941, given to her by Eleni. It featured Jane Russell on the cover, standing self-assured in front of an elegant sofa with a nonchalant glare at her pink scarf. The cover girl was the definition of beauty in Anna's eyes. Her long yellow evening dress caressed her curves, shimmering all the way to the floor and beyond like the dappled sunshine Anna was so familiar with. Its vibrant yellow glowed in the chest like stolen pirate treasure.

Tonight, I'm going to try translating the poem I wrote in Greek last week, she thought to herself, knowing it would be grammatically wrong. But as she sat in her bubble and played with her words, Anna could put herself first without guilt.

Eventually, when her eyes stung from the dimly lit oil lamp, turned to its minimum so as not to disturb her parents, she blew out the wick and watched the smoke rove towards Kate's bed, luminating her profile like a gentle crescent moon.

Oh God, please let her see sense, Anna thought, promising to make more time for her little sister. She can barely speak English and George doesn't speak any English at all. How will they survive if they go to England? They have no money. But for now, she had to sleep before the beginning of another working week.

Early the following day, Christina came rushing into the girls' bedroom.

Chapter 3 – 1945

"Get up now you two, you have to start early today, I have to catch the first bus to Varosi so I won't be here to make the haloumi… Anna you'll have to do that. Kate, the apricots need picking before the birds finish them off, and don't forget to slam the chicken house door shut when you collect the eggs. That wretched fox has been trying to get in again. Don't forget to take a plate to yiayia Stavrou as soon as possible, she's been complaining more lately. I swear she thinks I do nothing all day long." And with that she fled towards the gate in a cloud of dust.

"Wait!" shouted Anna, confused and rubbing her eyes, wondering if she was still asleep. "Why are you going to Varosi, has something happened?" she yelled after her mother.

"No," Christina replied as she fumbled in her bag. "It's the damned English again! Now the war in Europe has ended they want us all to register at the main municipality, like sheep. Damn crooks and spies, the lot of them!" She could just about be heard shrieking as the gate shut behind her with a thud.

The two sisters looked at each other mischievously. With their mother absent they could indulge with breakfast in bed.

"Do you think she's going to buy us some shoes?" asked Kate, sipping her hot tea.

"No way, she's got no money, we'll have to make do for at least another year. Anyway, she didn't measure our feet with twigs, did she?"

"I hope she brings back treats from that fancy bakery." Kate grinned, biting into her sesame bread. "Anyway, if she was to buy shoes, it would probably be just for you... Princess Anna! I just get your hand me downs, don't I?"

"Do you remember the stories of big cars, and shops the size of mountains she teased us with?" Anna tried to lighten Kate's mood as they continued to discuss their mother's ritualistic visits to town before the war, and how she would board the bus with the same worn-out plastic bags that doubled as a barrier to prevent cockroaches entering the larder.

"And... I was the one who put the plastic bags back in the larder," complained Kate. "Mother was never satisfied, she always told me I didn't pack them tight enough into the wall and would re arrange them herself. I don't know why she didn't do it herself in the first place!"

Kate's lack of restful sleep was clearly affecting her mood, thought Anna. She decided to give her a wide berth and steer clear of the subject of George for a while. The girls got dressed in silence and Anna set off to meet her father in the field. With her headscarf on her shoulders, she took advantage of the early morning breeze before the day's mix of sun and wind ravaged her skin; and it wasn't even summer. She despised her work clothes. She imagined herself in Jane Russell's beautiful yellow satin dress and wondered if she could ever look as elegant as a cover girl, but reality reared its ugly head and reminded her of all the extra jobs she had to do since Vasili left.

Chapter 3 – 1945

Everyone suspected things would get worse on the island, for now there was talk of threats from Turks and extremist groups. But Anna had been living with threats all her life. She now took it in her stride and worried that she didn't worry at all! She was more concerned about her younger sister.

"Make sure you take the route past yiayia Stavrou's house," her father demanded almost daily.

Anna walked past yiayia Stavrou's house just as she did every morning and saw her standing, dressed in black, leaning over her walking stick, with a tin cup in her hand. Her eyes were transfixed on Anna approaching. It made Anna anxious. What tricks is she conjuring today to delay me, she wondered. What will she complain about today?

Anna approached her grandmother's cottage along the ramp carved by heavy boots over many years.

"Where were you yesterday? Why didn't you bring my food?" she groaned.

"Yiayia, yesterday was Sunday, mother brings you dinner on Sundays. Don't you remember?"

"It was cold!"

"Yiayia, we bring it to you as soon as we cook it."

"Get your brother to run faster," she shrieked, waving her walking stick suggesting there might be consequences otherwise.

"Yiayia I told you, Vasili went to England three months ago," Anna said and sighed.

"Tell him he's a selfish boy and I want my dinners hot!"

she yelled as Anna started making her escape.

Anna walked hurriedly, looking back at her grandmother, still shouting about her selfish grandchildren not helping her, as she did every day. She waved goodbye to her and surreptitiously watched her collect drinking water from the clay pot outside. The sediment would have settled by now, and the water would be fresh, thought Anna, reassured her grandmother wouldn't go thirsty.

Anna recalled how her spirited grandmother used to chase her and Vasili around the whitewashed circular hut, waving her stick at their shenanigans and screaming, "Go home, you wicked children!" Anna knew it was cruel to antagonize her grandmother, but as a six-year-old, she just couldn't help herself.

Yiayia Stavrou's hut was one of just a handful of traditional homes, preserved and dotted around the village. Having fallen out of fashion, they were now only occupied by old ladies in black; widows armed with the greatest secrets and most valuable treasures in the form of myths and legends. Nowadays they sat in their doorways waiting for loved ones to return from the war.

The place yiayia Stavrou observed from day by day had become her prison as well as her haven, and every day she watched an inexplicable world go by, not knowing who to trust.

CHAPTER 4

1948

Summer of 1948 brought an unseasonable weather pattern causing storms and high winds in the village. At the age of twenty-one, Anna felt as far removed from Jane Russell as it was possible to be. Like the trampling of hoofs, thunder clattered all night long bringing ribbons of rain racing down from every roof. Even fireflies were unable to hold on to their lanterns. Dishevelled and bedraggled as a gypsy whose begging has left her high and dry, Anna went outside with a painted smile. She was delighted to find the chickens had laid eggs that morning.

Feeling mellower, she wrapped the eggs in her apron and turned from the chicken run to go back inside the house, when rain suddenly splashed directly into her face from high winds. She caught her breath and waited for reprieve under an old fig tree that leant its exhausted branches against the fence. She held tight to her apron.

The rain gushed through the dusty streets, twisting and turning its fierce swell into a river of mud, sweeping up everything in its angry path. It was the worst summer storm the elders could remember, with thunder that could wake the Gods and crack open the heavens. Nothing could make Anna feel more grotesque that day.

Suddenly, she heard raucous laughter through the din of falling rain and turned from the rickety fence. She peeked through the slats to see what the commotion was about; and there before her, drenched and taking refuge from the deluge in a derelict stone arch opposite Anna's house, stood three young soldiers. Anna was curious. She watched in secret as they placed their rifles on the ground and took off their shirts, wrung them tight and swung them in the air, flicking each other like children. A moment later, they sat down and took off their heavy boots.

"Jeez, Jim, yer fuckin feet stink," laughed the stoutest soldier.

"Yeah, and yer a fuckin smelly bastard!" the other roared with laughter, pouring the wet contents of his boots over the other man's head, then dodged away from his fury.

It was the first time Anna had seen soldiers so close to her house. Knowing they were stationed nearby and seeing them in the distance was quite different to having them on her doorstep. A moment later, the rain stopped as suddenly as it started. The soldiers climbed down from the shelter. But just for an instant, the tallest soldier turned and saw Anna; soaked and shivering, stuck between the fence and the fig tree.

She squealed, as a sharp branch nicked her arm. Anna leant forward to protect the eggs in her apron pocket but tripped on a thick tree root. Through her peripheral vision, she saw him walk towards her, squinting at the unexpected plight of a young woman.

"Are you OK?" he asked, lifting her effortlessly to her feet. She felt the heat and pressure of his strong hands around her waist and panicked, pulling away from him.

"I…I…" Anna didn't know what to say, but for a split second, their eyes locked. Her eyes scrutinized the contours of his face with fierce attention and with all her senses quickened; she watched a few rogue raindrops fall on his young face. His tired, bright eyes shone, highlighting their different colours. It was something Anna hadn't seen before and as she took a deep breath, she was consumed by his resemblance to a heroic Lord Mountbatten. His blonde curly hair was darkened with rain and mud.

"Thang yoo… I…" Her eyes became transfixed for an instant while her heart raced around her chest and leaped to her throat like it wanted to choke her. The soldier smiled a radiant beam like the sunshine.

Anna wasn't sure how long they stared at each other. His intense scrutiny felt like a glimpse into a deeper truth within her, and in that fleeting moment, she belonged to him.

Already ahead, his colleagues turned around, bewildered as to what was holding him up.

"Ed!" one of them called out. "Eddie, c'mon man!" he yelled louder.

Ed's smile widened as he stared back at Anna, then ran to meet his colleagues. Anna heard the slush of his boots disappear. She stared in silence, paused, and wondered what just happened.

Anna was spellbound and for the next few days and could think of nothing else. At night she lay on her bed, staring at the ceiling, wondering if she would ever see him again. A phrase from Shakespeare's *Taming of the Shrew* suddenly had new meaning for her.

'To watch the night in storms, the day in cold,' defined her turbulent thoughts. The words resounded in her head, confusing and robbing her of precious sleep.

But why are their uniforms different? Anna pondered. Could they be here on a special mission? She'd heard cousin Yanni talk about extremist who wanted to get rid of the British. Maybe they're here to flush them out she thought, eventually falling asleep to the gentle whistle of the wind.

Anna knew it was forbidden to speak to the troops and her father would have beaten her black and blue if he knew she had feelings for an English soldier, so she tried to comfort herself with the absurdity of the situation. Even if I was allowed to talk to him, what would I say? she thought, trying to sleep while Kate snored in the bed next to her.

For weeks she wondered if she would ever see him again. However, this particular regiment was beginning to frequent the village and when possible, her surreptitious glances scoured the main streets. She didn't see him, but he was everywhere in her thoughts.

Chapter 4 – 1948

Then, about three months later, Anna was queuing at the post office to collect the family mail. She waited in silence to see if her family name was called, but on that day no mail arrived for them, so she turned to leave. As she walked out of the building that doubled as municipal offices and, on occasion, a court room and sometimes a clinic, she heard a group of soldiers speaking English and immediately identified his voice from the day of the storm. Her eyes panicked while her heart jumped hard and loud as if it wanted to leave her body and explode in mid-air. Anna looked around and there he was, the English soldier with different coloured eyes, gazing right at her with a childish, guilty grin.

"Yasso," he uttered, with a glow in his eyes. "How's your arm?"

Anna stared for a few seconds. She wanted to answer but had no voice. Her throat was dry with everything she wanted to say. He was truly the most enchanting creature she'd ever seen. More handsome than Paul Newman, and every glamorous man she'd seen in her copy of *Vogue*. Nevertheless, she couldn't risk talking to or even looking at him. She bolted home as fast as she could, turning once to see him still standing there. Pleased she wasn't wearing her work clothes that day, her pulse raced, and her heart throbbed at the thought of having to forget someone she didn't know but would always remember.

As Anna approached her gate, panting and out of breath, Azra was in her doorway, smiling, trying to make eye contact to greet her. Anna purposefully looked away in case her expression gave away her disgraceful behaviour and continued briskly to her room. Sweating profusely from the heat, Anna lay on her bed, wondering how she was ever going to rid herself of this unfamiliar pain. Suddenly, the door burst open and Kate walked in. Her loud dramatic sighs of disdain suggested more strife with their mother.

"I'm done for the day," she complained, slowly taking off her boots, unaware of Anna's tears.

"If she wants anything else done, she can do it herself!"

That Sunday after church, Anna took a slow stroll up to Koukles on her own, overlooking the splendours of her surroundings. Once on the mountain, she looked out at the inseparable blues between ocean and horizon, then closed her eyes, quietly inhaling the fragrance that seemed like celestial incense.

Up there, Anna felt the freedom to indulge in visions of her imaginary life with the English solder. She drummed up an array of situations with him by her side and wondered what the words 'I love you' would sound like if they fell from his lips. But the tumble from her dream back to reality became all the more painful in just a heartbeat.

She sat on one of the rocks, staring at the delicate buttercups growing wild along the clifftop. She remembered how, as children, she and Kate would pick the tiny flower heads to make dolls' eyes.

I don't know what I want anymore, she thought, feeling sorry for herself. I just know I don't want to marry

Grigori. I hate the way he looks at me, and the way his ears stick out from the mass of curls on his head. I know I could never get to love him in time, like mother suggests. Please God, don't let them force me. But before she could stop them, tears appeared on her cheeks. She thought of her mother's words.

"People are beginning to talk! You should be married by now. Don't you realise how lucky you are to have Grigori asking for your hand? And he had an education. There's hardly any eligible men left and you're toying with those foolish ideas in your head!"

In the midst of her misery, she looked down and was surprised to see a remnant of fabric from years gone by, saved from the ravages of hungry mountain goats. This had been one of her favourites. She remembered the day she and Kate acquired it. They'd had the rare privilege of Eleni's attention while Mr. Leos's fiancé and her mother were in the shop, swooning over beautiful silk and lace like lost doves who'd finally found each other. Without looking at the two girls, Eleni pointed to a box of scraps pushed into the corner of her small front room that doubled as a shop.

"Help yourselves to two pieces each; but don't leave a mess!" she demanded in her professional voice.

Anna and Kate could barely contain their delight. They rushed to the corner and rummaged through a treasure trove of beautiful prints, remnants of dresses worn by lucky women in the village and even neighbouring villages, come for the rare indulgence of a custom-made dress.

As a little girl, Anna compared Eleni to the goddess Athena, who turned people into spiders if they dared pretend to be better than her at her craft. It was one of the first mythological stories she had learned and since that day, she had become a little less afraid of spiders in case they were once budding seamstresses.

Were the women who wore her dresses headed for bigger and brighter destinies than small mountain villages? Anna could only imagine. Did any of them look as beautiful as Jane Russell? She wondered, picturing them at fashionable parties with their figures adorned, parading with like-minded people who sipped instead of drank their tea.

She took a deep breath and looked away from the sun as it descended, glowing with blinding orange and yellows as a reminder it was time to go home.

Anna walked dreamily in the dusky half-light. As she approached the first house at the edge of the village, she could hear raised voices. She knew the family well; their son Alex was Vasili's best friend and the boys used to get into trouble as a pair. Slowly getting closer, she saw half a dozen or so men, including her father, huddled around a small transistor radio trying to listen to news with big smiles on their faces.

"King Paul of Greece has declared Cyprus desires union with Greece… the UN have accepted the petition… ENOSIS is now an international issue."

"We've done it!" she heard Yanni delight as he jumped on the small table, trying to dance to the background music from the news. “We will unite with Greece this time… We will… and it won’t be long now. Then these British bastards can leave and stop pretending to the world they’re here to protect us.”

Anna heard the men rejoicing as though their dreams had come true. They helped themselves to her father’s zivania and mulberry wine and danced as if they’d won a war.

CHAPTER 5

1950

"You're twenty-three years old now! if you wait any longer, you'll be a spinster," yelled Christina. "Grigori has been waiting for you since you were fourteen years old!" she yelled louder, waving her arms in the air. "We'll be the laughingstock of the village; terrible gossip will spread about our family…and what do you think this is doing to your father?" Christina continued to rage; her puffy eyes nestled deep in their sockets.

Anna lay faced down on her bed and screamed into her blanket.

"I don't want him!" she confessed, pushing boundaries.

"Then who…? Who are you going to marry?" Christina demanded to know. "Because you cannot stay single. That's not an option!"

"I don't know!" screamed Anna. I just want to go to England and stay with Vasili."

"Why? So you can marry an Englishman?" Christina's words hit like bullets.

"No… I… I don't know what I want," Anna lied to her mother.

Chapter 5 – 1950

"Well... Now we're going to unify with Greece, maybe... maybe things will get better," Anna proclaimed.

Her mother slowly shook her head in disgust.

"Anna, sometimes I think you're the brightest girl I've ever known, and sometimes I can't believe how stupid you can be."

Christina went to the window and opened the shutters. The evening breeze crept into the small room as if to liberate Anna. Temporarily rescued by its vitality, Anna remained quiet, hoping her mother and the subject of marriage would all go away. As the light touched Christina's face, Anna could see her mother's sun-ravaged skin. Lines previously unnoticed became discernible for the first time; they made Anna think of a road map, a map to a life of duty and tradition, woven together in the same common thread that led to her strength, stamina and assertiveness. Like a collection of roads in a busy city, each dependent on one other to reach a common objective... Anna's thoughts were drifting out of control again.

Seething with frustration, Christina let her headscarf slip halfway down her head revealing coarse, wispy grey hair, poking in all directions like the breast of a dishevelled wheatear bird. "Your father's just as passive as you. I suppose I'll have to make all the arrangements," she grunted quietly.

"What arrangements? Mother, what do you mean?"

Christina abruptly left the room.

"Mother, what are you going to do?" Anna called out,

as her mother stepped out into the courtyard and sat in her favourite chair. Anna went back to her bed and continued to cry into her pillow.

The following day, Anna left the house early, hoping to find out what her mother was planning. She didn't have to go far, for Aliki was on her way to Anna's house to pick up more embroidery thread. Aliki also had news. "Anna, she can't match you up with Grigori anymore. My cousin told me he's getting engaged to Melina."

"Do you mean Alex's sister?" asked Anna.

"Yes, she's wanted him for years, she's been watching you, hoping you wouldn't marry him." Aliki looked sympathetically at her friend. "Anna, you could've had him, he waited so long for you, everyone knows it."

All of a sudden, Kate came running towards them with a huge childlike smile; puffing and panting as if she'd run a marathon in search of her sister.

"Anna! Anna!" she yelled, waving a letter in her hand.

"This came for you. It's from England, it must be from Vasili," she said excitedly.

Anna opened the letter while the others looked on.

"What does he say, Anna? Did he marry Athena? Is he rich?" Aliki impatiently jumped up and down.

"It's not from Vasili." Anna's hands began to tremble. "It's from a women's magazine in London, they've published my poem." She stared wide-eyed at Aliki for a moment, then carefully folded the letter and opened the magazine. She flicked through pictures of Princess Elizabeth, women in twin suits and pearls, and adverts encouraging women to purchase warm underwear for their husbands. Then, lurking at the bottom of page nine, she saw a small square with her poem in print, under the title 'Our International Readers'.

The three girls stared at each other in amazement.

"I can't believe it... Anna... Anna, you're famous!" screeched Aliki, her eyebrows raised with new esteem for her best friend. The girls clenched each other tight and jumped up and down, squealing with delight.

Anna walked home, chatting incessantly to her sister.

"What are you going to tell Mother?" asked Kate, absorbed in her own thoughts.

Anna hadn't thought that far ahead, but a plan was beginning to hatch in her head.

By the time they got home, it was clear by their mother's expression that news of Grigori and Melina had spread. Anna cagily slipped away and tried to be invisible. She shut the bedroom door behind her as quietly as possible and began to calm the silent carnival spinning in her head. She needed a sophisticated plan to make this work; everything else was insignificant. She sat aloof on her lumpy horsehair mattress and began scheming.

That night she lay in bed staring at the ceiling and waited patiently for the sun to rise. She got up before her family and quietly slipped into her favourite dress, feeling brazen, sinful, and nervous. But it was something she had to do. She fixed her hair in the small vanity mirror on the dresser, taking advantage of the first stripey light as it peeped through the shutters. She was oblivious to the absence of the only photograph of her and her sister on the dresser. Anna tiptoed out to the sound of her sister's weird and wonderful snoring melody and walked to the bus stop.

As the bus screeched to a halt outside the schoolhouse, an angry man boarded quickly.

"You overslept again!" he shouted at the driver. Anna looked away; she recognized the man and couldn't risk being seen.

"Eh, so what! Why do you need to go anywhere this early in the morning anyway?" he yawned, revving the engine to prove he was awake. Two people boarded with Anna and paid their fare. She slipped away to a secluded seat at the back of the bus as the driver turned up the radio volume, trying to keep himself awake. Her insatiable craving to read the letter over and over again made blood rush to her head, leaving her dizzy with absurd, fanciful dreams.

'Our readers are so delighted and inspired by your beautiful poem that we would like to offer you a permanent spot in our monthly magazine.' She read it over and over again, savouring every word.

She sat staring out of the window with a permanent smile, enthralled as the day the English soldier helped her from the fall. Forty minutes later, the driver slammed on the brakes.

"Last stop!" he slurred, rushing to get out of the driver's seat and into the coffee shop.

Anna tried to walk elegantly in her Sunday best shoes.

Chapter 5 – 1950

It was hard enough walking in an elegant dress and trying to keep it crease-free. She walked the few hundred yards to the post office in full view of the small town and knew she had to act with caution in case she bumped into someone who knew her family and would question why she was out in the town without a chaperone.

"I'd like to mail this letter and register to receive mail at this branch," she told the clerk. The old man peered through the top of his thick greasy glasses and frowned.

"Young lady, you can't just receive mail anywhere you know!" he whistled, displaying a huge gap where his front teeth once resided. He looked her up and down and frowned even deeper, endorsing his authority. "Anyway, I need your husband or father's signature," he demanded, dismissively slamming his pen on the desk.

Just then, a colleague appeared and dumped a pile of files in front of him. The two men argued about the time and quantity of work, when Anna saw an opportune moment.

"My husband's been delayed at work, he's a policeman," she blurted. The two men continued to argue. "Did you hear me, sir?" Anna called out, confidently tapping on the counter. The clerk's face reddened, and his nostrils began to flare. With that, he slammed a piece of paper on the counter in front of her without making eye contact.

"Sign!" he yelled, turning to the growing queue and the clock above the door.

"What a great day!" Anna thought half an hour later, as she sat in a coffee shop, devouring a wonderful feeling of freedom. Passers-by stared at her drinking alone in a coffee shop, but she didn't mind. She took the letter and read it one more time when she suddenly heard heavy boots and the clinking of metal approach in her direction. The sound dulled into the background hub of a busy town, waking up to yet another crisp bright morning. But all of a sudden she heard a vaguely familiar voice approach her, and looked up from her tea glass.

"Good morning ma'am," her English soldier whispered with the sweetest, kindest smile Anna had ever seen. With her newly found confidence, Anna was prepared. This time she wasn't going to run away, or stutter, or make a fool of herself.

"Oh, er, good mornink sir, Mr..." she mumbled, smiling at the sight of his blazing eyes that pierced through her. She felt her cheeks flush with the redness and heat of the bell peppers in her mother's vegetable field but wouldn't, couldn't look away from the diamonds in his eyes, hoping one day she could tell him how valuable they were.

"You're beautiful," he said slowly, staring at her smooth skin that glowed in the shade of grape vines. "My name is Ed, short for Edward. What's yours?" he asked, slowly holding out his hand.

"My name iz Hannah," she said, with a croaky voice. Anna went to shake his hand but felt awkward. Speaking to him was bad enough, but to touch him was an insult to her family values. He was English after all, therefore a potential threat. No one trusted U.N. soldiers.

Chapter 5 – 1950

Covertly, Anna could see a few women across the street, beginning to stare. She couldn't risk them knowing her family, so once again, she bolted away as fast as she could, without shaking his hand and without saying goodbye.

When Anna got home it was late afternoon and she needed to be discreet about her day. Surreptitiously she snuck back into her room to get changed but noticed something was different. She looked at her dresser; it looked different somehow. Kate's drawer was slightly askew.

It's not like Kate to leave anything out of alignment, she thought, beginning to think the worst. Hesitantly, Anna opened the drawer; it was empty. She looked under Kate's bed; her Sunday best shoes were gone. She looked for the small case that once belonged to yiayia Stavrou; that was gone too. A frenzied inspection of cupboards confirmed Anna's worst nightmare. She sat on her bed with a great thump and stared at the roughly plastered wall, covering heavy stone slabs. How on earth was she going to explain to her parents that Kate was gone?

She went to the kitchen and found her mother with her head in her hands.

"Where on earth have you been?" she muttered slowly without looking at Anna.

"I… I…"

"Kate's gone!" she whispered. "My baby's gone!"

For the first time in her life, Anna felt sorry for her mother and pulled up a chair next to her, hoping somehow she could comfort her.

"Why? Why are my children leaving me, Anna? Is God punishing me, have I been a bad Christian?" Her mother cried hysterically on Anna's shoulder.

"No mother, you're a good Christian woman! Don't ever doubt that." Anna was surprised by her own words and the closeness of her mother. She felt awkward.

The following Sunday, Anna went to church with her mother and grandmother, dreading the gossip about Kate and George after the liturgy. She helped her yiayia to her seat.

"I can manage perfectly well on my own!" complained yiayia Stavrou, nudging her granddaughter to stop fussing. "Who are these people talking about, Anna?" she shouted, in case the congregation was deaf.

"Shhh yiayia, they're talking about the new family that moved here last month," Anna whispered into her grandmother's ear.

"Ahhh, I see them all the time, they're smelly Turks!" she wailed, waving her stick in the air, accidently hitting the man in front.

"Yiayia you can't say that!" Anna apologized to the man in front.

"Why? I can say what I like, girl. I hate those smelly Turks… I hate them all! They'll rob us one day, you mark my words, they're going to kill us in our beds!"

Anna escorted her agitated grandmother to the back of the church to be with her peers. Six of them, including Eleni senior, the dressmaker's mother, sat together making more noise than a tittering of magpies.

"Sssshhhh!" insisted the priest, staring at them with the authority of God. Now the women took heed.

After the sermon when everyone stepped outside, Anna was keen to disappear before gossip of her sister got underway although she was surprised it wasn't about her sister. News of the new family superseded Kate's departure.

"I heard that new family came here from Kyrenia," said cousin Stella. "My father went to Kyrenia once to get a new fishing net, it took him ten hours to get there in the tractor."

"Why would anyone leave their village at a time like this?" asked the baker, his clothes oozing with a foul stench of old yeast, as he headed towards his bike and attempted to balance his huge body across the saddle. "I know they only have one child though," he shouted, as the bike wobbled down the hill.

"The man is called Pavlo" said Menelao, climbing onto his father's old tractor as they vanished into a cloud of dust and diesel fumes.

Yiayia Stavrou and her best friend were eager to continue their conversation over a brandy and some olives. Aided with their walking sticks, the two women shuffled away, deliberating who had the worst bone ache that week.

When Anna arrived at the coffee shop, her father was seated in his favourite spot, reading a newspaper. She sat next to him, waiting to be reprimanded for not stopping Kate from leaving. There was an uncomfortable silence.

"It's not my fault, father!" she exclaimed, convinced that everyone blamed her. "I didn't know she was actually going to leave."

Christophoro listened to his daughter behind his newspaper for a while. Then, he slowly folded his newspaper and Anna could see his true expression.

"Child, I don't care for gossip, religion or excuses. I'm a simple man with few expectations. Unlike your mother, I know she's safe with that fishmonger." A sly grin began to emerge.

"You knew, didn't you…? You actually knew!" Anna jumped up in surprise.

"Of course I knew, where do you think they got the money to go?" he laughed, tossing the newspaper towards Anna. "Read the headlines."

Anna read: 'Violence erupted in the streets of Nicosia as campaign against colonial power escalates'.

"I don't understand, what does this mean?"

"It means things are going to get worse for us," he said. "It was the best thing for Kate, George and Vasili to leave the island."

"But why didn't you say anything to me or mother?" Anna was angry at her father.

"And face your mother's wrath! Trust me, it's better this way," he said, winking at her.

Anna rolled her eyes, drank a cup of tea with her father then got up to leave. An unfamiliar man was just entering. The short, stout man nodded politely at Christophoro then went to tune the hissing transistor radio on Harri's cracked Formica counter. Apart from the two men, the coffee shop was empty; for no one liked being out in that heat.

The two men watched Harri polishing glasses with a threadbare linen tea towel infused with unidentifiable odours. His arthritic fingers fumbled with a fresh bag of coffee, releasing the aroma of sweet roasted chestnuts.

"It's very temperamental and the volume button doesn't always work," cried Christophoro.

The man eventually found a news station.

"I haven't seen you before," enquired Christophoro. "Come and join me."

The two men started to talk. Both had tales of woe about wayward children, and an ever-growing list of things to do, and it wasn't long before the two men realized quite how much they had in common.

"We're from Kyrenia," said Pavlo. "And I know what people are saying about us. We're not spies, and we're not murderers. We came here because it's closer to our son's boarding school. It's that simple!" he grinned slowly.

Christophoro was embarrassed, knowing that his own wife was one of the biggest gossips in the village.

"I have a son too," bragged Christophoro, though with a heavy heart. "His name is Vasili, I sent him to England to get away from the troubles. It's the only way to keep our young men safe and prevent them from getting caught up in this ENOSIS chaos. A union with Greece is never going to happen if you ask me. They have their own troubles with all those communists running around, why would they take on more problems for themselves? If we did unite, they may force communism on us. Doesn't anyone on this island have a brain cell to use? Last year we thought the union with Greece would happen overnight and our prayers would be answered. How quickly things change."

Pavlo sighed and was a little intimidated by Christoforo's depth of knowledge.

A little later, the men were still talking when Anna walked past with a basket full of mulberries she'd collected from her plot.

"Ah Pavlo, this is my daughter, Anna!" said Christophoro, proudly beckoning her back in.

Then all of a sudden, the unmistakable sound of army boots could be heard. Anna stopped in her tracks. Christophoro and Pavlo turned cautiously to see a clean-shaven British army sergeant enter the square. They watched him proceed to the counter and adjust his hat to wipe his brow before removing it. He looked for a clean section of counter to place it, then turned his nose up at countless cups and glasses waiting to be dunked in Harri's washing up bowl.

"Beer!" he demanded, slamming his money on the counter. Harry continued with his back to the sergeant. "I said beer!" repeated the sergeant, getting agitated.

Harri turned around, got close to the sergeant's face, and retorted slowly and clearly.

"Your...money...isn't...welcome...here!"

Chapter 5 – 1950

The sergeant's clean-cut features and the way his hand moved close to his holster scared Anna. She dropped her basket. Christophoro put his arm in front of her in a protective gesture.

"Fucking peasants," the sergeant tittered slowly, making sure his venomous words had maximum meaning. "You think we're here for pleasure? You're never going to unite with Greece, not if we can help it." He laughed callously and added, "I hope the fucking Turks annihilate you one day!"

He cast an eye on Christophoro's table and slowly turned away, spitting on the ground as he left. Anna's heart beat faster. Her hands were shaking, and she burst into tears.

"What's he talking about, Dad?" She trembled, afraid of the sergeant's words.

"He doesn't know what he's talking about, girl!" Christophoro said dismissively looking at Pavlo's worried expression.

CHAPTER 6

1951

"Sit down father, you've been up since sunrise," Anna fussed.

"I'm fine, this is where I rest and get away from your mother."

With hands stained red as a maple leaf in autumn, he continued like an obsessed lover with no control over his actions.

Anna watched her father empty mulberries into an oak barrel, ready to press.

"Dad you shouldn't be doing this on your own," she said, offering her assistance.

"Don't worry yourself, Pavlo is coming to help me," Christophoro affirmed, preoccupied with optimism. "Ahhhh! This is the best crop we've had for a long time." He smiled, squeezing the little red berries between his fingers. "Deep red berries make the sweetest wine and cousin Yanni will build you a house on that plot one day, but the mulberry tree will always be mine, just remember that!" He laughed.

A few minutes later Anna left the bunker, happy to see her father in good spirits. She entered the courtyard to Old Red crowing and looked towards the front gate where Pavlo and a young man were struggling with the latch. Anna went to assist and greeted their guests with pleasantries. As Pavlo entered, Anna could see his tight shirt buttons ready to pop.

"This is my son, Petro," he proudly revealed.

Anna shook hands and led them to a table in the shady covered terrace that surrounded the courtyard. The cobbles were cooling in the evening breeze and the two men sat, relieved from the day's heat. Meanwhile Anna went to fetch her father, leaving Pavlo admiring the pillars that held up the arches along the terrace where he sat. He sat back and relaxed now he was out of the villainous sun, and observed chickens running around strategically placed fruit trees. A surge of deep pink bougainvillea climbed up each pilar, then fell into disarray, as it swayed in the breeze, just missing his cheek. A ray of white sunlight scattered final colours for the day as sunset approached.

Pavlo sat back in his chair with a sense of calm, peace and tranquillity. Anna went inside when her father joined the guests but could overhear them talking.

"Ah, you're here!" Christophoro brought a bottle and three glasses from his cellar and sat down to drink with his guests. They sat with their backs against the open shutters from the house, trying to snatch the evening breeze. Pavlo slowly opened up the week-old newspaper he had tucked under his arm.

He sighed discreetly, then read aloud.

"Three thousand men of the 16th parachute brigade, the largest single contingent of British troops to arrive in Cyprus in peacetime, arrived aboard the aircraft carrier today. With the island's recently augmented garrison, the total number of British troops stands at about ten thousand." He put down the newspaper and continued. "They've taken over Harri's place."

"Whaaaat!" yelled Christophoro, slamming his glass on the table.

"Harri just told me we're only allowed in there at the weekends now. He doesn't want any trouble, Christophoro… Don't try anything, they're armed, remember! He's thinking of closing down the coffee shop altogether, so he doesn't have to serve them."

"Why is he serving them in the first place?" screamed Christophoro.

"He has no choice, man!"

Anna returned with three glasses of water and a traditional dessert of preserved quince, aware of the sudden change of conversation. It was obvious to her that her something had upset her father. She smiled and listened quietly for a while, uninterested in unravelling or becoming privy to the conversation. All she was interested in was expressing herself through poetry and whether or not she would see her soldier again. She tried to slip away.

"Er, Anna, don't go yet, this is Petro. He's home for the Easter holidays. He graduates from Nicosia boarding school in a few months." Her father had simmered down and was trying hard to get back on track as to the reason why he had invited Pavlo and Petro to the house.

She observed Petro's sturdy profile and listened as he bragged about the countless times he had outsmarted his school masters and got the highest marks in his class and was complimented for looking like Cary Grant. Pavlo grinned and gently nodded his head in acknowledgment of his son's brilliance, but Petro's fluid and articulate enunciation made Anna apprehensive. She wasn't interested in talking to him; he made her uncomfortable.

A few months later, Petro graduated from school with flying colours. His excellent command of the English language landed him a job as a driver at the British military base nearby. Petro couldn't believe his luck. There he was, driving beautiful Land Rovers and receiving perks no one else in the village had; and he was being paid. He chatted endlessly to the British soldiers while driving them around; in turn they rewarded him with gifts. Rothmans cigarettes and sometimes Cadbury's chocolate made him the most popular man in the village; although he never could get rid of the English tea and didn't want to give it back in case he offended the soldiers. Life was good for Petro and he wasn't too shy to flaunt it. Petro was also privy to information no other individual outside the base was.

"You know your people's right fuckin' ignorant, don'cha?" the soldier who offered him tea blurted, in a bold Cockney accent, taking a long drag from his cigarette. Petro carefully looked up from the Land Rover bonnet with his head tilted to protect his hair.

"What do you mean, sir"

"Don'cha fuckin' idiots know?" he hissed. "You people wan' us gone, don'cha? Know wass gonna 'appen t' ya fackin' peasants if we leave? Oo's gonna protect ya… the Greek commies? The Turks?" He laughed sarcastically and hopped off the vehicle, flicking his cigarette into the dusty road ahead. "We was in the war ya know… and naa we jus' wanna go 'ome! But we's stuck ere wiv you fackin' lot."

"We don't all believe in the same things sir."

"You shoulda seen the fuckin orror's of Hitler," he interjected, getting himself worked up.

"Fucking lucky bastards, yer don't know when yer well off!" he snatched the car keys from Petro. They got back into the Land Rover and drove in silence.

Back at base, Petro got to type documents for the soldier who gave him Rothmans; he was by far Petro's favourite and over the weeks they had become good friends. It wasn't just the countless packs of cigarettes Petro got to share with his friends, he also enjoyed the stories of life in the English countryside. Stories about hunting and shooting weekends at his father's lodge in Scotland, and boarding school stories similar to Petro's own. The two had an affinity that fuelled Petro's dream of going to England.

One Saturday, Anna's mother brought her a cup of tea in bed. Not only had she never done this before; she was also smiling, something Anna hadn't seen for a long time. Anna sat up, rubbing the sleep from her eyes and frowned. Something wasn't right.

"Anna my dear," she said softly, looking into her daughter's beautiful green eyes. "You are twenty-four years old now and people are beginning to talk!" she said frankly.

Anna began to dread what was coming next.

"So, your father and I have decided you're to marry Petro."

Anna's eyes opened wide with horror. In all her twenty-four years, she had never spoken back to her mother, or questioned her decisions or judgements, but this was unbearable!

"Mother, you can't be serious?" she choked on her words as her guts began to wrench. "Petro is just a boy… I don't even like him, he's arrogant and I don't know anything about him… Please mother, don't do this." She went to grab her mother's hand hoping she would understand the absurdity of the arrangement, but her mother pulled away.

"It's already been arranged, Anna. You had plenty of chances, but you turned them all down. We gave you choices because you have a pretty face, now it's too late; your father and I want you married before the end of the year."

"Mother… please!!" Anna wailed in vain.

"Look child, we don't know what's going to happen to us. People think there's a war coming, then what will you do? All the men will be gone, and you will end up a spinster with no children… That isn't an option for us." Christina did her best to appear sympathetic.

"But we're going to unite with Greece just like they promised. Then I can go…" Anna couldn't finish her sentence and their eyes met.

"Go where, Anna? Leave your father and go to England with no husband, like your selfish sister? Do you really want to be the one to completely break your father's heart?"

Anna howled like an animal that had lost a limb. An animal in so much pain that her voice diminished into the same void as her mother's the night Kate disappeared.

"Anna… none of us get what we want, we just have to weigh up what's best for us. Petro can give you a good life. He's educated and can get a job anywhere. You'll find love with him, Anna, I promise. Love doesn't follow you around or fall from the sky. The kind you read about in your silly English magazines isn't real." She paused for a while, realizing her daughter's pain.

"Look, you're a good girl, Anna, you will grow to love him like the rest of us did when we were first wed. Just work together and keep God in your heart. There is nothing else in life, Anna, nothing! However hard you search."

Anna continued to howl, nevertheless she listened to every word her mother said. Christina got up slowly, took a deep breath and squeezed her daughter's hand with joy. Anna lay on her back, contemplating Shakespeare's *Taming of the Shrew*: 'There's small choice in rotten apples.'

In her mind's eye, this was the beginning of a journey she had to learn to embrace. She lay on her bed, eyes red and puffy, crafting Machiavellian plans to continue writing poems for the magazine. For now it was going be difficult, but one day in the future, she was convinced it wouldn't be.

Chapter 6 – 1951

On the day of Anna's wedding, Christina woke early. Anna had little say in the arrangements.

If I don't make a fuss, maybe it'll just go away! She fantasized, pulling the blanket over her head, but Christina was excited. First came the ritualistic tea in bed which always signified something ominous.

"I've made it extra sweet today, Anna, so you can keep your strength up."

"Who's that giggling in the courtyard?" Anna asked with a lump in her throat.

"Aliki, cousin Stella and all our friends, of course! They're here to help, silly girl! Just come to my room for a moment, I have something for you," Christina shouted above the din of squawking young women outside.

Christina went to her heavy wooden wardrobe and opened the rasping door. Mothballs fell to the ground and filled the air with their overwhelming odour. She rummaged beneath the beautifully starched, embroidered linens, all neatly folded and piled high, then took out a little leather drawstring pouch. Carefully, Christina put her fingers inside as if extracting crown jewels from a dust bag and took out a lipstick and small bottle of perfume.

"I have no need for these anymore," she whispered, offering her daughter the most feminine things she owned. Anna remembered seeing her mother sneaking them out of the wardrobe for cousin Stella's wedding, almost five years ago. It was the only time she saw her mother wearing lipstick.

"Now let's see you in that beautiful dress," she urged in the most comforting voice she could muster, acknowledging her daughter's fragile disposition.

The two women returned to Anna's room, overwhelmed by friends and family that came in droves.

"Ouuuut!" shouted Christina, ushering the women away and closing the door behind them.

Anna took the white protection sheet off the dress. Until now, she hadn't seen it finished. She gasped, breathless for a second, then smiled for the first time that day.

The dress was even more enchanting than Jane Russell's floating gold ensemble. It was more beautiful than the dresses worn by Queen Elizabeth's maids of honour at her coronation just months earlier. Her green eyes reflected the brilliant, luminous jewels adorning the bodice, blinding her with their radiance. She ran her fingers down the glimmering white silk gown but felt the rough skin from her fingers chafing and catching. She was mortified at the thought of damaging such an exquisite work of art and touched it again with caution. Slowly and tenderly, she ran her fingers down the dress like a mother stroking her new-born child. As she gazed at the emerald green rhinestones stitched meticulously on the sleeves, a fresh potential raised her spirits.

"I know how much you like the colour of the marble in the church," said her mother affectionately. "So I asked Eleni to sew some on your dress."

"Eleni made it?" asked Anna, with fervent enthusiasm.

"Nothing but the best! Your father insisted." Christina was getting emotional. Anna stepped into her dress with her mother's help. It was the most tender moment they would ever share together. Anna looked at herself in the mirror.

"I… I… look beautiful," she said softly, staring at her reflection in detail.

"Yes, you do," agreed her mother, no longer able to contain the women outside.

"Finally!" complained Aliki, bursting in with the red sash ready to tie around Anna's waist.

"You can't go to the church without it, the priest won't marry you without proof of your virginity anymore," whispered cousin Stella.

"Yeah, I heard he's getting very strict these days. He says we're getting too influenced by the British and forgetting our traditions. Let's hope he's in a good mood today," said one of the bridesmaids.

Anna stepped into the courtyard and waited for Petro and his entourage to arrive.

She always assumed this moment would feel different; be different somehow; nonetheless, she'd come to an impasse from which there was no backing down. This ceremony was her mother's and not hers. It was a silent sacrifice for her father's yearning and her culture's desire;

it went against her goals and dreams, but the marriage had to work.

Filled with doubt, she watched Petro and his family enter the courtyard with a violinist, hoping her mother was right. Hoping more than hope that she would forget about the English soldier and how heavy her heart felt that day.

Anna had only met Petro a few times and although he was about to become her husband, she was too embarrassed to look him in the eye. He approached her in the crowded courtyard.

The Brylcreem in his hair shone as strongly as it smelt and resemble the wing of a raven after a spring shower. A nervous chortle leaked from his well-defined lips. His black suit was immaculate with barely a dust mark from his walk to her house. His impeccable sense of dress was one of the few features Anna knew about him. They stood in awkward silence for a few minutes, waiting for Christophoro and Pavlo to finish their ouzo, and Christina and Katerina to stop gossiping and take yiayia Stavrou's walking stick before she rammed it into someone thinking they were Turkish.

The two families walked to church while bride and groom prepared to walk down the aisle together. Anna was embarrassed and uncomfortable at the attention she was receiving; she was a private person, preferring instead to merge into the background rather than be in the limelight.

However, bewilderment changed in a heartbeat when, looking down the aisle in the front row, Anna saw her soul mate, fledgling and best friend. Kate sat looking more radiant and more grown up than ever in a fawn-coloured cardigan and string of silky pearls. With her hair tucked into a French bun, she was more beautiful than Lauren Bacall in *To Have and Have Not*. Her eyes were glassy with secret excitement she no longer had to contain. Seated comfortably next to George, Vasili and Athena, she mimed “Yassou,” to her older sister.

Anna didn’t need to look at her father’s face, she knew that all he wanted was there that day.

CHAPTER 7

1954

"Go home and let us get on with our work, old man!" Yanni demanded.

"Just make sure your tools are gone by the end of the day. They're moving in tomorrow," said Christophoro, surreptitiously inspecting his younger cousin's workmanship.

"Stop fussing, or I'll cut down that damned mulberry tree and use it for firewood!" yelled Yanni.

"Here, look at this." He turned the kitchen tap on and watched his cousin's face marvel at the never-ending stream of water that gushed into the stone sink like a mini waterfall.

It took Christophoro's breath away. "Is it safe?" he asked, looking in all directions in case of a flood.

Yanni rolled his eyes and hurried into the bedroom to test the electric light while Christophoro checked the sink, the plug, the pipes, and the cooker with its full tank of gas.

"She's the only one along this street with indoor running water!" shouted Yanni.

Christophoro went to the back door and scrutinized the hinges and door frame. Precisely and cautiously, he stepped onto the concrete steps, inspecting the smooth porcelain finish. From the top step he could see the mud hut in the back yard, the only surviving remnant of the arid land he purchased so many years ago. Now it was a perfect enclosure for the goats. Christophoro swept up the final debris, then turned to his idol: a natural sculpture created by nature's own handiwork. Elevated in the middle of the yard with long sprawling branches, the last mulberry tree in the village was safe from Yanni's construction work.

Cautious not to disturb wildflowers growing between friable, chalky soil, he swept the fallen berries into the compost, to discourage hungry critters from feasting on dark red soup and potentially damaging its roots.

Dry, brittle knuckles swayed towards the ground in a naked dance, waiting for a blanket of fresh spring leaves to save them. Christophoro pampered the tree and nursed it as always, while listening to the soothing hum of thrush nightingales and bluethroats.

"Are you still here, old man?" shouted Yanni.

"Ah well, I guess I should go home now," Christophoro murmured, rubbing his sore back.

He left via the side gate, admiring the new curved fence that surrounded the property, and strolled home exhausted. It had been a long day, and he still hadn't ploughed the field ready for new carob trees. He was gasping for a drink and decided to take a detour towards Harri's as it was a Saturday and safe to do so.

The raucous banter and repartee coming from the coffee shop broke his tranquil state of mind.

In the evening light, Christophoro caught a glimpse of a young soldier standing unsteadily on a table, as if giving a theatrical comedy performance.

"What d'ya call a soldier who's survived a mustard gas attack?" he spluttered into a wrapped-up napkin. The table wobbled; the soldier tried desperately not to fall. The ten or so men called obscenities and hurled nuts at him, howling with laughter.

"A seasoned veteran, yer fucking morons!" he stammered, drooling into his beer.

Christophoro caught sight of his son-in-law talking to Harri at the bar.

"Come, join us!" shouted Petro awkwardly, beckoning his father-in-law to participate. Christophoro knew it was his son-in-law's job to mix; he'd been thinking about it a lot recently. Refusing the invitation, Christophoro put up his hand, shook his head and went on his way.

Later that week, Anna and Petro moved into their new home, and in the summer of 1955, Anna gave birth to her first daughter.

"Aah, that's a beautiful daughter you have, Anna," the self-appointed village midwife wrapped the baby in swaddling and handed her to Anna. "I had eight sons before I was finally blessed with a daughter," she smirked.

Anna was overwhelmed by the miracle of her newborn baby daughter and finally began to reconcile with her path in life.

Chapter 7 – 1954

"I've waited a long time for a grandson," shared Christina, peering lovingly into the baby's face.

"But a granddaughter will do just fine!" The women were in good spirits at the birth of a healthy baby when they suddenly heard someone entering the house.

"We're in here, Petro!" Anna joyfully shouted. But instead of Petro, it was Azra.

"Can I see the baby?" she asked shyly, not sure if she was welcome.

"Oh…er…yes." Anna was surprised to see her Turkish friend show up like that, but Christina flew into a rage.

"Get out of my house you filthy Turk!" she raged, chasing Azra out the door. Then, with eyes as fiery as a picture of the devil Anna had seen in one of her schoolbooks, she turned to Anna.

"Are you still friends with that woman?"

"Ye…no…er, oh mother stop it! you've made the baby cry with all that shouting" Anna avoided her mother's scrutiny.

Meanwhile, Aliki caught up with Petro as he was about to finish work on the other side of the village.

"Your wife's just given you a daughter," she proclaimed, proud to be a bearer of good news. Petro sat outside the British base, smoking and drinking whisky with Dimitri the butcher, and stared at the ashtray.

"Oh," he sighed, moving his chair into the shade, preoccupied with his thoughts.

"Are you going to name her Katerina, after your

mother?" asked Dimitri with great interest and a smile.

"Dunno," mumbled Petro, flicking his ash to the ground.

Dimitri stood up. "Well…err.. thanks for the cigarettes. I'm off."

He left Petro deep in thought. As the sun diminished, Petro got up, ran his long slim fingers through his hair and took a deep breath.

"Aint ya gotta ome ter go te?" mocked the tea soldier as he left the building.

Petro staggered home to see his newborn daughter. He stumbled through the front door, followed by the reek of alcohol and a trail of Christina's scorn.

"Look! Look, Petro, isn't she beautiful?" cried Anna from the bedroom, holding their daughter to her breast. Her cheeks were still glowing with fatigue and sweat. She stared at her baby's tiny face and could think of nothing else. Petro shuffled into the living room, lay on the couch and fell asleep.

The next day, Petro left for work to the sound of his baby crying. When he got to the base he was met with a friendly face.

"New serg wants ya…pronto!" demanded one of the newer soldiers to join their base. Petro cautiously went to the sergeant's office.

"Name's Jones!" he trumpeted, rummaging through drawers looking for something in a hurry. Without looking at Petro, Jones found the file he was looking for and frantically flicked through it.

Chapter 7 – 1954

"You wanted to see me sir?" Petro felt uneasy.

Sergeant Jones peered over his glasses and looked directly into Petro's face. With the early morning sun eager to ascend, Petro discerned beads of sweat forming on the man's bald head. He recognized the sergeant immediately but remained calm.

"Read!" he demanded, hurling a newspaper at Petro.

Petro read.

'A right-wing nationalist guerrilla organisation (EOKA) has begun an armed campaign in support of the end of British colonial rule. Their aim to unify with Greece (ENOSIS) has led to the formation of the Turkish Resistance Organisation (TMT) in support of the partition of Cyprus.'

"D'ya know any of these clowns?" he bellowed.

"No sir."

"You suspect, you come and tell me and me only!" he barked, his bulbous eyes staring deeper into Petro's face. Without blinking he got up from his chair and carefully propped his rifle next to the filing cabinet.

"Er… yes… sir," Petro said nervously.

"Now get to work, you fucking peasant!" He slammed the door behind Petro and continued his search through drawers and cupboards.

Walking to his station, Petro felt a silent panic. His hands trembled as he examined the clipboard with the day's agenda. However, the words became blurred and disorganized, deflecting from his duties. He was perturbed by the ferocity of memories flooding back, on top of an already challenging situation. He stood tall, took a deep breath, and looked towards the sergeant's office. Then, without further hesitation, he went to Rothman's cabinet and carefully took a file, a carton of cigarettes and walked out the building for the last time.

Bewildered and humiliated, he wasn't sure which was worse; the shock of what just happened, or the forthcoming mockery from friends. It was clear in Petro's mind that he couldn't return and risk being recognized from the scene of the most horrific incident he had ever encountered.

That Sunday after church, Christina invited friends and family over to introduce them to the new baby. The celebration of a new life was a joyful occasion.

Petro sat under the mulberry tree with his pals.

"Are you going to work with Christophoro now?" asked his friend Nico.

Petro closed his eyes and took a long silent breath.

"Yes," he sighed.

"I'm glad you came to your senses. You're lucky no one's calling you a traitor," mocked Tasso, the village policeman. He took the last sip of Christophoro's zivania and slowly savoured it with his eyes shut. "Aaaaaah! No one makes zivania like your father-in-law."

"Thank you," said Christophoro, approaching with another bottle. "Petro, tomorrow you can plough the north field and prepare it for root crops." He was relieved to finally get help.

Chapter 7 – 1954

A few minutes later people started to leave the party; Petro watched Nico leave through the side gate.

"Wait! Nico... hold on!"

"What is it, what's wrong?" asked Nico.

"I... er... Well... Nothing," croaked Petro, suddenly changing his mind and absconding into the house. He stared at his work shirt and trousers hanging listless on the wardrobe door. They were no longer a celebration of his success.

"What's the matter son?" Pavlo watched him from the doorway.

"Nothing...nothing I'm fine." Petro sighed, looking at the ground.

"I don't believe you, son. What happened at the base? Did you see someone?" But before Peter could answer, Katerina walked into the room with baby Ariadne and Christina.

"She's got your eyes, Petro." Katerina smiled and buried her face into the baby's swaddling, making her giggle.

A short time later more people were leaving. Tasso was one of the last, finding a quiet moment to discuss more sensitive information with the men. "It's too dangerous for women to go out alone. Even if they walk with us. There are snipers on the edge of the village and the cowards are even targeting women now," he warned. "There's no way of telling if they're rebels, Turks, or British." He adjusted his belt, ready to ride out his shift at the coffee shop.

"God help us all; they'll kill us in our sleep!" said yiayia Stavrou who was listening nearby, and with that, she rushed into the kitchen for a knife.

"Mother, what are you doing?" shouted Christina.

"I'm going to kill the Turks!" she screeched hysterically, waving the knife around. "I'll kill them all with my own two hands."

"Calm down old woman, we'll make sure you're safe!" fumed Christophoro, hoping his words would stay true. "Petro, walk this crazy old woman home before she kills someone!" he hollered. Petro went to help yiayia Stavrou collect her belongings.

"Who are you? Don't touch me, get away… I know you're a spy. I've never seen you before. I'll kill you if you touch me!"

Christina was at the end of her patience.

"Dear God when will this old woman stop…? I guess I'll have to make up a bed for you and you can stay here tonight," she sighed, not wanting to agitate her mother any further. "But stay away from the kitchen, OK, old woman? You promise?" She took the knife away from her mother.

The family slept peacefully that night but the next day brought unaccustomed and unwelcome security measures.

A few weeks later, Christophoro went to meet Petro at his house so they could walk to the north field together, but when he entered the house there was no sign of him.

It was sunrise and Anna was overwhelmed with exhaustion from Ariadne's crying.

"Didn't that lazy scoundrel come home last night?"

Christophoro asked, becoming increasingly impatient.

"I haven't seen him for two days," she revealed, accustomed to her husband's antics. She cradled Ariadne in her arms.

"That boy needs talking to!" he said fiercely. "He knows we have lots to do this week. Tell him to come as soon as he gets home!" Christophoro stormed out of the house. "And don't forget to lock the door behind me!"

"But I'm home today."

"Especially when you're home!"

Christophoro walked past yiayia Stavrou's house, scanning her property for anything suspicious, then ran north towards his field as she appeared from inside.

After her father left, Anna had just managed to get Ariadne off to sleep when there was a knock at the door. Surreptitiously peeking through the window, she saw a somewhat familiar face, and she called from the window, "Do I know you sir?"

"My name is Lucas," he said softly. "I was at school with Petro."

"Ah yes, I've seen you with Petro, please come in."

His clean, neatly pressed trousers and white shirt fit him perfectly, suggesting an income worthy of indulgence and a job of high ranking. He entered the house slowly, looking around in awe.

"You have a lovely home," he said politely.

"Thank you," said Anna curiously. "But I need to ask why you've come here?"

The man sighed and looked at Anna's tired, worried face.

"I… Erm, I… saw Petro yesterday. He was boarding the bus for the port."

"What bus… what port?" Her voice began to tremble.

"He's gone to England!"

He looked down at the marble floor, unable to look her in the eye. Anna gasped.

"What... what are you talking about?! He can't… he…"

The man interrupted her as she grasped for words. "That's all he said. Now I must go. He said something about sending money when he can." The man left in an instant.

Anna stared behind him in case he should come back and inform her it was all a mistake, a silly practical joke.

She was dumbstruck. She'd learned to love him as much as she possibly could; albeit, to what end? She always assumed having done her part, everything would fall into place. Confused, angry and hurt, Anna turned to the newest love in her life.

CHAPTER 8
1956-1960

"Now, try this. This... is the wine of kings!" bragged Christophoro, proudly handing Anna a small sample. Anna sipped the wine and listened to her father's anecdotes. "Didn't they teach you anything in that school? An English king got married in in Limassol. He fell in love with this wine and called it 'the wine of kings and the king of wines.' Silly man had no taste! It's a woman's wine... far too sweet!" he declared, engrossed in his own secret kingdom.

He went outside to adjust the dry palm leaves on the bunker roof.

"That blasted sun always finds a way in!"

Anna felt the coarseness of her father's hand as she handed him a gigantic palm leaf.

"Sometimes I think these leaves are helping to add a sweet earthy taste," he uttered, reaching across the roof. Anna was glad to be outside and away from the acrid air of the bunker. She watched her ageing father climb down strategically stacked rocks, wedged comfortably into the vertical hillside.

"I'll have to adjust the racks, or the bottles will get too warm and explode," he muttered to himself, tweaking a wall fabricated from thick olive branches and willow twine.

Anna looked down at Ari sleeping peacefully in a sling.

"And remember, Anna..."

"Yes father, I know! You don't have to keep telling me. I won't tell anyone how you make your wine," she yawned.

"You need to get to bed, girl." He watched his exhausted daughter adjust her sling. "Take the baby home and I'll see you tomorrow."

Anna walked home in the gentle evening breeze to a blended scarlet and yellow sunset.

Deep in thought, she smiled mischievously, wondering if she should revise her latest poem, inspired by last winter's storm, when rain flushed through the village and cascaded over ledges; kissing the ground before selfishly and effortlessly drenching the land. Anna recited every word in her head and sneakily went to see Azra before going home. The look on Azra's face at the sight of a visitor was staggering. Anna could feel the warmth from her kindred spirit at a glance. Anna didn't often go inside Azra's house, for she couldn't put up with her mother's anger if she found out. "Azra, don't you have any lamps at all?" Anna asked, looking around at the dimly lit hut as four of her six children huddled in the corner like rats.

"It's OK, we're used to it!" she said. Anna could see he whites of her eldest son's eyes staring at her. Now around fourteen years old, Baruk made her feel uncomfortable.

"Have you ever thought about moving to a village with more Turkish Cypriots, Azra? It breaks my heart to see people treat you like this."

"Leave? Goodness, I could never do that. What if the Kallikantzaro got me on the way there and stole my children? What if my husband came back looking for us? No! We will stay and face our fate."

Anna left the hut with a vision of the boy's troubled eyes in her thoughts but exhaustion took over and she rushed home to put Ari to bed.

As soon as she started to warm her hands on a hot cup of aniseed tea, Anna heard a noise on the front porch.

Concealed behind the curtain with her back to the wall, she peeped through the window with her heart pounding in her chest, terrified that someone might be trying to break in. She froze for a moment; for there in the moonlight, she caught sight of a familiar silhouette. Petro was slowly pacing up and down, smoking nervously. For a moment, she wondered whether to let him in; he had been gone for six months with no letter or money and in that time, she had no idea if he was still alive.

"Wait!" she called, quietly unbolting the security locks.

She stared at her husband in the dim light. His hair was tousled, and he smelled of whiskey.

Dark circles under his eyes were enhanced by the lustre of moonlight.

"Aren't you gonna let me in?" he grinned, tossing his cigarette into the front yard.

A surge of adrenaline pumped though Anna's veins.

"Why should I? You're a liar and a cheat! You... you've damaged my father's name! You..."

"Please let me explain. There's something you don't know." He barged his way in. Anna watched him shuffle across the cool marble floor.

"Well? I'm waiting." She stared at him with tight lips.

Petro lay on the sofa where he often slept after a night of drinking. He hesitated.

"I... I missed you and Ari."

Anna glared with disdain.

"You know something? For an educated man you really are stupid! Now, tell me where you were, who you were with and why you came back, or you won't be staying here anymore."

"I...I was in London, Lucas told you, didn't he? I tried to find us a home so we can get away from this mess, I really tried Anna honestly I did, but London is so expensive, I ran out of money...and it's so cold there!" He laughed, trying to make light of the situation.

"So, you decided not to tell me and let me worry... You really are the most selfish creature I have ever come across."

"But I... I wrote to you, Anna; didn't you get my letter... letters?"

Any respect she'd nurtured for him in the short time they'd been married died that night.

The next day Anna woke early and ordered Petro stay in the house while she went to her parents to make excuses for him, afraid of what her father might do. Christophoro was furious. The man he had helped set up a life with his precious daughter was humiliating the family. He stood from the kitchen table, leaving his morning coffee, and rushed to find Pavlo.

He encountered him on his way to the blacksmith's and approached him with righteous indignation and a head full of steam. "I'll be the laughingstock of the village!" he fumed, unleashing his red-hot temper.

Just at that moment cousin Yanni approached with his donkey, on his way to work.

"Hey… Cousin, stop!" he yelled at Christophoro. "This isn't going to solve anything is it?"

"If your boy puts one more step out of place, I'll beat him myself!" Shouted Christophoro, waving his fist in Pavlo's face.

Pavlo's lip trembled. "You have my word, Christophoro; he'll step up and be a man from now on."

Soon after, Petro got a job at the local municipal offices and kept his head down. He tried to win back his father-in-law's respect; but more important for him was to avoid Sergeant Jones, who was still stationed in the village. Every morning, he took the long route to work and was constantly looking over his shoulder. He worked hard and kept to himself. His behaviour seemed dull in comparison to the old days, but Anna began to enjoy the more mature Petro. Maybe he had mended his ways and maybe he really was sorry for what he did? Although his conduct was often erratic, she put that down to his boarding school experience.

Shortly after Ariadne's first birthday, in November 1957, Anna gave birth to a son. Petro's lack of interest led her to choose another name from her side of the family, so she named him Theo after her grandfather.

Anna worked tirelessly, looking after her children, her house and her animals.

Just before Christmas that year, while walking to her parents' house with baby Theo in her arms and Ari skipping along happily, she walked past the blacksmith's workshop. Glancing towards a clearing past the square, between two fig trees, she caught sight of Petro talking to his friend, Nico. She halted for a second, furtively listening to their conversation.

"I've been waiting for him to fix a blade on my father's plough for weeks, he's finally finished!" announced Nico, gently running his finger down the edge of the blade. "Anyway, you never told me why you came back."

"Well... it was very hard." Petro became sheepish. "I couldn't raise enough money."

"I thought you had it all worked out?" Nico was curious.

"Well, I didn't know London was so expensive, no one talks to you and I didn't know what to do with the fi…" he hesitated. "And I… It's so, so cold there. Some days you couldn't see your hand in front of your face from all that smog."

Anna slipped away quietly; her husband was back,

and she didn't want to upset her father by asking awkward questions, so she was happy to carry on as normal.

Sixteen months later, In March 1958, Anna went into labour with her third child. Aliki and her mother were by her side again.

"I didn't see the mad sisters on my way here," said Aliki, curiously. "A bit strange for a Saturday, they're usually walking up and down telling people they're going to hell."

"Ooohh, those three are the devil himself! Does anyone even know how long they've lived on God's earth?" said Christina.

An hour later, Anna delivered another baby girl into the world. The three women celebrated with a glass of Christophoro's best stash of mulberry wine.

"I'll tell your father he drank this batch last year. The stubborn goat will never remember."

The women laughed and raised their glasses to baby Anastasia.

"Here's to my third and last baby!" saluted Anna.

"Huh, we'll see!" Aliki laughed. "Now, I'd better get going! I'll be back to help you tomorrow, Anna." She kissed her best friend on the forehead. "Aristo and the twins will starve if I don't prepare their food."

Aliki walked home past the coffee shop, and to her surprise, almost all the men from the village were huddled around Harri's transistor radio waiting for lunchtime news. It being a Saturday meant British troops could show up any minute. She stood behind the pergola, intimidated by so many men intently fixated on the tiny radio, and listened.

"News just come in that a 17-year-old boy who got caught up in an altercation with a British Grenadier in Cyprus has been shot in the head," intoned the announcer.

Alex's dad yelled, kicking chairs away from under the table. "I'll fight the bastards to death! I'll join the boys of EOKA and fight the bastards till we rid them and the Turks from our home!"

"Was that Stavro's boy?" Aliki heard her father quietly asking Harri.

"I don't know, it's hard to tell."

Tempers flared and discussions became heated. The men raged; trying to piece together gaps in the news and calculate the exact location of the incident.

Aliki paused for a moment, trying to process the implications, then rushed home, feeling unsafe for the first time in her life.

The next two years became fraught with danger all over the island. Doors were kept locked at all times, women were warned not to go anywhere alone, and Tasso was given instructions by a higher authority to report any suspicious behaviour.

Tensions became so high that one Sunday, the priest invited Tasso to make a speech after the liturgy.

"If you've signed up with EOKA, you are putting everyone here at risk!" he declared across the congregation, waving his arms as a mark of his authority. "They don't care who they shoot, and who they recruit!" he continued. The congregation were astonished to hear him speak against EOKA.

"Do you want the British to stay here and continue to bully and murder us? To take all our money and call it tax? To rape our women and think it's OK?" shouted Menelao. His elderly father walked towards him and joined in. The baker and his two sons followed suit.

"Whose side are you on anyway?" roared Harri, and in a flash the atmosphere changed.

"TRAITOR!" they shouted, charging towards the podium.

"ENOUGH!" shouted the priest. "This is the house of God!"

But without hesitation the men charged towards Tasso and wrestled him to the ground in a crazed frenzy.

"ENOUGH!" roared the priest even louder, trying to prize the men apart. "This is the house of God; he is watching us! Now leave my church… immediately… all of you!" His command resounded like the thunderous wrath of Zeus. The men stopped fighting and left the church in silence. The priest went to help Tasso to his feet.

"Leave me, I'm not a child!" Tasso shrugged the priest away and charged after the men while the three mad sisters got on their knees and rocked back and forth, begging for forgiveness. Christina rushed to her elderly mother and took her to Anna's house nearby.

"Why did you bring me here straight after church?" complained yiayia Stavrou. "What have you done with all my friends? Is it him… did he take them away?" she prodded Petro as they all sat down to eat.

"No, yiayia. We're not allowed to gather outside the church anymore!" sighed Anna. "Anyway, didn't you hear the trouble inside?"

"Turks, the lot of them! They're going to steal my water, aren't they?" she panicked.

"Yiayia, no one's going to steal your water."

"They're going to kill me. They know where I live, they're coming for me…" She became hysterical. Anna sat closer to her grandmother and put one arm across her shoulder.

"Why is she crying, Muma? Did the gypsies take her money?" three-year-old Ari asked her mother.

"No darling, don't worry yourself, now go and play with your brother and sister. Here yiayia, have a glass of Dad's special batch, it'll calm you down." Anna nonchalantly passed a glass to her trembling grandmother.

The next day, Anna could hear the slow clip-clop of the cheese man's donkey walking towards her house. She flagged him down.

"This is my last visit to your village," he yowled in his strange accent, pouring kefir into Anna's clay pot. "They've told us we can't trade on our donkeys anymore."

"Why?"

"Why? Why do they do anything?" He chuckled. "They're cheats. They think I'm a millionaire and they want taxes and licenses."

Chapter 8 – 1956-1960

Anna watched him place the cover back on his churn and effortlessly secure the strap. His small frame was not much taller than the donkey's saddle, and he had the same coarse grey hair as his companion. He'd been coming to the village once a month since Anna was a baby and she never even knew his name. She glared at the countless lines on his face while he adjusted the saddle. As she got closer, Anna could see the depth of the wrinkles on his forehead, evidence of his family's bohemian, roaming heritage. She stared at his rough clothing and wondered why she'd never asked about his walks through northern villages in all weather. But somehow, it was too late. Anna's heart felt heavy, knowing this would be the last time she saw him.

"What will you do?" she enquired, looking into his nameless brown eyes. The man shrugged his shoulders.

"They tell me God will provide, but I don't see him anywhere, do you, child? Say goodbye to your mother for me."

Stroking his donkey's mane, the two synchronized as if their existence depended on each other. She watched the old man limp with the soul of a wolf; his presence lingering long after his physical departure.

A few hours later, cousin Stella arrived to help Anna.

"Mum's bus to Varosi was cancelled again yesterday. The one before was stopped and searched by that nasty sergeant and his men!" she said, taking cups from the cupboard for kefir.

"Even the mail has stopped. They're not allowing any large vehicles in, just in case they're smuggling people.

What does God have planned for us?" sighed Stella, passing cups to Anna's children.

"Who knows!" replied Anna, sipping. "Everyone's behaving suspiciously – it's like they're being followed. I can't stand it anymore. I feel like a prisoner in my own home."

"At least you and Petro could go to England and stay with Vasili."

Anna had wanted to go for so long, but not under these circumstances.

"I can't leave my father. He's getting old and there's no one left to help him. Anyway, I have three children to take care of."

Stella started to lay the table for dinner.

"You need to start thinking about yourself and the children Anna. That husband of yours isn't..."

Just then Petro rushed in with a big smile, jingling a bunch of keys.

"Look outside," he smirked.

The women looked at each other then went to the window. They saw a green and white Ford Fairline, parked outside the house.

"Whose is it?" asked Anna.

"Mine... ours! Of course." He grinned, putting his arm across Anna's shoulders.

"But we owe money! We have nothing, and you go and buy a car!"

Anna was furious; Stella thought it best to leave.

"Where did you get the money!" she shouted, knowing full well they had none. Petro ignored her and went outside with a handful of soot to smooth away rust from the passenger door.

From then on, his new toy kept him occupied most evenings and reinstated his popularity.

In February of 1960, Anna sent word to the municipal offices where Petro worked, informing him of the birth of his fourth child. Another daughter.

For two days, nobody had seen or heard from him; and once again, Anna was left with the luxury of choosing a name for her daughter, so she named her Christina, shortening it to Tina, after her mother.

Luckily, transport to and from the village had been restored as a result of Zurich paving the way for peace talks, so Anna could catch the bus to Varosi to register Tina's birth. While her mother looked after the children, Anna relaxed on the bus, excited to get her magazine and money at the same time. What excuse would she use to register Tina's birth alone this time? Maybe since talks were swaying in favour of independence from the British, creating a cheery atmosphere, the government official would be in good spirits and not question her too much. Anna had become used to thinking on her feet.

"I've come to register my daughter's birth," remarked Anna to the clerk behind the desk, in the same building she collected her mail.

"Where's the father?" questioned the clerk, astonished to see a lone woman embarking on such an important enterprise.

"He's... he's a policeman, and he's still at work."

"Lady, we have strict rules here!" recalled a tall thin man, pushing his glasses back up his horsey nose. "What if you weren't married...hmmm...what then?"

Anna looked at the clock above the wall; it was ten minutes to one. Unfortunately, there wasn't a queue of people this time.

"Look there he is!" she announced, pointing to a policeman outside who was talking to the senior clerk. "Do you want me to call him in, away from your boss?" she asked, assertively staring back at him.

"Oh, er... no! I'll get the paperwork."

After registering her baby's birth, Anna went for a cup of tea in a nearby café, weary from raising four young children. A day to herself was a very welcome treat even though It was the middle of February and cold, so the place was almost empty. Anna sat inside with a hot glass of tea and tried to relax but her peripheral vision revealed a group of men staring in her direction. One was shaking his head and tutting. She looked on, feeling confident he didn't know her family so she didn't care.

As she began to unwind and flick through her magazine with excitement, Anna looked through the grimy window at the street outside and saw what looked like Petro's car. She leaned forward, making sure not to touch the glass, and saw a tall, grey-haired man getting out. Anna put down her magazine and rushed out of the café.

"What are you doing with my husband's car?" she asked the middle-aged man sternly. Something wasn't right, he looked too old to have stolen it. Anna's heart suddenly raced at the prospect of Petro having disappeared again. For as much as she wanted to know the answer, another part of her dreaded hearing it.

"What are you talking about, lady? This is my car. I bought it yesterday from a man who said he was going to England. Are you calling me a thief, woman?

"No… no I'm not. Did he say when he was going? Did he have bags wi…?"

The man laughed in her face then looked at his elderly mother who was struggling to get out of the passenger side and went to help her. "And if you see that crook again, tell him I want my money back!" he shouted at Anna. She went back inside the coffee shop to collect her magazine and saw the half dozen or so men laughing at her; it wasn't the first time she had been laughed at. She walked to the bus stop feeling like her insides had been ripped from her body. Yet again he betrayed her. Yet again she felt like a fool, and yet again she would have to face the humiliation towards her family.

The following day, Christophoro went to confront Pavlo, incensed by the situation. With the ferocity of a barbarian on a mission, he headed towards Pavlo's cottage. He felt his thick handlebar moustache twitch with rage. Determined to beat Pavlo if he had to, Christophoro approached the cottage at the edge of the village, oblivious to the caked mud on his boots and legs from wading through puddles.

Reaching the small courtyard, he heard the nanny goat bleating in desperation, under the shelter of an orange tree. A family of rats scurried away at the sound of Christophoro's heavy boots while hungry chickens shuffled in a frenzy, desperately searching for food. Christophoro rigorously pushed the front door with his stick, but the cottage was empty. Katerina and Pavlo had taken all their possessions and fled like thieves in the night, as swiftly as they had arrived, and with no explanation. Christophoro punched the door repeatedly, swearing he'd find both father and son and break their legs.

He spent the next few days in his wine bunker, trying to avoid more gossip about his family.

"Dad, it's not your fault!" called Anna, picking the dry palm leaves from puddles outside.

"GO AWAY!" He shouted loud and clear.

"Father please, there... there's other news... It's good news, it's about..."

"GO AWAY," he shouted even louder. Anna left her father to calm down.

The next few months saw a ray of light. Talks were leaning in favour of independence and the village waited patiently for more news.

However, Anna was beginning to question her own future. She'd been feeling lonelier lately and there was only one person in the village who could empathize with her situation.

Bedraggled and sleep deprived, Anna got up early the next morning and walked discreetly to Azra's house, hoping they were still friends after the turmoil between Greek and Turkish Cypriots. To her, Azra wasn't an enemy or a spy or an evil spirit. She was her friend. But as she brushed past overgrown vines to the entrance where the young woman often stood, smiling and trying to befriend people, she heard a voice.

"Are you looking for Azra?"

"Oh! Yes!" yelped Anna, surprised to see one of the mad sisters there. The old lady was picking young prickly pear flowers to decorate the church.

"She went to Turkey, she went to Turkey…" the mad sister repeated, cackling at the sound of her own voice. "God will punish her; he will punish all of us; he is here!" Her sister suddenly appeared from behind the cactus and together they performed another epic religious rant about God's wrath towards all sinners. Anna thought it best to go home.

In August 1960 there was cause for celebration all over the island.

"I never thought this day would come!" Harri seemed positively merry. "I don't have to serve those damn animals in my shop anymore." His body was now almost completely disabled, but it didn't stop him from climbing on tables to hang decorations.

"What in God's name are those?" asked Mr Onassis, now retired and living alone in Pavlo and Katerina's old cottage.

"Aaah, you youngsters have no idea about making do! You think money grows on trees! I spent hours making this chain from classical linen. Anyway, I hope everyone comes today, I need to sell all this beer I bought," he mumbled, weaving the tattered linen bunting between vines and draping it across the counter.

Later that afternoon, Anna's family went to the celebrations; even Christophoro found the courage to look his friends and neighbours in the eye without the burden of quiet humiliation on such a historic day.

"Ah Christophoro, who knew we were going to finally rid our shores of those British bastards!" Said Yanni. "Come and share one of Harri's disgusting beers with me, the old fool's watered it down, he thinks we haven't noticed."

Yanni embraced his cousin.

"You never finished those steps in Anna's house," he reminded Yanni.

"Now! Now, you old fool! You think now is a good time to talk about the steps? We've just won independence from the British and you want to talk to me about steps!"

Anna watched them and tried to think of a time they were together, without an argument.

"Can you believe it?" said cousin Stella, beaming. "Harri's giving away free coffee today!"

"That because there's not many of us here!" Aliki's

father interjected. "The stingy old goat knows most people are celebrating in the capital."

"Aaaaah, independence!" affirmed Yanni, slowly sipping his beer and smiling nostalgically at his cousin. "Look old man, I promise I'll go there tomorrow and fix it."

He grabbed Christophoro's head and kissed him loudly on the forehead. Christophoro rolled his eyes.

"We have to look forward now," said Christophoro, immersing himself in the conversation, relieved no one was interested in his family affairs.

The priest sat nurturing his coffee in the corner, listening to the conversation. Tasso came on duty and sat next to him with a beer; he pulled his chair closer.

"So how long do you think independence will last?" he whispered.

"Only God knows. But Father Alexander from St Nicholas tells me some of his congregation still want to fight for ENOSIS. They think it's only a matter of time before Turkey invades. We've left ourselves wide open!"

The priest watched them dance into the early hours of the morning, eager to listen to anything and everything they had to say. He went home praying peace would last and begged the Lord for no blood to be spilled in his village; now and in the future.

CHAPTER 9

1962-63

"I don't want to get stung… Mumma, the bees are angry, I don't want to get nearer!" Seven-year-old Ari stood back from the hives, nervously pacing on the spot.

"Don't worry, you're protected. We can't leave Azra's hives – if we don't take the honey, someone else will. Besides, it fetches a good price at the market!" Anna's muffled voice could just about be heard behind her mask.

"But bapoo Christophoro sells bottles and bottles of his red juice. Isn't that enough?"

"No, it's not! Come here, take the frame so we can put the lid back on the hive; quickly before the bees get agitated."

Quickly and nervously, Ari got closer to the hives in what used to be Azra's yard. Anna left her to drain the honey while she went her mother's house collect a fresh batch of her delicious spinach pies and olive bread.

"Father, have you packed the wine yet?

"I'll be ready by sunrise tomorrow… Just be on time or we'll miss the morning's rush," he shouted from the stable. "I don't know where people are getting money from these days, but make sure you take plenty of your mother's pies this time. We ran out last week."

"OK, I'll, see you tomorrow."

Early the next morning, Christina arrived to look after the children while Anna and her father made their way to the newly prospering Varosi. Anna enjoyed going to the market. Her life was finally taking a turn for the better. Being financially self-sufficient from selling so much honey and her own recipe for koupes, meant she was in charge of her own life for once. I don't understand why no one has put koupes on a stick before, she sniggered to herself. I may try koftes on a stick next time to see if they sell as well. Annas confidence was soaring for the very first time in her life and she had no time to listen to gossip and rumours about where her rightful place should be.

Anna and her father arrived at the market as the sun was beginning to warm the earth. The town square was filled with traders from neighbouring villages. People unloaded donkey saddles, tractors and hand pulled carts, taking advantage of the sudden upturn in the economy. Anna marvelled at the sight and sound of people from ethnic backgrounds she had no idea were living on the island. She could see different Muslims sects, Christians and even the occasional Yazidi group, originally from Kurdistan, celebrating their food and crafts. It reminded her of the bazar in the Ali Baba illustrations she once saw in her early reading books.

At the end of a busy day, timing it to perfection to get the best deals, Anna took some money from her apron.

"Father, wait for me before packing up," she said in a hurry.

Her father rolled his eyes.

"Don't rob them like you did last week, girl!"

"They're tired, father! Besides, they don't want to take all that stock back home, do they? I'll offer them a fair price, I promise!"

Twenty minutes later, Anna came back with an arm full of books, flour, fresh fish and a winter coat for Tina.

"You're sinful, girl!" her father laughed.

Their load home was far lighter, in more ways than one. The void Anna once felt impossible to crawl out of, had vanished. Now she was consumed with hope for the future and instead of breathing with her heart, she was venturing with her head. They got back late that evening, exhausted but content.

"I've decided to buy a cot for baby Tina with some of my profit," Christophoro said softly. "She needs a bed, your mother can wait for the linen."

A few days later, Anna was scurrying to make space for the cot when she heard something roll along the bedroom floor. She looked down and saw her old butter tin. Surprised, she carefully picked it up and pulled out the roll of papers. She found the first poem she ever wrote for the English soldier; it seemed crude in comparison to her capabilities now. Remembering every moment and every emotion as she read, Anna affectionately put it back in the tin and found a better hiding place in the house she had grown to love.

Chapter 9 – 1962-63

The next day, Aliki arrived to help Anna with the morning routine.

"Oh… finally, your four-year-old has a bed. You have room in your bed to turn at night," laughed Aliki. She went to the kitchen to help Anna with breakfast. "Do you even know where Petro is these days?" she enquired quietly.

Anna sheepishly carried laundry through to the kitchen.

"Aren't you angry, Anna? It's been almost four years!" Aliki suddenly changed the conversation when four hungry children came barging in for tea and toast.

"What about your poems and stories?"

Anna shook her head.

"They fired me, said they weren't receiving my mail regularly."

"For heaven's sake! Don't they realize the troubles we've had here?" Aliki seethed.

"I guess they don't care," sighed Anna.

"I'll see the children get ready for school," said Aliki.

And with the kind of exhaustion that had nothing to do with sleep but everything to do with her situation, Anna took four-year-old Tina by the hand and departed for her mother's house.

On arrival she could see cousin Yanni sitting in her father's favourite chair in the courtyard.

"This is very strange," he mumbled to himself, staring at a newspaper. He sipped his tea and waited for Christophoro to join him with a bowl of bread and olives.

"What is?"

"There's a description of a village here that sounds like ours. How did these people know about the riot in our church? There's also something here about a missing file. The description really sounds like our village!" he retorted, frowning as he read on.

"How about using that wild imagination to solve my roof problem instead!" complained Christophoro, spitting olive pips out onto the cobbles.

"Stop telling me what to do, old man! I told you I'll get around to it!" Yanni suddenly exploded.

"You've been saying that for months." Christophoro's moustache began to twitch.

"Then do it yourself, selfish old man!" Yanni stood abruptly, scraping the chair legs on the cobbles, and left the cosy courtyard. Christina rolled her eyes.

"You two are worse than gypsy boys!"

"Aha! I know why you're here, poking your nose into my business! You're looking out for those gypsies, aren't you? What do you think they're going to do to you? They just want food, tell them to go away if they come begging!" Said Christophoro.

"What's going on?" Anna enquired, out of breath from the brisk walk. Christophoro laughed heartily and beckoned his granddaughter to sit on his lap.

"It's winter solstice, and the damn gypsies work for the Kallikantzaro, you know that!" Christina looked at her husband with scorn. "They'll come from underground and steal our grandchildren if we're not careful." She looked at

Tina with a smidgeon of affection.

"For heaven's sake, old woman! Do you still believe in that nonsense? Sometimes I think independence has made this village backward!"

He stormed off to his bunker with Tina over his shoulder. Meanwhile, with Anna's help, Christina continued to fill her basket with fallen leaves and orange blossom, ready for the compost heap.

Moments later, with Tina still over his shoulder, Christophoro emerged again.

"I'm going to collect the birds for dinner," he said playfully, cherishing the time with his granddaughter. Tina giggled from his shoulder, staring at the distant ground below.

As they approached a clearing in the trees, Christophoro looked up.

"There… there they are… Ahhh, we timed it just right! We have a great catch!" He pointed to a handful of sticks, wedged discreetly amongst the branches.

"What bapoo, what did you catch?" Tina looked high into the trees.

"Look closely!" he whispered. "See there?"

"Where bapoo?"

"There between the leaves" He pointed excitedly.

Tina looked up and saw four dead birds, hanging upside down on a perch.

"How did you do that bapoo? Do you have magic like yiayia?"

"No, it's not magic, it's my sticky sticks that catch the birds. You just have to know when and where to put them. Now, reach up and grab them!"

Tina manoeuvred herself into the expanse above the lowest branches. She looked around the half-tree, half-sky world and marvelled at the freedom to look at the heavens and possibly touch an angel at night when no one was looking.

"Hurry! you're getting heavy," her grandfather grunted.

"They keep sticking to my fingers bapoo. I can't get them off... Help me, they're going to pull my fingers off, bapoo help!" she screamed.

"Don't panic! They're not going to pull your fingers off, silly girl," he chuckled. "It's just gum from the trees I wrapped on the sticks; it won't hurt you. It traps the birds so they can't get away and we can eat them for dinner."

Tina briskly shook her hands, enabling a dead quail to plummet onto her leg.

"Aaaahhh, bapoo they're attacking me! Help me!" She wriggled in her panic. Christophoro couldn't stop laughing and lost control. The two fell to the ground, laughing hysterically.

"Is it because I used my left hand bapoo?"

"No, don't believe that nonsense your grandmother tells you!" he declared, packing the birds into his pouch.

"Here, jump back up." He lifted her back on his shoulders and they went home singing songs they didn't know the words to.

Chapter 9 – 1962-63

The next day, the morning ritual began over again in Anna's house.

"OK, I fed the chickens and there's a bowl of beautifully ripe peppers on the table. I'll just finish these dishes before leaving," cousin Stella said hurriedly.

"Oh, thanks Stella… Theo, stop! Anastasia, where's your... Hurry up or you'll be late for school, you three!" she shrieked.

"Mumma, do I have to go to yiayia Christina's today?" whined Tina.

"Of course you do. How else am I going to work?" Anna knelt down and buttoned Tina's cardigan.

"Can I come with you instead, please Mumma?"

"Tina, we go through this every morning… Now stop! I have to work."

"Can I go to school instead then? Please Mumma?"

"Tina stop, I have to go now," she implored, wishing more than anything to be with her children rather than harvesting carob syrup.

Tina despised the walk to yiayia Christina's house.

"But Tasso's dog always tries to eat me!" She started to cry as everyone fled from the house and went in different directions.

Tina dawdled towards her grandmother's house. Tasso's German Shepherd had taunted her ever since the day she set eyes on him as a puppy; even then he was on a leash. She mooched around the curving fence, walking through muddy paths and silt, and tried to be brave.

This time I'm going to be really quiet, so he won't hear me, she thought as she tiptoed towards the narrow alley behind Tasso's back yard. His reinforced fence, strengthened to protect his family during the days of unrest, had become synonymous with danger for Tina.

She took off her shoes and walked timidly; anxious not to wake the monster. But somehow, the psychic dog heard her…again! Terrified, she let out a strangulated whimper and froze with her back against the fence, where he couldn't see her. She remained frozen for an age, listening to his wet nose sniff along the bottom of the fence, hungry to get to her. Tina sat on the ground as quiet as she could possibly be and waited. The silky dust on the ground felt comforting against her cheek and slowly her eyes began to close.

Sometime later, she woke to the sound of mysterious chanting by old ladies dressed in black, looking over her. She'd only heard this type of chanting once before, at a memorial service in the cemetery, where people made strange gestures between the coffin and the sky, wailing like injured animals. Tina was mystified. Had she died? If so, was this heaven or hell?

"Aaah, thank Jesus and Mary you're alright!" Christina sputtered, wiping sweat, mud and mucus from Tina's face.

This is nice, thought Tina.

"She's alive!" She heard great-grandmother Stavrou's, high-pitched voice screech across the room as she hobbled towards the bed with her walking stick and a bottle of olive oil. "Let's thank the Lord and praise him!" she shouted, looking towards the sky, while yiayia Christina painted the sign of the cross with olive oil on Tina's forehead. Aliki's mum came rushing in from the kitchen.

"Praise the Lord and all his glorious work!" she rejoiced, stroking a confused four-year-old's hand. Tina daren't tell them she felt fine, they might smack her for making fun of them. So, she decided to spend the morning in her grandmother's bed being pampered like a goddess.

A little while later, she heard yiayia Christina walking across the courtyard; Tina stopped looking out the window and pounced back into bed just as the chunky wooden door opened and let in a sharp beam of light.

"Here, drink this," Christina said and smiled, holding a bowl of bean and spinach soup. Tina stared at the soup, then looked to her grandmother's wrinkles, fascinated by the lines that appeared and disappeared as she went from speech to silence.

"Oh, er, yiayia, I'm feeling much better now!"

"Well, that's great news. I'll leave the bowl here and you can come to the kitchen when you're ready, my sweet child."

Tina turned her nose up at the soup. She was bored. She got out of bed and slowly walked through the courtyard to the kitchen. She could hear her grandfather's voice as he prepared to depart.

"Damn it, woman, why did you leave my boots outside? The stupid chickens have been pecking at them and destroyed the laces!"

Tina sat at the table trying to look sickly, but she was thirsty. Her grandfather's lunch sat wrapped in a linen tea towel, next to a bottle of water. Without asking, Tina pulled off the cork and gulped a huge mouthful. But an overwhelming flood of coughing and spluttering choked her. Christophoro let out a thunderous laugh.

"It serves you right for not asking!" he roared from the door behind her.

Christina raced into the room. "Dear virgin Mary!" she yelled at the top of her voice. You think it's funny to let her drink ouzo? You're a disgrace, now get out of my sight!" she screamed, shoving her giant husband out of the room.

Christophoro picked up his lunch and went to work. Christina could still hear his raucous laughter down the street.

"And don't come home till you grow up!" She screamed.

"Here baby girl, have some orange preserve, it'll help take the taste away." Christina sympathetically passed Tina a plate of her favourite dessert.

This has been a really nice day! thought Tina.

After a rare day of luxury, she eventually had to leave her grandmother's house. But it meant she had to cross the courtyard and bypass 'Big Red the Second' to get to the gate. Her ploy was to wait until he was at the far end of the courtyard then run to the gate as fast as possible. She stared at the cockerel for an eternity, waiting for him to strut to the far side; then she braced herself. A rush of adrenalin spurred her across the courtyard, past clucking hens and aiming for safety. But Big Red was too fast for her and yiayia Christina came the rescue for a third time that day. She belted the aggressive cockeral away in true heroic, yiayia style, grabbed her granddaughter and took her into the house.

"Perhaps the day wasn't so good after all," thought Tina. Half an hour later, it really was time to leave.

"Right, now you can walk slowly and he won't hurt you, he's asleep in the corner."

"But yiayia he will see me, he hates me." Tina cried.

"Learn to face your fears child! Now go. If he runs after you kick him hard."

Tina tiptoed across the dusty courtyard but at the halfway point, she heard the cockerel fly towards her, as angry as she was scared. He landed on her shoulder and flapped his wings in her face and against her back in a frenzied attack. Tina screamed so loud the cockerel became startled and with one brisk punch, Tina pushed him away and fled home with scratches on her arms and face.

A few minutes later, Tina was relieved to approach her own house. She could see her mother frantically coming towards her from the opposite direction. Tina's eyes lit up as she skipped towards her mother. But Anna seemed disconcerted and started to run. With haste, she took Tina by the hand and rushed into the house.

"I've told her a million times to get rid of that wretched beast!" she said angrily, examining Tina's scratches. But something more pressing prioritised her actions. She went into the kitchen and took bread, butter, mint, aniseed and a small coffee pot. "We need to go outside the mud hut and wait for your brother and sisters to get home from school," she said hastily. "Now go, if it's been flooded take no notice, it can't harm you!"

Tina rushed to the garden and poked her head inside the dark, dank hut. She sat on a stool, away from the yellowish-brown puddles; though confused, she wasn't afraid, for her mother was there (and from then on, the smell of sodden earth brought back a fond memory of that day).

"I'll light the fire and we can make toast," said Anna nervously.

In lieu of an explanation, her mother made aniseed and mint tea with extra sugar. Tina didn't understand what was happening but didn't ask questions when it meant she could have yet another sweet treat. She sat quietly and drank every drop of sweet tea, watching a small beam of late afternoon light peek through the window, detecting yellowish puddles with remnants of decaying orange peel that once hung from the ceiling to dry. A faint whisper of citrus tried to reach her.

Her mother once told her, "The secret is to cut the peel in a continuous spiral. Then I'll hang it up in the hut to dry. We can add it to your bath water to smell nice, and if we put it in the drawers, it'll make your clothes smell nice too. If we're lucky, yiayia Christina will make some of her special orange and honey cake with it."

Soon her siblings arrived, and the family remained in the hut toasting bread and drinking tea. Tina was so comfortable to be surrounded by the people she loved, she quietly fell sleep with her head on Anastasia's lap. But it wasn't long before they heard a resounding thump on the front door of the main house. Anna dropped the toasting bread and rushed to the front door.

"All of you stay here!" she demanded; her voice trembled.

The children looked at each other in wonder, waiting for their mother to return. Anna rushed up the back steps to the kitchen and went through the house. The knocking became so persistent, she thought it would break the door down.

The children listened to undertones of unfamiliar voices that quickly escalated in a crescendo of hysteria. Eventually Ariadne and Theo went to investigate. Anastasia dusted the toasted bread from the floor and nibbled between the soggy parts.

"What's happening?" asked Tina, suddenly awake and rubbing her eyes.

"I don't know," Anastasia said with a mouth full of toast. The two girls looked at each and followed their siblings into the main house and hid under the dining table.

Tina saw three dark, emaciated women at the door. Their sweaty, leathery skin resembled the hide of weather-beaten animals that roamed the streets. In true nomadic style, the women wore ragged clothing, each layer covering holes in the one beneath. Tina had been warned by her mother and grandmother about gypsies who stole children and threw them in quilts over their shoulders, and sure enough, their quilts bulged to exactly the size of a small child.

Anna believed stories of gypsies from south of the island venturing north when they were hungry, to feed their addiction for human flesh. To her knowledge, this was the first time they had passed through her village. The women were dishevelled, barefoot and hungry.

"Give us food and shelter or you will go to hell!" the eldest woman demanded in a strange Romany accent. Anna refused and tried to push the door shut. But the more she refused them, the angrier the women became, squealing and howling like banshees, cursing her and her family.

"You'll burn in hell if you don't let us in, lady!" shrieked the tallest. But as the gypsy moved her haggard body towards Anna, Ariadne's head overflowed with wild seething and she rushed to her mother's aid and stood by her side, ready to protect her.

Anna's fear and anger rapidly reared to the surface at the sight of her daughter.

"Go to hell and stay there, daughters of Satan!" she screeched at the top of her voice, punching the woman hard with a tight fist and drawing blood. Unaware of her suppressed emotions, she ignited into a rage like a volcanic eruption.

"You'll never take my children!" she shouted, chasing them down the street with a broomstick. Anna's gentle personality unleashed a mysterious force she had no control over. She kicked and threw stones at the gypsies to safeguard her children.

"I'll kill you if you come near my children again, you cannibals!"

She yelled so loud, the neighbours came out to witness the scene.

"Mum stop!" cried Theo tugging at her dress. The gypsies fled down the street looking confused and angry.

By now the mulberry tree was so big that its branches reached onto Anna's small front porch. Its branches that were like a red and green waterfall in summer were now transformed by winter into bare, spindly, witch-like knuckles, swaying majestically towards the ground. Its infinite wisdom and grace absorbed village gossip while young spies listened from their bedroom window at night. Christophoro and his friends sat on the porch, listening for news between the radio's hissing and screeching.

Tina lay in her bed watching her siblings pretend they could understand the discussions outside, then stared into the sky, entranced by the millions of stars and wondered, "Do they have stars in England?" as she fell asleep to the words Greece, Turkey, and war.

CHAPTER 10
1964

"Mamma…where's my father?" Theo constantly questioned his mother.

"He's working abroad."

"Where? Where, is he working? Why isn't he here to take care of us like Alexi's dad? Was he killed by British soldiers?"

"Where did you get that idea?"

"The boys at school are calling him a traitor. I hate him!"

Theo, now eight years old, needed answers.

"What! Your father's not a traitor; you go and tell them that!" she scolded.

"I saw soldiers with guns outside the school gates again. Are they looking for him? Why don't you tell me anything?" he screamed at his mother.

Anna was at a loss. Theo stormed out the back door and slammed it shut.

"They're not looking for your father, they're here to keep peace!" she yelled behind him, wondering how her eight-year-old could understand a situation even she didn't understand.

Chapter 10 – 1964

"What's all the shouting about?" Christophoro approached with freshly baked bread and a newspaper, but before Anna could answer, he felt compelled to warn her of a subject more pressing. "Trouble's brewing again... There's rumour of extremist EOKA snipers hiding in the mountains, blackmailing people into joining. They're threatening anyone who might tell the authorities. Also, Yanni just told me the U.N. have made the decision to shut down all markets and public gatherings in case there are riots."

"Oh, dear God, not again! How will we make a living?"

"I don't know what to tell you! I'm just an old man who has to work until the day he dies. Unless they kill me first!" He thumped into a chair, stretched his aching back and rotated his shoulders.

"Do you think Theo could be targeted?"

"Don't be ridiculous, girl, he's eight years old... Anyway, I'll talk to him later."

Later that day, cousin Stella and Aliki sat with Anna on her porch preparing vegetables for dinner.

"I'm really worried about my father," Stella whispered.

"What do you mean?" Anna stared down at her bowl of aubergines, making sure she cut them as thin as possible.

"Well... he's behaving very strangely lately. Sometimes I see him sneaking out the house at night!" They stopped and looked at each other. A stony silence fell between them. Stella quickly changed the subject. "How are you coping anyway?"

"We have very little food left so I have to sell the goats. This is the last of the vegetable crop for the season," sighed Anna.

"Oh dear, I hadn't realized it was that bad," Aliki empathized, returning from the kitchen. "I'll walk you to yiayia Stavrou's house if you need to take her some food."

"Thanks, my father would go mad if he heard I walked alone after five o'clock."

The three women finished prepping their vegetables and placed their trays in Anna's oven.

"It's my turn bake tomorrow. Do you have enough flour, Stella?" Aliki enquired.

"Yes, I think so. I have to bake a bit extra for my mother though." Stella closed the oven door with caution. "I don't think I could ever get used to these modern gas ovens, Anna. I prefer the old clay dome outside. I can see exactly what's inside without opening a door and being blasted by a cloud of heat. What if it catches fire? It's inside your house. Don't you worry?"

"No, not at all!" Anna laughed. "It's much better, it means I can stay inside when it's raining."

The women walked to yiayia Stavrou's house, alert and brimming with unfounded confidence. They found yiayia Stavrou, now in her eighties, sitting next to her water urn outside the hut.

"Yiayia, why are you outside, sitting here alone…? It's not safe, now go inside!"

"What?"

Chapter 10 – 1964

"I said it's not safe," Anna repeated louder, gently taking her grandmother by the arm.

"I don't want those smelly Turks stealing my water!" she aimed her stick in the direction of her water urn. "And I'm not moving in with your mother! You can't make me! The woman's impossible." She pulled away from Anna and walked inside.

"I'm not, yiayia, I've brought your dinner."

"Who are those two women with you?" she shrieked. "Are they spies?" She shuffled towards a tin she left by her bedside. They can't have my bread!" She clasped her tin close to her chest.

"No yiayia, it's your great-niece Stella and Aliki... You remember Aliki, don't you? You taught her how to embroider. You told her she was as good as you!" The girls laughed.

"Well, she looks like a spy... Tell her to leave!" Anna took her confused grandmother's hand, sat her at the table with a fresh plate of food and kissed her cheek.

"Don't worry, you're safe, yiayia, now get some hot food in you. I'm leaving now, do you need anything else before I go?"

"What?"

"I said I'm leaving now. Do you need anything else?"

"Where's Vasili? Why hasn't he come to see me? Selfish boy!"

Anna rolled her eyes while her spirited grandmother mumbled between mouthfuls of food.

"OK then… I'll see you tomorrow, yiayia."

The women walked the short distance back to Anna's house, listening to the soothing liturgy of an afternoon service. Anna instinctively glanced towards her old childhood secret mountain hideout but was puzzled; her rocks looked different. Instead of three rocks side by side with a wistful breeze and childish dreams whispering between them, she saw a mound of soil between them, with what looked like the shadow of a man trying – not very successfully – to hide.

"Did you see that?" she asked the girls, pointing to the mountain.

"See what?" Stella looked around, suddenly alert.

"I thought I saw someone up there…looking down at us."

They stood staring for a moment.

"I don't see anything, is it that wild imagination of yours, Anna?" Aliki laughed. The girls looked away and strolled back home in silence.

When Anna's three eldest children left for school the next day, she had a busy day of chores lined up.

"I'm sorry Tina, but I have to sell mamma goat and her three kids. There's a man on his way to collect them."

"But Roz is my best friend!" Tina's eyes began to water.

"I'm sorry, baby, she has to go with the other three. We need the money."

"But Roz is pink, she's a magical goat." Tina cried, referring to the colour of the kid's skin. "Who will I play with when she's gone?" She rushed outside and found Roz grazing under the mulberry tree.

"Come… come on," Tina whispered, quietly trying to shoo Roz to the back of the mud hut and hide her away so she could stay. Roz, clearly preferring to chew tasty morsels from the ground, refused to budge. Anna watched Tina from the kitchen window and went outside.

"You're starting school in a few days, now go and practice your numbers! You know they won't let you in if you can't count to twenty!"

"Yes, Mamma. And I'm picking things up with my right hand now, honest I am! Yiayia said only the devil uses his left hand to write with. I don't know how the devil can see me; doesn't he have bad people to look at instead?"

Anna tried hard not to laugh. She sat in the shade of the mulberry tree waiting for the buyer, enjoying a short reprieve in her tireless endeavours to provide food for her family. She closed her eyes for a moment and thought about her mother's archaic superstitions.

"If you don't smack her left hand, then I will! She'll soon learn!" Christina kept insisting.

"Mother, I'm not smacking my child, those days are gone, no one cares if people write left-handed anymore!"

"Then I'll do it myself, as no one cares anymore!" She would sulk and walk away in a huff.

"You will NOT smack my child… Do you hear me?" Anna had yelled back, observing how much like yiayia Stavrou her mother was becoming. Still, her mother wouldn't heed her words and Tina kept coming home with a sore left hand.

Moments later, Tina watched from the kitchen window as a man in a suit herded their four hungry goats away. Partial to the flare on his trousers, he struggled to usher them away with his foot and keep his clothes intact. Anna went inside the house with a handful of money.

Darn, she thought, I forgot to take the oil lamp to yiayia Stavrou, and the nights are getting longer. Someone has to take it before she goes into a rage. With everything that went on that day, Anna forgot about the curfew.

"Tina can you take the lamp from the kitchen table to yiayia Stavrou's house? But you must come straight back, I think there's a storm coming."

"How can you tell, Mamma? Do you have special powers like yiayia Christina?"

Anna scooped her four-year-old in her arms, took her outside and pointed to the sky.

"See that grey cloud? It's a long way from the blue sky at the moment, but it's moving. Now hurry up before it gets here!"

Tina rushed to the kitchen table, took the lamp safely in her arms and bolted to her great-grandmother's house.

She skipped happily for a while with thoughts of starting school, then suddenly became distracted by the chatter and whirring of sewing machines from Eleni's shop. A young woman came out of the building and dumped scraps in a pile by the water urn. With the sun still shining and warming her face, Tina waited for her to go back inside; then the mesmerizing colours beckoned her. First she placed the lamp carefully on the ground, then went to examine them.

Without warning, a thunderous crash echoed across the sky as if it was about to fall and crush her to death. The sky darkened with angry clouds, pushing and racing above her head.

She grabbed the lamp, but it slipped from her tiny fingers and shattered on a rock.

Not sure which was scarier; her mother's wrath or the dark clouds, Tina picked up pieces of broken glass and started to run. But the darkness and heavy rain made everything look different.

"It's him!" she thought, as tears ran down her cheeks and merged with the rain that bounced off her face, feeling like a horseman's whip. "He knows I've been lying… he knows I'm still left-handed!" Blinded by a storm of tears, she ran through puddles, occasionally looking up at the angry clouds, hoping the devil would spare her from being swallowed whole.

Meanwhile, as soon as Tina had left, Anna had taken the money to her father's house and placed it on the table.

"Well done!" he whispered. "You got a good price for the goats!"

"No, it cost me more than that in guilt!" she whispered back.

"What?"

"I said take the money for flour and corn."

Christophoro tied the money in a handkerchief and put it in his pocket.

"Tina's starting school in a few days," she spoke emptily.

"Yes, I know, but Anna, we have to face facts. We may have to leave the island."

"Oh, not again! Father, I don't know what to think anymore. What will be will be, I'm tired of fighting. I'm tired of gossip about Petro and I'm tired of the thought of another war. I'm tired of doing it all myself. I'm tired of being stuck in the middle. What do they want this time? Our souls? Our children? This is a small island, why does everyone want a piece of it?"

"Hush, girl! The neighbours can hear you."

"I don't care… I don't care about any of it anymore!"

She looked at the headlines in her father's newspaper.

'Turkey's military invasion averted as robust warning comes from USA. President Lyndon Johnson fears such action would lead to war between Turkey and Greece.'

Rain began to fall, Anna looked up at the sky. It's come earlier than I expected, she thought, then suddenly remembered the curfew. I have to check if Tina's back. Oh God, I should've gone myself.

She stood abruptly without telling her father, knowing he would be angry at her forgetfulness, and hurtled out the gate. The rain rapidly turned torrential, the sky darkening by the second. Something didn't feel right. Anna stood in the middle of the road, drenched and gasping for breath.

Chapter 10 – 1964

"TINA…TINA!" she screamed at the top of her lungs then started to run.

Ashamed of her bad judgement and forgetfulness, she reminded herself to breathe. Was her child lost? Taken by gypsies before winter solstice? Stolen by marauders in uniforms after curfew?

As the rain tapped on her head and trickled into her hands, she ran even faster like Demeter in search of Persephone, and she would run farther than hell if she had to.

At last, she heard the sweet sound of her four-year-old's cry in an abandoned tractor outside the church. Anna found her under the canopy, curled in a foetal position, clasping the lamp. Her arms, face and legs were covered in blood and mud. Tina looked up at her mother.

"Mamma, I'm so sorry... I… broke it," she confessed, shivering in a mini swamp where there was once a seat.

Anna held out her arms and tenderly picked up her child.

"It doesn't matter anymore, she doesn't need it." Anna burned with guilt, releasing broken glass from Tina's right hand.

Anna didn't speak of the incident to anyone; but the next day, she took Tina to visit the weekly doctor. Ashamed she might be seen and have to provide answers, Anna arrived early. She found him setting up surgery behind a screen in a corner of the post office.

"Come in, come in," he ushered, squeezing past filing cabinets filled with criminal records, births, deaths and overdue taxes.

"How did this child get such an injury?" he asked, sipping on his coffee.

"I… Er, I can't pay you!" Anna quickly changed the subject.

"So what's new in this backward village?!" he retorted, having come from Varosi. "Here, I'll dress her wound. Now keep it clean, I know that's hard for you people, but do as I tell you, and give her a spoonful of cod liver oil every day." He picked out a fresh bottle from his stash.

"Not again!" Anna was curious "Do you even have any medicines in that big bag of yours?"

The doctor choked on his coffee.

"Well, I'm glad I didn't pay you… You think you can cure the world with that damn cod liver oil, you're a useless doctor!"

The doctor coughed and spluttered in dismay. No one had ever spoken to him that way before.

"Take some cod liver oil, that'll stop you coughing!" she yelled at the top of her voice then took her daughter and left.

CHAPTER 11

The Attack

"Will I have to count in front of the class, Theo?"

"Yes, and if you get it wrong, you'll get spanked in front of the class," Theo teased.

"Take no notice of him," said Anna, casting a look at Theo, then she took her youngest by the hand.

As they entered the schoolroom, the young teacher hailed Tina to a vacant seat. "Ah, we have a new student today. It's Tina isn't it? Come and sit in the front row for now."

Having sensed Tina's anxiety, Anna signalled the teacher into the corridor and stood with her back against the classroom door.

"Sir, I just wanted to say… my daughter is left-handed, she can't help it, she has tried her best to use her right hand, but she can't. She also has an inj…"

The teacher's solemn expression changed into a look of horror as he raised his left eyebrow.

"Madam, it is your job to steer your child into a good Orthodox community, not mine. If she is left-handed that's between you and God to resolve! Now, if you'll excuse me, I'll do my job and you can do yours!"

Anna pushed her back against the classroom door to stop him from leaving.

"Sir… if you spank my child… or punish her in any way, I will come after you myself with a stick. Do you hear me?" she said slowly and clearly.

The children heard every word and gasped. No one spoke to teachers like that; not even men. With passive aggression he pushed past her, slamming the door in her face.

Anna's short walk home, usually comforted by the familiar bouquet of unspoiled wild wildflowers, herbs and trees saturating her senses, suddenly felt unnaturally silent. She looked into the distance and noticed three army trucks.

Then, without warning, a bloodcurdling scream, like the scream she imagined Harri unleashing when his thigh was cut away from the bone, filled the air. Anna quickly looked to the source but was surprised by a rustling in the trees and bushes nearby. The profile of a familiar face, tearing through the field like a rabbit escaping a trap, was dappled by the shadows of olive trees. It was Burak, Azra's eldest boy. Anna couldn't mistake the sudden flash of his eyes she'd seen before. She saw him running in the thicket then he disappeared from view like Hermes in his winged sandals.

Bewildered and aghast, she felt a knot forming in her stomach. She heard the scream again even louder, and as Anna strained to see through the bright morning rays of sun, she made out the form of cousin Stella, howling as she ran barefoot in her nightdress. Anna bolted to Stella's house, and there on the ground, on his own front porch, lay Stella's father, motionless and covered in blood. The alarm had been raised and people started gathering.

Loud shots were suddenly heard from the village square, shaking the ground with a resounding explosion. People took cover under Stella's porch.

"We're under attack!" yelled one of the women.

Anna gazed at the empty sky ahead. Something whispered in her heart that wasn't even a word and for the briefest and most surreal moment, a voice entered her body, bidding farewell then slowly dwindled.

She charged past an unmarked truck speeding down the narrow street. Its wing mirror cut into her arm, but she continued to run, ignoring the deep gash oozing blood down her sleeve. Unable to stop herself, Anna entered the square, beckoned by a sixth sense. Shattered glass lay strewn across the cobbles in a scene of carnage. She analysed the scene with the sound of her pulse ringing in her ears. Confused by the hullabaloo, she pushed past a small crowd, gawping and weeping over her father's body. Suddenly the brightness of her eyes dimmed with the darkness of a broken universe. She felt like she was drowning. She clasped her father's blood-stained head between her hands and caressed his right cheek, unsure if the scene was real or just an apparition. Christophoro slowly opened his eyes.

"Make… it… ri…" He took his last breath.

"What, Father, what…?" Her fractured voice couldn't continue.

"Did anyone see what happened?" shouted Tasso, barging his way through the crowd.

Anna carefully wiped the blood from his face and howled like an animal. Harri limped toward her and with the help of Yanni, they pulled her away from her father's dead body, almost tripping over the body of a young man on the ground next to him. Anna could hear the young man's mother approach like fire fuelled by wind. She pushed past helpers to get to her son and threw herself onto the ground. Anna leant to the ground to touch her father's blood on the cobbles but Harri and Yanni carried her away. The last thing she remembered about that day was a limb hanging from a nearby tree with what looked like the remains of a man's body on the ground. Everything else was a blur after that.

A few days later, Anna had barely spoken a word. She hadn't seen her mother and when she was a little more coherent, Stella came to visit her in bed; confused and bewildered.

"Anna, your mother… she…"

"Where are my children? Where is my mother?" Anna's voice was dry and raspy. She sat up and sipped the sweet tea.

"The children are fine, they're with me. But your mother, she left yesterday with mine. They went to join the convent in the mountains."

Anna looked at her cousin, baffled.

"But… but... why would she do that?"

"They're taking vows to live the rest of their lives as Orthodox nuns. My mother has been talking about it for some time, I guess she feels like now is the time. She started behaving very strangely when my father was killed. Now I've lost both of them."

"Does anyone know what happened? Why were we attacked?

"Tasso told us they thought we had a lot of EOKA members here in the village and this was the quickest way they could flush them out."

"But my father wasn't a member… I… I know that for a fact! He didn't like the way they bullied people into joining. Why Stella, why…"

"I don't know, Anna! maybe he was just in the wrong place at the wrong time." There was a moment's silence as the women tried to absorb the severity of the situation. "Anna, yesterday when I was here, you said your father told you to 'make it right,' what did he mean by that?"

"He meant I need to restore our family and our honour," said Anna. "It means I have to find Petro... I have to make it right, Stella, for our family honour. I just have to!"

"Well, as long as you're sure, Anna. But that means you really have to go to England now."

"I've never been surer of anything in my life," Anna confirmed.

CHAPTER 12

The Journey

"I think he lives in a castle with servants." Passionately animated, Tina ran around in circles fantasizing about her rich father whom she'd never seen. "And I think he's going to make me a dolls' house..." she babbled, carefully packing the last of her toys. "This bag is very heavy, Mamma. Do I have to carry it all the way to England?"

"You won't be carrying it all the time, just to and from the boat and trains," Anna explained with heightened anxiety.

A few hours later, Anna locked the front door, stepped back, and took a final glance at her house. Under an orange sky in early September, the mulberry tree fluttered and danced in the morning breeze and for a moment, she understood why her father loved it so much. She took her last glimpse of the mulberry tree standing proud and composed, enticing her to return one day.

Anna walked away with four young children, accompanied by reflections of her recent aspirations to breed silkworms and produce the finest silk the village had ever seen, so she could sell it to Eleni and raise money for Ariadne's education. She had it all worked out. Ariadne would be the first girl to attend secondary school and make history; it was a battle Anna had been gearing up for. But for now, she had buses, boats and trains to focus on.

They walked to the bus stop loaded with bags and waited for the bus to take them to the port. Anna stood with her four children between the ages of five and ten, slipped the house key into her bag and saw it nestle comfortably in the depths of linen.

By sunset, they'd boarded a boat from Kyrenia and set sail to Greece.

"Is this my bed?" asked Tina, jumping on a lower bunk.

"You'll have to share with your sisters," replied Anna, yawning and massaging her aching shoulders. "Theo and I will have the top bunk." She climbed up and collapsed with exhaustion.

"Let's go and explore!" whispered Theo, mischievously.

"My hand hurts," squealed Tina, running to keep up with her siblings. She skipped behind them and then sat on a creaking bench, swaying to the rhythm of the sea. It seemed like half the island was on board, greeting each other as if they were still neighbours. Anna spoke to a woman much older than her, sitting alone, divided only by a fraying curtain between their cabins.

"Are you going to England as well?" asked Anna, feeling sorry for the woman.

The woman looked round and watched as Anna stuffed

her bags in the tiny cabin.

"I'm going to Greece to live with my nephew. I have nothing left here now my husband was arrested." The woman turned to face the wall and curled into her bed in a foetal position. She wasn't in a mood to talk. Anna looked in the other direction, trying to assess the situation. Families just like hers were leaving the island. Is this what independence has done? She thought to herself. Why had it all broken down? Why did so many parties want such a small, insignificant island? What made them feel they had any say in her homeland in the first place? Anna was so tired that she couldn't begin to feel the anger deep inside.

Meanwhile, out on deck, Anastasia saw her younger sister sitting alone.

"What's wrong?" she asked Tina.

"I don't know!" groaned Tina, rubbing the cut on her right hand. Seven-year-old Anastasia gawked at the pus and blood in her sisters hand and rushed to get their mother. Anna raced up and down the deck with Tina crying and dripping blood, when a porter pointed to a small door.

"She has a serious infection," said a young ship's doctor, adjusting his white coat. Anna could barely understand his Athenian accent. "If we don't lance it now, it could get worse and she could lose her hand – or go blind. But I don't have any pain relief." He continued to rummage through drawers and cabinets. By now Tina was semi-conscious with pain and fever.

"I don't have enough money to pay you!" cried Anna.

The doctor looked at Anna and her children.

"Ah well… Think of it as a favour," he replied, taking a small scalpel from his big brown leather bag. "Besides, I'm bored. There's nothing for me to do on this heap. Now hold her down!"

"What?"

"Hold her down, I told you I don't have anything to numb the pain." He looked at Theo. "Boy…help your mother hold her down."

Anna and Theo held down the tiny body of a malnourished, hysterical five-year-old, pleading with her mother to stop. Anna closed her eyes and bit her lip until it bled, for what seemed like an eternity.

"There! We're finished," said the doctor, wrapping the last of her bandages.

"Bring her in first thing tomorrow so I can examine her and change the bandages."

"Thank you," Anna sniffled, trying desperately to comfort her hyperventilating child.

A few hours later, Tina joined the other children on deck with her right hand held out, stiff and still throbbing. She watched an elderly priest, surrounded by an eager group of boys, laughing and jeering over a magazine. The priest established eye contact with Tina.

"Would you like to see?" he leered, sliding the magazine along the bench. Tina was horrified; she'd never seen pornographic images before. She glared at the priest for a second, then swiped the magazine to the ground with her left hand, and watched the wind blow it into the air like a bird. Panic stricken, the priest jumped from the bench and chased after it like a butterfly collector without his net.

That night was stormy and as people entered the dining room, Anna took her children to their cabin. Fumbling in her overstuffed bag, she pulled out four pieces of bread and four boiled eggs and they sat curled up in their bunks eating dinner.

"Not boiled eggs again!" moaned Theo, holding his nose but eating voraciously.

As they sat eating in their cabin an almighty gale raged like a frenzied poltergeist causing waves to crash against the boat, tossing and swaying as it rose and fell in the swells.

Tumbling back and forth, Anna checked Tina's bandages then snuggled into her bunk with Theo for the night, wondering how many more storms lay ahead.

"Where are we going to stay when we get there?" whispered Ariadne, still trying to piece things together.

"With your father, of course!" Anna whispered back.

"But I don't know him. Will he recognize us? How do you know where he is?" The questions kept pouring from Ariadne.

"There are lots of Greek Cypriots like us going to London, everyone knows each other. Anyway, Vasili gave me his address and I wrote and told him we are coming. Everything will be fine, now go to sleep!"

The next day, the boat's foghorn sounded loud and clear.

Children ran on deck to witness a small tugboat slowly and precisely pulling their large boat through the Corinth canal. Tina couldn't believe it was real. She looked at the bridge above, and innocent of the theory of perspective, believed she was watching tiny people walking above her, so that when a year later her schoolteacher read *Gulliver's Travels* to the class, Tina raised her hand to tell everyone she'd travelled through Lilliput to get to England.

By the time they reached the final leg of their journey, a train to Victoria station, Anna was emotionally and physically drained. Victoria station was light, bright and enjoying a brisk September chill. The air smelled fresh, like the aftermath of semi-tropical rainfall in the village.

With aching limbs and empty bellies that grumbled for anything but boiled eggs and dry bread, Anna looked around for her estranged husband, hoping he would be there to meet them. The only hope she had to cling on to was that Vasili spoke to him and made him see sense.

Tina had never been further than her grandmother's house before. She looked around excitedly, watching people rush around getting on and off trains. Doors slammed and people yelled while others looked as serious as the village priest. Others held umbrellas, even though it wasn't raining. A woman tugged at her sagging beehive trying to restore it from the morning mist. Another stood in line for a train wearing white stilettos and, oblivious to her surroundings, took out a tiny mirror and carefully added more lipstick.

Tina was shocked and quickly looked away.

Two women walked briskly past her, laughing as they drew smoke from lipstick-stained cigarettes. Their beautiful dresses and cardigans matched the brightness of yiayia's basket of oranges and lemons.

"Blimey, these stockings don't arf ladder quick, Bren," complained one, as they ran for their train.

With eyes open wide like an owl in search of prey, Anna looked around for her husband; she barely remembered what he looked like. A man that looks like Cary Grant, she thought to herself, making sure her children were close. A fleeting pause between commuters unveiled a short man with jet black hair and olive skin, amidst a sea of tall chalky men with skin like alabaster.

"Ahhh, there he is!" she yelled, waving frantically in case he missed a woman with four young children, numerous bags, cases and parcels in Victoria station during the morning rush hour.

Finally, at the age of five, Tina saw her father for the very first time. She'd heard stories about him from her mother and grandparents, although she didn't always understand the words bapoo Christophoro used to describe him. The monumental moment she had been waiting for, the image she'd carved in her mind of what a father should look like, the man who'd made her mother cry so many times with the power of his absence, was finally here in front of her. Tina took her first glance at him, and then looked to the ground in case he thought it impertinent to stare. Besides, this was a good opportunity to look for that gold the streets were paved with. Tina had been looking forward to that just as much.

Grinning like a schoolboy, Petro hugged his wife and welcomed his family.

"Dad!" Theo's eyes lit up as he held on to his arm with affection. The two eldest girls stood close to each other in silence, blushing at their father's compliments.

"And this must be Tina," he whispered with a voice like warm honey. Now Tina had to look at him. Her heart tickled, like the ants she played with in yiayia Christina's porch.

Gently and slowly, he gave Tina her first hug. She felt the softness of his tan suede jacket as it touched her small body. His Brylcreemed hair was thick, dark and swept back across his head with perfection. He was groomed like the picture of an English gentleman Tina once saw on the cover of a magazine in the village shop, a magazine that sat upright and alone on a rack next to boot polish, sewing thread and out of date newspapers.

Tina smelled his shiny wet-looking hair. It smelled like a hundred flowers picked from the mountain next to yiayia Christina's house on a day when they'd had plenty to drink. It smelled even better than the cologne her mother inherited on her wedding day and tried to hide in her wardrobe. Petro lifted eight-year-old Theo and threw him over his shoulder.

"You smell like yiayia's spice cupboard," Theo squealed with delight.

"How was your journey?" he asked a blushing Anna.

"Oh, er…fine." She yawned, noticing his accent had changed slightly. "Actually, I'm very tired and the children are hungry." She wasn't sure where to look.

"I'm so sorry about your father, Anna, he was a good man."

Anna looked at him, wondering how they had four healthy children together, yet she barely knew him.

Petro led his family to a grey Ford Cortina parked outside the station. Theo jumped onto the back seat and marvelled at its beautiful red vinyl interior. Petro helped his daughters into the car while Anna lifted the heavy bags into the boot.

"They're so beautiful," he smirked, smiling at his daughters.

"Yes… yes they are. Look, I didn't know whether you received my letter, you didn't reply…"

"Oh, that's fine, I knew you were coming." Petro interrupted her and adjusted his rear-view mirror.

They drove south towards Brixton, watching buildings rush by. Ariadne and Anastasia fell asleep almost immediately, whereas Tina watched men on both sides of the street with hair like her father's. She watched people of all colours walking and getting on and off buses. People kissed on pavements, the buildings were tall, and occasionally they passed billboards with bright, psychedelic colours, parading like kaleidoscopes with pictures of happy people.

"Why do Englishmen go outside with wet hair? Don't they get colds?" she whispered to Theo, confused by so much Brylcreem.

"No silly, they don't have time to wait. They're very busy," Theo said.

"How long does it take for English hair to dry?" she asked her brother.

"It takes them a long time because it rains every day. Don't you know anything Tina?" Theo rolled his eyes at his little sister.

"I have a great place for us to live, Anna," said Petro proudly.

"Yes, Vasili told me you have a restaurant of your own. Why…"

"Somewhere with three bedrooms and a bathroom, all to ourselves!" he added fervently.

Anna managed a tentative smile.

"I'm so happy you're all here," he said convincingly.

Half an hour later, the car stopped outside a restaurant on a busy road opposite Brockwell Park. As the children got out of the car, Petro discreetly dusted the seats with a handkerchief he kept in the small pocket of his suede jacket.

Tina continued to inspect the ground. Her eyes followed the line of grey paving stones up the street, mirroring the colour of her father's car. It was late morning, and the sun was deciding whether to go or stay, as it flashed on tiny silver speckles in the concrete. Tina was confused. Her friends told her she'd see streets paved with gold. They said you could pick it up and keep it. Tina even promised to save some for them when they came to visit.

"Is this it?" she agonized, feeling cheated as the family walked over the speckled jewels, embedded forever in concrete. Still looking on the ground, Tina felt dejected, and with a sullen expression, devoid of joy, she wondered: what other lies have they told me?

The family entered into a lobby with one door leading into the restaurant and another going upstairs to the flat above. They went up the narrow staircase to the first floor.

"This is our room." Petro opened the door to a large room with the highest ceiling Anna had ever seen and although it smelled of damp, she was grateful to have a roof over her head. "And here's the bathroom," he said, and showed her an indoor toilet next to a room with an enamel white tub in the shape of a coffin.

"What... what's this?" Anna backed away.

"It's a bathtub, silly woman! You fill it with water and get in to wash yourself." Petro laughed at his wife's ignorance.

"But why does it need to be so big? No one needs to waste that much water to wash themselves." Petro rolled his eyes and shut the door. Anna looked around at the large dark lobby between her new bedroom and the bathroom. "What is this space used for?"

"I think they used to store coats and boots here. Anyway, there are two small bedrooms upstairs, the children can share."

Anna was delighted to have so much space and spent the afternoon unpacking her meagre belongings while the children ran up and down the stairs exploring their new home.

During her first week, Anna tried to get acquainted with her new surroundings. Secretly relieved that Petro actually turned up to collect them from the station, she still felt suffocated by the constant grey of the sky and the restraints of always having to be inside a building. However many layers of clothing she wore, she always felt cold – and it wasn't even winter. She felt lost without friends and family around her, but her choices were limited.

When she wasn't washing up, preparing vegetables for the restaurant, or tending to her children, Anna found it hard to sleep and spent many lonely hours listening to the occasional car racing to catch the green traffic light outside. Some nights Petro would sleep next to her and some nights he would disappear but Anna never questioned him.

Downstairs in the restaurant she found a perfect sun trap in front of the shop window where she could watch the world go by and feel the early autumn sun on her face. It penetrated through her closed eyes and into her lungs like the reunion of a lost love. She watched women getting off the bus outside with bags of groceries and wondered how they could carry fruit and vegetables without squashing them at the bottom of their bags. What about eggs? She thought to herself. How do they carry eggs on a bus? Anna dismissed her thoughts and got up from her table to go into the kitchen. She brushed her fingers across the red flock wallpaper and flinched unexpectedly, like she'd touched a prickly pear cactus. The intensity of sun through glass had bleached the avocado green carpet in a long streak and as she weaved between white starched tablecloths Anna could hear her children arguing upstairs.

She entered the small kitchen at the back of the restaurant through strips of vinyl acting as a curtain and examined the large cooker along the back wall. With six burners it looked big enough to cook food for the entire village; although she couldn't explain why the large fridge felt so intimidating. Could it be because it looked big enough to trap a small child inside?

CHAPTER 13

September 1965

As the city paused and the moon vanished from sight, the family slept long and deep.

Clouds drifted across a dark sky, gliding through the mist until chirping swallows broke its silence. Daylight came with a bitter sun, pale as a lemon, weaving shadows through stirring trees. Anna woke to the smell of crisp, cold air. She turned to the large window and looked at the treetops in the park across the street, peeking between the short curtains and window ledge. The busy road between her new home and the park woke with its usual rev and roar of engines. Suddenly she was disturbed by a powerful knock on the front door downstairs.

Who could possibly be knocking at the door this early, she thought? Anna looked out the window feeling like she was on top of a mountain, but to her delight, she saw her sister Kate looking up at her with a peachy smile.

Like wind over leaves, Anna rushed down the narrow staircase, ignoring the blanket falling from her shoulders. She fumbled with the cumbersome lock then swung open the door, as wide as her hug. Not even a bitter September morning would rob her of this moment.

"But you're…"

"Pregnant? Yes!" beamed Kate, grinning with a healthy glow.

"Didn't the doctor tell you it wasn't possible?"

"Yes, he did. I don't know what happened, we just stopped worrying and it happened."

Anna led her sister out of the cold and into the kitchen downstairs, behind the restaurant.

"Vasili told me you were coming; I couldn't wait to see you!"

The sisters sat in the cold, draughty kitchen and talked as if no time had passed between them.

"I haven't seen you since my wedding, it's been far too long." Anna couldn't stop kissing and hugging her little sister.

"I feel terrible for leaving you all those years ago, but it was the only way George and I could be together. Mother would never have approved."

"Why didn't you tell me Father gave you the money to leave? I thought we were close, Kate. You didn't even tell me at my wedding."

"I tried to tell you at the wedding, truly I did, but Mother was watching me like a hawk. I think she wanted to keep us as apart in case I persuaded you to come to England. As for Father, he made me promise not to tell you in case you told her. You know how intimidating she could be."

Anna thought for a moment. "She eventually stopped talking about you, as if you didn't exist." The sisters continued to talk and drink hot tea for a while, trying to keep warm in the draughty kitchen. Eventually the unavoidable subject of their father arose, and the mood changed.

"Surely someone saw who did it?" whispered Kate. Sheets of rain fell in the tiny courtyard behind them.

"I really don't know… Stella told me we had a lot of extremist EOKA members in our village. That was the rumour anyway, but I don't know. What I do know is that Azra's son may have had something to do with it. I saw him running in the fields that day…"

"Do you mean Baruk? Anna, you have to tell someone! He may be a spy, or…"

"Tell who Kate? Who, and what am I going to tell them? To think, I befriended Azra when everyone shunned her like a dirty dog."

"Well, maybe she didn't know anything about her son's activities? I… I really don't know what to say or what to think." Kate held her head in her hands. "I feel awful for not being there." She sighed.

They talked until human activity stirred upstairs and when copious cups of tea had been drunk, Kate changed the subject.

"We've been offered a council house on a brand-new development in Brighton! And George has a job as head chef at an exclusive golf resort nearby." She carefully placed her teacup on the workbench next to the large cooker.

Suddenly, Petro appeared with a small parcel in his hand. He went outside into the courtyard and fumbled around between the potato peeling machine and some old iron, then came back inside empty handed.

"Hello brother-in-law," Kate chuckled uncomfortably with a friendly grin.

"Morning," he mumbled.

Kate continued her chatter in the icy kitchen, while discreetly watching his movements.

"Er, if it's a boy we're going to name him after Father. Well... Umm... I'd better not miss the bus, service is terrible on Sundays," Kate added hastily, casting a worried glance at her sister. She left in a hurry.

"I don't want her here all the time," Petro growled.

"But I haven't seen her for years, and she needs me now she's having a baby."

"This is my house, and I will tell you who can and can't come here!"

Anna was too tired to argue and felt she was need upstairs.

A few days later was Anna's 38th birthday and as it was her first birthday since they were back together, she secretly hoped Petro might remember and maybe, just maybe, he might buy her a present; but she spent the morning rummaging through her belongings trying to improvise school clothes and equipment.

"I've spoken to the school and there's room for all of them at Rosendale Primary," Petro called.

"I'll draw Ari and Theo a map so you can walk there tomorrow," he said, rushing out the door.

"But how will I get back if you don't take us?"

"Just reverse the map!" He frowned at her with contempt then slammed the door behind him.

"Mamma, will I get smacked for using my left hand?" asked Tina, watching her father strut to the Ford Cortina.

"I don't know, Tina! Now come here and let me change your bandages."

"Ouch Mamma, that hurts, it's stuck to my hand!"

"Well hold still, I have a clean handkerchief I want to use instead. Ahh, it's looking much better, it's healing really well." Anna was delighted at a bit of good news on her birthday.

The next day they woke to the sound of crows screeching in the trees outside. Tina quickly put on her dark green wool dress to try and keep warm.

"This is so scratchy, Mamma, I hate it!" she complained, bouncing around.

"Sorry, baby, but it's the only warm dress that fits you… Ari, can you understand this map?" asked Anna, her heart beating so fast she could barely speak.

"Don't worry, Mum, we'll find it. Anyway, you're almost fluent in English, why are you worried?" Ari sensed her mother's anxiety.

They walked along Norwood Road and eventually stumbled upon a group of boisterous children. Tina watched girls with long blonde braids skip past her with brightly coloured ribbons in their hair. A girl with freckles ran past her, with hair the colour of sunset, reminiscent of the flames from yiayia's winter fire.

Feeling particularly dowdy, Tina became distracted by her luxuriant surroundings.

"What does that sign say, Mamma?" She pointed curiously.

"It says 'for sale'."

Tina pulled a face.

What do they mean, she thought? You can't sell houses, they're built by bapoos, aren't they? She was confused before she even set foot in the classroom.

Twenty minutes later, they arrived at the gates of the Victorian school. Anna observed a tall, middle-aged woman with an enormous chest float towards her.

"Aaahh! You must be the new family. We've been expecting you," she assured kindly, looking over her thin glasses. "The children have missed two weeks of school; did you know that?" she asked sternly.

The three eldest were led away by her nervous assistant who stood a few paces behind. Tina suddenly felt a huge void in her stomach.

"Where are they going, Mamma? Why aren't we going with them?"

"Can you translate to the child that the infants' class is over here?" she said and pointed, sensing Tina's confusion.

Every step closer to the classroom tightened the knot in Tina's stomach. The headmistress took them to a cabin, inside which was a huge room with chairs stacked on tables and a group of children occupying the far end.

Chapter 13 – September 1965

"This room doubles as our dining room at twelve thirty sharp! I'll introduce her to the class; you should probably leave now," she urged Anna, trying to take Tina by the hand.

"Where are you going, Mamma?"

"I have to go now. You're starting school, Tina."

"There there, now… It's time to meet the other children!" The headmistress began to lose patience.

"Mamma, why are you leaving me here?" Tina screamed so loud the other children turned and stared. Feeling her mother's fingers slip away, she kicked and howled like an incensed demon.

An hour later, hyperventilating alone in a corner, Tina casually stared out the window; determined not to mix with children who spoke in riddles.

"Come and join us Tina, we're doing puzzles." The teacher pointed to a group of raucous children seated in a circle on the floor. Tina felt abandoned and refused to sit with the other children and watched the calming presence of a ginger cat outside instead. The cat jumped off the sill with an ethereal grace and without thinking, Tina ran to the door and chased after her nimble feline friend.

She got as far as the main road and when suddenly she felt someone swoop her into the air, just like her grandfather used to do. But instead, Mrs. Barnett's long skinny fingers let loose a short sharp slap, penetrating Tina's skin, like the sting of Azra's bees.

"Don't you EVER do that again!" she gnarled.

The next day, Tina watched the children march, dance,

twirl and hop merrily with a type of exuberance she hadn't seen before. Mesmerised and spurred on by the urge to participate, she joined in and forgot about the cat.

With the first week of school over, Anna's children arrived home to find an unknown lady in their kitchen.

"Ello kids," she said, slowly painting her nails. The children looked at each other, wondering who she was.

Their father walked in, looking sheepish. "Er, this is Pamela… and I want you to be nice to her!" he exclaimed.

Confused and hungry, the children rushed upstairs to look for their mother. They found her sitting quietly, reading.

"Mamma, who's that woman downstairs?" Theo asked.

Anna didn't answer. She looked up from her book, silent as a mouse, with one eye resembling a ripe plum.

"What happened?" Theo gasped.

At that moment, Ariadne rushed in. "Go to your rooms," she told her younger siblings, then closed the door.

"Mum! You can't let him treat you like this. There must be something you can do?" Ari's eyes blazed with fierce indignation and rampant fury.

"What can I do, Ari? I promised your grandfather I would restore our family honour and that means I have to accept my fate," explained Anna, trying to soothe her eye with a cold flannel.

"You mustn't tell anyone about this Ari, you promise me?"

"I promise, Mum, but people will see it you know, you can't hide it!"

"It'll look fine in a few days, don't worry yourself. Anyway, it doesn't hurt, now go and do your homework."

The next morning, the children went down to the kitchen and found the woman seated in the same chair. She crossed her legs and sighed, rearranging her bedraggled beehive with the end of a pointy comb. She appeared to have a bad smell under her nose.

"What yer names again, kids?" she asked, looking into her hand mirror.

"I'm Ariadne," said Ari, watching the woman's purple and pink crimplene dress ride up her thigh, revealing a mass of white flesh.

"Ari… what?" she gasped. "Thass a bleedin boys name, aint it?" She laughed. "I'm gonna call ya… err, less see naa... I likes Fay… Yeah, I'm gonna call ya Fay, like Faye Dunaway."

She took a long drag from her cigarette and blew thick smoke into the air.

"Haa bout you, love?"

"I'm Theo!"

"Awe yeah, Pete told me bout yous. Yer name's short for Theo…theo sumink aint it? Can't member naa! Anyways, I'm gonna call ya Chris… Yeah, thass better!" She took another long drag from her cigarette and tried to blow smoke rings in the air.

"What bout you, love?" She pointed to Anastasia with a long pink fingernail.

"My name is Anastasia," she whispered slowly as if she

was being pushed into a corner and threatened by robbers.

"Ana...what... Bloody ell, I aint gonna call ya Anna, vass yer bleedin mum's name aint it?" She laughed. "Yer look like Leslie Caron... I'm gonna call ya Lesley," she gushed, rummaging through her make up bag.

"Haa bout you littlun?" she asked Tina.

"My name is Tina and I like my name!" Tina yelled; her eyes transfixed on the woman's hair. "Why does your hair look like candy floss?" She pointed to the woman's head. Instantaneously, Petro came in from the restaurant.

"Are they being rude?" he demanded.

"Naaa... iss nufink I can't andle, Pete lovee. Essept that littlun. Bit feisty aint she?"

"Pamela is our... er... guest, so we must show good manners. Anyway, she's kindly offered to take you to see *Pinocchio* at Brixton cinema," he announced, wondering why his children were being ungrateful.

"Is Mamma coming too?" asked Ari.

"Na she bleedin aint!" blurted the woman. "And I meant what I sez Pete luv. I can't be doin wiv vem foreign names!" She stubbed her cigarette out on the concrete floor while the children put on their coats. "C'mon kids. And yer better bleedin behave yerselves an all!" she added, ushering them out the door.

Anna watched from the upstairs window then took flight down the stairs like a woman possessed. A sharp flurry of October sleet endeavoured to cool her fury, but no amount of tonic could relieve her frustration.

Chapter 13 – September 1965

"Where you tek my children?" she screamed down the street.

"None yer blee..." but before the woman could finish, Anna approached in a whirlwind and swung her fist so hard that the woman fell to the ground like a sack of potatoes. Anna escorted her children back home to a bombardment of abuse behind her; just in time to witness Petro drive away.

By five o'clock, Tina was still looking out the window.

"Is Dad ever coming back?" she asked curiously, wondering if she wanted him to return.

"Don't worry, Mum...I'll help serve in the restaurant tonight," Ari declared.

"We can't open tonight; we'll never manage on our own," said Anna.

"Mum, please... Let's open. We have bookings tonight. Besides, I'm tall like bapoo Christophoro, I can easily pass for fifteen."

"I'll show Theo how to cut chips and Tina can wash dishes," joined Anastasia. "We can pretend we're preparing for Easter!"

"Well... Er, OK, if you're sure you can manage."

That night, as patrons came and went, Ari did her best not to mix up the orders. But in the midst of all the mayhem, Anna had forgotten they had no chicken, no carrots and very little steak left. She quickly improvised, offering customers some of the koftes she'd made earlier.

"Koff what? I don't want nuffin wiv bleedin coughin in it," an agitated customer screamed at Ari. "Call yerselvs a bleedin restaurant! Huh." The man and his wife got up and stormed out. Embarrassed and nervous, Ari walked between tables asking customers if the food was to their satisfaction. "Yes dear, these meatballs are divine," an elderly lady with a blue rinse and fox fur around her shoulders said, smiling at Ari. Then she turned to her party and continued to discuss the horror of the Moors Murders.

When all the customers had gone, Tina and Anastasia could barely keep their eyes open.

"Is Dad ever coming back, Mamma?" Tina yawned.

"I really don't know. I'm sorry but I don't know what to tell you."

"Good, I don't like it when he's here. I don't like that lady with the big white legs either."

Anna couldn't help but laugh out loud.

"Phew... I'm exhausted!" said Ari. She took off her shoes and rubbed her aching feet. "I'm going to bed now." She staggered up the stairs and fell into her bed. Drained and weary, the children all fell asleep within seconds of getting into bed.

It was almost 1.30 a.m. and as the universe slept, Anna poured herself a glass of wine, wondering if it would taste like her father's mulberry wine. She found it surprisingly good and poured another. She stared at the day's takings. One thing she had become adept at since working with her father at the market in Varosi, was adding up. She counted the day's takings and went to bed with ingenious, creative ideas on how she could change her life for the better.

Chapter 13 – September 1965

Six hours later, she woke to an overwhelming smell of alcohol. Petro had come home in the small hours and slept silently next to her. She didn't care where he'd been, who he'd been with, or how long he would stay. It was Sunday, and that meant church.

The Greek Orthodox church in Camberwell Green had become her saviour and every Sunday morning, Anna took the number 68 bus all the way to what was then the only Greek church in South London.

"Vasili!" she called, waving to her brother in the church courtyard. Thrilled to see his sister, Vasili zigzagged between the crowds to greet her.

"What…the…hell has he done to you?" Vasili stared at Anna's purple, yellow and red eye.

"Everyone know how he treats you Anna, I won't stand for it… I won't. If he lays another finger on you, I'll kill him… I swear I will!" Vasili's face reddened.

"You'll do no such thing!" ordered Anna. "He's the father of my children."

"Why do you defend him, Anna? You make me so angry when you do that! He's not worthy of you and the children! Come and stay with us; you don't have to put up with that useless shit anymore!"

"Trust me, it won't be forever, I have a plan. Anyway, the children love their schools, I can't keep moving them."

Anna looked away; she didn't want to discuss Petro anymore. Instead, she caught sight of a familiar face nearby.

"Pardon me for staring, but have we met before? Are

you from Varosi?" the lady enquired.

"No, but I had a market stall there with my father."

"Ahh, that's where I've seen you… Your father made that delicious mulberry wine, didn't he? My brother couldn't get enough of it." She laughed heartily and held out her hand.

"I'm Sophia Alexandrou."

Anna and Sophia chatted incessantly at the back of the church. Both women were delighted to have found each other in such a transient and hostile place like London. Anna couldn't believe how happy the new friendship made her feel.

After the service, Vasili dropped Anna home in his gleaming new Jaguar before going back to his own restaurant in Clapham Common.

"I don't want you to come in just in case he's home," Anna demanded.

She opened the door, went upstairs to the flat and checked on the children.

"Have you all finished your homework?" Anna smiled.

"Yes, and I'm starving!" Theo shouted from his room.

Anna ushered her children downstairs to the kitchen and had just opened the mammoth fridge door when Petro unexpectedly showed up and stared vacantly into her eyes.

"What the hell do you think you're doing? Shut the fridge door… now! That food isn't for you. There's bread and cheese on the shelf; now take it upstairs," he demanded, taking another parcel out into the courtyard.

Chapter 13 – September 1965

The children grabbed their food and rushed to the top of the stairs, listening to their parents arguing yet again.

Anna suddenly yearned to be heard. She stood still and released a fragile smile.

"Listen to me. I don't care about your women… I don't even care if you verbally abuse me! But don't you dare deny my children food!" she screamed.

Petro stared at her black eye for a moment.

"Well… OK then, I… I'll give you three pounds every Saturday and you can go to Brixton market to get their food. But don't let them go through the kitchen cupboards again!"

Anna nodded, and was quite pleased with the outcome. I can meet Sophia and we can go to the café for a cup of tea every Saturday, she thought.

CHAPTER 14

1968

"Put your coat on, we're going to Brixton."

Tina loved to hear those words, which meant quality time with her mother while her siblings did their homework.

Meticulous timing took them to Electric Avenue by 9.35 a.m. where they could walk through the arcade, out of the cold, and find rare fresh produce unavailable in the supermarkets.

With evidence of its previous glory in faded whitewash, the arcade entrance had become tired and worn. Husky chips of old paint kept dropping to the ground and remained there like solid snowflakes.

They entered through a maze-like alley, staring at the colourful vendors, listening to the sounds of Desmond Dekker, Judge Dread, and Dave and Ansell Collins in the background. A man with long dreadlocks and two gold teeth watched Tina stare at a barrel of undecipherable meat.

"Das pig tails me darlan. Go nd tell yer mother dey mek good soup!" He laughed.

A huge sweaty woman stood next to him, chopping pigs' legs on a butcher's block.

"I'll give er a recipee me darlin," she exhaled, adjusting her money apron.

Barrels and trays of salt fish, yams, okra and taro lined the alley, which seemed to Tina like a winding, hollow caterpillar; but the best part for Tina was that not a single blue-eyed blonde girl with ribbons in her hair could be seen.

"Stay close, I'm just getting some taro." Anna looked around, leaving Tina to soak up a jamboree of accents, rhythms, dialects and colours, all melting into a symphonic orchestra, conducted and designed to delight only those who could hear its magic.

"Fresh mullet – come and get it!" yelled another man, gutting the last of his stock into the storm gully. While perplexed by the concoction of rancid and exotic smells from putrid fish scales and guts, Tina found it strangely reassuring. It was better than the choking smell of carbolic soap in the girls' toilets at school; better than the smell of overcooked cabbage in the school's cafeteria; and nicer than the smell of her father's Brylcreem hair that had once dazzled her.

"Bloody flies!" waved an angry greengrocer, performing his own version of the jitterbug, imitating violent dance moves in a fist fight with an invisible opponent.

Tina closed her eyes and felt liberated in this world filled with cosy contentment and spontaneity where she could explore and be with other outcasts and loners like her. It was a world where she wasn't mocked, ridiculed or judged. Tina walked deeper into the caterpillar and watched in amazement as colourful African headdresses bobbed in a frenzy of activity, stacking fabric against the caterpillar wall. Bales of fabric in rich, bold, earthy colours, like illustrations in Mrs. Barnett's library, promised tales of wonderment and adventure.

"Come un browse me darlin, we won't charge yer." The eldest lady laughed. "Come me darlin, I'll show ye ow to wear a gele!" she insisted, noticing Tina stare at her headdress.

With Bob Marley and the Wailers blaring through the tunnel, Tina sat on an upturned barrel ecstatically waiting to be adorned like an African princess, fighting the urge to dance. She'd found her paradise. A paradise where no one looked her up and down because her clothes were different, and no one gave her the 'how do you spell your last name again?' squint.

A few minutes later, Anna found her daughter giggling in a heart-warming congregation of spirited people, pampering her.

"Girl, ya look like a tiny princess ya know!" A man with yellow teeth and dreadlocks puffed smoke from his pipe, smiling.

"You can ave dat piece but if yer wan matching agbada, I give yer cheap, got plenty o fabric me dear."

"Thang you madam," Anna replied as she blushed and quickly took Tina's hand. She gathered her bags and rushed to the café on Coldharbour Lane where Sophia was waiting.

"What's that?" asked Anna, pointing to a tin in Sophia's bag, as she flopped wearily into a chair.

Chapter 14 – 1968

"Oh, it's called spam," Sophia said and laughed. "I think it's a type of English meat, the kids love it, and we can't afford real meat."

"What's that on top?"

"Oh, that's a special key you need to open it. The tin's perfect for growing herbs in afterwards, I've already got a collection of parsley and oregano growing on the kitchen window."

Anna stared at the tin, thinking the meat inside must be very special if one needed a special key to access it.

"Anyway, what do you think about English tea? Can you believe they add milk!" Sophia was disgusted, while Anna almost choked on her third cup.

"Oh…er, I love it actually. It took some getting used to though. They have these strange things called tea bags now, I haven't tried them, but I don't like the idea of sucking tea from a bag." Anna shuddered. Meanwhile Tina was becoming uncomfortable from the stares and laughs she was getting from people in the café. She carefully unravelled the gele and examined the curious animals in the print, wondering if she could draw them.

Anna and Sophia continued to talk. They each had their own palette of emotions and expressed their undiluted feelings in the rosy warmth of friendship.

Sophia remembered, "Ah! I know what I had to tell you. I just read about something called 'The Open University' where people can study in their own time. Maybe you can get a degree in English, then you can get a job and leave that brute husband of yours!"

"Aren't you forgetting something, Sophia?"

"Forgetting what?"

"Well, for starters, I'm a woman!"

"But that's just it, Anna, it's for everyone."

Anna looked perplexed. "Really?"

"Yes, everyone!" Sophia blurted with excitement.

Anna glanced at the clock on the wall behind the bustling counter and sighed.

"Oh, let him manage without you for once. You look exhausted Anna!"

They talked a while longer, then Anna departed to the bus stop with Tina holding tight onto her African remnant. Anna stood at the bus stop contemplating the idea of studying between getting children to school, working in the restaurant, cleaning the flat, doing the laundry and getting a little sleep. If my mother could work that hard, then surely I can too, she thought. The idea of finally being able to study in England, filled her with hope.

They boarded a crowded bus and got home to find Petro chatting to a professional young gentleman on the landing outside Anna's bedroom.

"Ahh… and here's my wife, Anna!" Petro grinned.

"Yassas, ti kanete?" replied the man in a high-class Greek accent, reaching out to shake her hand.

"Er… yassas," said Anna, shaking his spotlessly clean hand.

"My name is Stelios." His voice was warm and soft.

Chapter 14 – 1968

"I've just started working as a consultant at King's College Hospital, and your husband's kindly agreed to rent one of your rooms to me. I'm very grateful, ma'am," he said, tilting his hat. As he leant over to pick up his case, Anna could see his white shirt collar starched to perfection.

Tina watched him smile at her mother, then ran to her room.

"He's having our room," announced Petro. "Anna, can you help Stelios get settled in? I have work to do," he said and dashed off.

"Wait... What... where are we sleeping?" she whispered, not wishing to cause a scene.

"I've put our things in the boot lobby next to the bathroom, remember, we talked about this, Anna." Petros tone had an edge of hostility that only she recognised.

Anna took the stranger to her old bedroom, her eyes discreetly scouring the room in case Petro had left any of her personal belongings behind.

Stelios laid his small case on the bed and stared up at the Victorian mouldings that surrounded the high ceiling. "This is a beautiful room!" he remarked, walking towards the window. As he stood in the light that streamed through the window, Anna noticed a sumptuous luminosity in his fine wool suit. It reminded her of the changing sapphires in the Mediterranean Sea.

"I guess you get used to the sound of traffic," he muttered.

"Yes, it's not too bad... Well, let me know if you

need anything." Anna's eyes skimmed his face, noticing his resemblance to Anthony Quinn. His deep brown eyes deepened even more as he smiled to say, "Thank you."

Anna left the room and looked to the boot lobby next door. It was just big enough to fit her mattress and a few piles of possessions. She would just have to make sure the curtain across the front was always drawn. Petro had spent the morning fixing a screen to one side, allowing customers to squeeze past and access the toilets.

Anna buried her face under the candlewick bedspread and thought about Sophia's idea. She wasn't weak, or afraid, so why did she feel so fragile, so wretched?

A few days later, while the children were at school, Anna was cleaning upstairs when there was knock at the door. Petro rushed from the kitchen to open it.

"Hellooo, I'm Frank." A stout Scotsman with a red face and booming voice stood in the doorway. "And this is my… my wife, Aileen." A small pregnant girl stood by his side.

"Oh, you're early… I'll, er, show you to your room," Petro fussed, trying to avoid eye contact with Anna. "I hope you don't mind sharing a bathroom with eight other people?" Petro laughed, pointing to the cold Victorian bathroom next to his screened off bedroom. "Hot water comes and goes," he confessed as they continued. "Sorry, it's on the second floor." Petro rushed the couple up the stairs and having just cleared his sons' belongings into the girls' room, he offered it to the couple.

A few weeks later, and after numerous attempts to fix the hot water, Anna needed to speak up. "It's been two weeks since the children had baths, and there's no hot water again!" she complained. Not wanting to hear any more excuses, she took a shilling from the till before Petro could confront her. "I'm taking them to the public baths. I told Sophia I'd go and see her as she's still recovering from the accident, so you'll have to pick them up at four!" she yelled, making sure Petro heard her.

An hour and two buses later, they reached the concrete steps of Manor Place Baths in Walworth. An elderly lady resembling Freda Kahlo opened the door to the large, ornate, red brick, Victorian building.

"Aint no charge luvvy," she said, with a cigarette hanging from her lips.

"Ari..."

"Yes, Mum, I know, Dad's picking us up. Now go and take care of Sophia."

The children were shown to individual brick and concrete cubicles, each with a calcium-stained bathtub sitting in the corner of a cold cell.

"Ere littlun, I'll elp ya!" The warden put Tina's belongings on a chair and turned the tap on just as the choking smell of chlorine crept into Tina's lungs.

"I'll be back in twenty minutes luvvy." Her lip was tilted from the permanent fixture of a Players cigarette. "Don forget ter turn yer tap off will ya luvvy?" She left the cubicle and slammed the heavy door behind her.

Tina heard the clanking of keys as the warden grappled with the cumbersome lock. She was trapped in a cell without her sisters. Hoping she wouldn't be abandoned like the first day of school, she glared at the water pouring into the tub. It flowed so fast that for a moment her heart beat faster, and she swore she would drown. Tina watched and listened to it roar like a lion and backed away as far as she could, in case it leaped out of the bath and drowned her in the cell.

Hearing her hysterical scream above the thunderous sound of flowing water, the warden came rushing back in.

"You gotta turn it off when its alf full darlin!" she explained, frantically turning the tap off.

"We don't wanna flood ere do we luvvy?" She smiled kindly.

Eventually Tina stepped into the bath and felt pacified by the soft buzz of white noise from moving water in the building. It didn't matter that the fresh bar of carbolic soap made her skin feel tight and flaky afterwards, she felt safe for now, and that was all that mattered.

With the water cooling by the second, she stayed below the surface with her head high, trying desperately to stay warm in the draughty cell.

It was almost dark by the time the children were all dressed and out the door. But as instructed, they waited at the entrance for their father. They waited until the sun hid behind big buildings and left them in almost total darkness. They waited until they tired of playing hopscotch on the old Victorian steps, and every white car had been counted in the light, and they waited until their stomachs hurt like they were being ripped out of their throats because of the hunger; then they sat quietly on the steps with collars turned up and their hands in pockets.

As Tina looked at Anastasia's lips turning blue, she saw a grey Ford Cortina speeding towards them.

CHAPTER 15

1969

"Move the aerial to the left."

"Oh yeah, I can see Bob Wilson… Quick Dad, or we'll miss the match!"

The crowds cheered as Arsenal played Swindon Town in the league cup.

"C'mon Arsenal!" shouted Theo on tiptoes with the aerial in one hand, balancing like a novice ballerina. "Wow, Dad, I can't believe we've got a television."

"Hold it… right there!" Petro frantically twiddled knobs and buttons.

Meanwhile, Tina meandered back and forth, trying to discover the mystery of how little people got inside a box smaller than her. And how did they keep changing in size? Were they the same little people who walked across the Corinth canal? She snuck behind the cumbersome box for clues then looked around the front, even more mystified than before.

"You see how I look after you," joked Petro.

Ariadne looked away and went upstairs to find her mother filling in forms. She sat close and leant her head on

Anna's shoulder. Then all of a sudden, an almighty scream pierced its way down from the attic.

"That's Aileen, isn't it? Her labour must've started." Anna rushed upstairs and found Aileen huddled in a corner of the room like a scared, abandoned child. Her waters had broken, and labour was well under way.

"Where's Frank, is he at work?" Anna asked calmly, releasing the warm stench through a small dormer window.

Treading carefully between debris, Anna went to take Aileen's hand to comfort her but discovered her clenched fist holding a crumpled note.

A shaft of cloudless early evening sunlight revealed a lost child in a grownup world. Her frightened blue eyes and fair freckly skin were contorted in agony, partially blanketed by strands of unwashed hair.

Aileen unclenched her fist as an invitation for Anna to read the note. Anna brushed clothes, food packaging and refuse from the bed then gingerly sat down.

'Gone to Glasgow for a few days, urgent. Back by weekend. Love, Frank.'

"Aileen, how… how long have you had this note?" Anna asked, helping Aileen onto the bed as contractions came and went.

"I… I can't do this… I'm scared! My mother said it just happens naturally. I don't know what to do..."

"Mothers do that, dear, but don't worry, this love will make all other love irrelevant. It will hurt for while, but it's worth it, I promise," encouraged Anna, brushing Aileen's hair from her face.

Her contractions continued for hours. Anna sat with her, holding her hand and encouraging her to be strong. Close to midnight, Aileen looked so pale Anna was getting worried. "Ariadne, go downstairs and ask your father if you can call an ambulance. Tell him it's an emergency." She spoke in English, so Aileen knew what was going on. But before the ambulance arrived, Aileen had the most ferocious contraction, letting out a scream worthy of waking the dead, then all of a sudden Anna saw the baby's head. A moment later, a baby girl was born. Aileen's terror immediately turned to delirious joy. Anna panicked for a moment; for although she'd had four children of her own, she had never actually cut the cord before. She looked around for a pair of scissors or a knife but there was nothing available. Whilst she tried to think of something, Anna was relieved at the thumping of an ambulance crew running up the stairs.

"I'm going to call her Jean, after Jean Simmons. She's my favourite actress. Aye, she was bonnie in *Spartacus*!" Aileen's eyes gleamed.

"Bonnie?" Anna hadn't heard this word before. There was a short silence as Aileen continued to marvel at her baby and the ambulance crew checked her blood pressure.

"Hold her like this so she can latch on to the breast," Anna said, nestling the baby across Aileen's tummy.

"But I want to bottle feed her. All the magazines say it's better for the wee baby."

Chapter 15 – 1969

"We don't have any formula, dear, and your baby is hungry."

Suddenly, the din of paramedics preparing to take her down the stairs made Aileen panic.

"Can I... I don't have anywhere... Can I come back here, please?" she begged as they wheeled her into the back of the ambulance.

"Of course you can. Where else would you go?" Anna laughed.

Across the street, Anna could see Stelios getting off the bus after a shift at the hospital. The moonlight caught his silhouette.

"Ahh, good timing!" he said nervously.

Anna had her arms crossed. She shivered and laughed at the same time and turned to go back inside. She felt his cheeky half-smile caress her back as they walked up the dark, creaky staircase.

"I'm sure you would've done a much better job!" she said shyly.

"Oh, I don't think so, I'm a heart doctor, remember!" he jested in his educated, high-class Greek accent Anna could just about understand.

They stood awkwardly on the draughty landing for a long split-second. Absorbed by a surreal moment in time, Anna looked into his dark chocolate brown eyes then looked away to a void between the floorboards. She felt flustered and ran up the stairs to the children's bedroom.

"Good night, Anna." He blinked slowly, inhaling her

floating scent as she tripped over the hem of her skirt.

Blast – another job to do! she said to herself, checking to see if he had witnessed her clumsiness.

When he closed the door to his room, Anna crept back downstairs and fell into her bed. It was very late and she was exhausted.

The next day after the morning routine, Anna went into Aileen's room and shut the door behind her. The place was a sea of squalor, and Anna spent the next few hours scrubbing, folding, cleaning and sweeping until the room and her thoughts were clear of anything untoward.

Lastly, she reached on top of the wardrobe to store a blanket, disturbing some papers. Newspaper clippings, cards and notes fell like a handful of sycamore seeds floating on the air, then dispersed on the floor. Anna took a deep breath and picked up a birthday card with 'Happy Fourteenth Birthday' splashed across the front in glitter. She gathered up the faded clippings from 1963 and noticed bold text reading 'Train robbers' and '£2m pounds in used notes,' Her thoughts were suddenly deflected from the previous day's events. She was a little worried, wondering what relevance these things had, but quickly put them back in their original place.

When Aileen returned from the hospital there was still no sign of Frank. Eventually, a malnourished Aileen began to thrive on lentils, beans, fruit and vegetables like the rest of the family.

"Will you go back to your family?" Anna asked in confidence.

"No… They've already said they'll disown me if I have this baby."

"But why?"

Aileen looked awkward for a moment, then realised Anna was the only person in the world who could help her. "Well… and please don't judge me – please!" she said quietly looking away. "Frank and I aren't married."

"Well it's not end of world! You can get married now baby's here, can't you?"

"You don't understand. He's already married: to someone else. You see, he was my boss, he told me he loved me and that he would leave his wife. But I think he's gone back to her!" She started to cry. Anna tried to comfort Aileen with funny baby stories of her own, but it was futile.

Anna looked into Aileen's face and saw a desperate creature, anguished by the loss of an imaginary love for a man who sailed in and out of her life, changing it forever.

On Sundays when the restaurant was closed, the group of eight – and sometimes nine when Stelios had a day off – sat in the kitchen watching television. Even the smell of Brussels sprouts and chip fat couldn't deter them from a night of *Opportunity Knocks* with Hughie Green.

"Stupid woman," blurted Petro at one of the contestants.

"But Dad, I thought you liked women," Tina asked curiously, having seen him with women on numerous occasions. For the first time, Tina saw her father blush. Stelios gasped, not knowing whether or not to laugh. Anna daren't look at her husband, for his embarrassment would reflect on her in front of their guests. He was, after all, her husband and she couldn't possibly feel any worse about his antics.

However, one afternoon a few weeks later, when Tina and Anastasia rushed home, excited to see baby Jean, the highlight of their day, Anna told them that Aileen had gone back to Scotland.

"Oh! Will she be coming back?" Anastasia was particularly upset.

"Probably not, sorry girls, but she needs her family's help right now and they have agreed to have her back."

Meanwhile, Stelios was sitting quietly, reading in his room. He heard the conversation and smiled to himself. After so many months, watching Anna from afar, he finally had a plan.

A few days after her forty-second birthday, Stelios waited for a creak on the third stair tread with bated breath. His meticulous timing meant he could open his door and meet her on the landing without startling her.

"I have a birthday gift for you," he uttered nervously.

"For me? How… how did you…"

"Wait there," he said excitedly. He went back into his room and took a small flat package, wrapped in gold paper. Anna was humbled, embarrassed and flattered at the same time.

"I know your birthday was a few days ago, but we had an emergency at the hospital, and I couldn't get time off. But please take, I mean… accept this as a small token from me."

He stared at her with his bright Anthony Quinn eyes, hoping and searching to meet hers halfway. Anna unwrapped the gift and was shocked to find a pair of silk tights, with a picture of a woman showing her entire leg, on the cover.

Her eyes filled with guilt as if she'd done something terribly wrong.

"I…I can't accept this!" she said emphatically, looking at Stelios's red face and wondering if her husband was nearby; much like the day she saw the soldier for the first time and wondered if her father was watching.

"Anna, come back to Greece with me," he begged, opening a flood barrier of uncontainable emotions. "I can give you a better life than him; you and the children. I see him with women in his car, I see how he treats you and the way he talks to you. He doesn't deserve a beautiful person like you!"

Anna was shocked. She handed back the tights and rushed upstairs.

"Why, Anna… why do you do this? You must know by now how I feel about you. I know you have feelings for me too!" he begged.

"Because...because I promised my father on his death-bed!" she whispered, hoping no one else could hear her.

For the next few weeks, Anna avoided Stelios. In fact, many weeks went by and Anna hadn't seen him. He hadn't been down to watch TV with the family, she didn't bump into him on the stairs, and despite watching for his routine return on the 68 bus from King's College, he was nowhere to be seen.

A few more days passed, and Anna became concerned for his welfare. She knocked on his door, but there was no answer. She tried the next day, and then again, a third day. Something was terribly wrong. This time she forced open the rusty lock and let herself in.

She entered the room with trepidation. Mould and damp had found its way into nooks and crevices, growing like an unstoppable disease in veins of dust and moisture, and produced a foul smell that gripped at her throat. The high ceiling and draughty Palladian window in the large Victorian room, the jewel of the entire apartment, meant it had an insatiable thirst for heat. Anna shivered and knew she had to take action. Stelios's assiduously arranged belongings bore no suggestion of his intentions, yet somehow Anna couldn't help feeling partly responsible for his disappearance.

A Savile Row suit made from the finest light wool was left in the wardrobe. Its navy silk lining, bright as the wing of a bird of paradise strutting for a mate, hung lifeless on a wire hanger.

Anna closed the wardrobe door and looked at her reflection. However infatuated she was by Stelios's charm, she knew she'd made the right decision. Feeling no guilt, and keen to rid the cobwebs, she began to pack his belongings before mould completely destroyed them. She cleaned the room until it was immaculate. This time, not even Petro could stop her moving back into her bedroom.

With a comfortable bed in a cosy room, she was able to continue with her Open University course in comfort, uninterrupted. She even found a way to get to the lectures every other week.

"Sophia has an important doctor's appointment and she's asked me to go with her," she'd lie.

"I don't like that woman! She takes up far too much of your time."

That was good enough for Anna! She had an arrangement with Ariadne. On the days she attended college, Ariadne would prepare her siblings for school and make sure they all got home safely.

"Mum, I'm fourteen, I know the drill," whispered Ariadne, rubbing her eyes. "Tina is nine now and perfectly capable of getting herself dressed, now go before you miss the bus."

"One day you'll be going to college with my blessing, and I'll want to hear all about it," whispered Anna, caressing her daughter's face.

"Go, mother!" Ari demanded.

Anna got on the number three bus from across the street and was filled with excitement. She felt at peace; just like she did at Koukles, all those years ago.

As the rain fell on the streets of South London, Anna smelled the musky scent of unwashed passengers, but it didn't matter. It was her time, and she could be alone with her thoughts. Sometimes she wondered what she would do if she bumped into the English soldier. She remembered his eyes and the smile he gave her with them, then wondered where he might be today.

With meticulous detail, Anna went over her plan to leave Petro. She had a stronghold on the family's finances. With Petro's erratic, irresponsible behaviour, surely her father would approve. Surely he could see she'd done everything possible to restore their family name. Even beyond life he was still her strength, her confidant and her hero.

"Are you OK luv?" enquired the lady sitting next to her with a strong Jamaican accent, seeing Anna's tears fall to the floor.

"Oh sorry… yez, I'm ogay" Anna exclaimed quickly.

"Downt apologise luv, da world is fulla ayte," the lady said and laughed a hearty laugh as she got off the bus in her black tweed coat and pink nylon headscarf.

Two young women in white PVC boots with matching accessories made their way down the middle aisle. Another wore purple shoes, with tights in exactly the same shade of purple.

Who has that much time to devote to colour matching, wondered Anna, stepping off the platform at Vauxhall.

Entering the large glass doors to the university, Anna felt her heart skip a beat; she belonged there. She approached the shiny lift along an uneven parkette floor, worn almost to concrete.

Being one of just two females on the course, Anna felt more comfortable at the front of the classroom. A middle-aged man in a brown shirt and knitted tank top sat next to her. He smelled of fresh spices and expensive soap.

"Hi, I'm Rich," he declared with a straight face.

Anna was astonished! Why on earth would a stranger tell her he was rich?

Noticing the confusion on Anna's face, the man held out his hand.

"The name's Richard, Rich for short." He chuckled.

"Oooh, I see… I'm Anna." She blushed and shook his hand.

A few minutes later their tutor entered the room.

"Good morning class, nice to see such a big turnout," he mumbled with a nervous laugh. He took off his wet duffel coat and hung it precariously on the back of his chair. "Lovely to see you all, my name is Andy Johnson, please call me Andy, we're all adults here." Another nervous laugh followed. He opened his heavy leather briefcase and took out a pile of papers. A dishevelled character smelling of tobacco and coffee, he bore a strong resemblance to John Lennon; even more so when he reached for his round glasses. Anna warmed to him like a sick puppy.

Turning to the chalkboard, a bald spot in the most inconvenient place on his corduroy trousers attracted amusement from the class.

An entire morning analysing English poetry was bliss for Anna. Her mind unhinged from everyday reality summoned her into another world.

"I'll see you all in the cafeteria for lunch," Andy said at

the end of their session.

Surprised by his casual relationship towards students, Anna wasn't sure how to respond.

"Just a minute, Anna," he called as she followed her colleagues out of the classroom. Anna turned back. "I want to talk to you about your story. It's full of grammatical errors." Anna was deeply embarrassed and upset; she'd put her heart and soul into her story. "But the bones are fantastic!"

Anna went from sad to overjoyed in a split second; she felt quite sick. "Thang you, Mr Andy sir."

"I want you to edit and add more atmosphere and descriptions," he suggested. "Then I want you to send it to my home address, not to the college. Our next session isn't for weeks, and if you want to pass the assessment, we need to make it perfect."

"Thang you again, Mr Andy sir!"

Her heart skipped a beat then began to pound in her ears as she ran down the corridor to catch up with her new friends. Even cafeteria tea tasted good that day.

At four o'clock, she caught the bus back home. It was dark and bitterly cold, but Anna didn't care. Highly motivated, she sat on the bus re-reading her story, holding onto Andy's address.

Absorbed with inspiration, Anna returned home to find her children up in their rooms and the candy floss woman sitting downstairs in the back kitchen again. Petro, surprised by Anna's entrance, turned his back to her and continued to marinate steak for the evening's menu.

The overpowering smell of the woman's hairspray masked the smell of fried onions. She sat in the same position as before with her dress riding high, revealing the elastic of her knickers. Her pure white legs glowed in the dimly lit kitchen. But Anna had come home with newfound confidence. She was no longer prepared to pretend that her bones were made of something inferior, or that the dust beneath her feet led somewhere invisible. Her voice mattered, and she was prepared to express herself clearly. So instead of quietly departing up to the flat, she walked to the fridge with a spring in her step and the woman's loathing stare burning into her back, but she stood tall. She took out a piece of cheese for her dinner, smiled at them both then went upstairs to tell the children her good news.

"Why is that woman here again? She keeps calling me Chris. I don't like it," complained Theo.

"She told me not to sit next to black children at school," Tina blurted, without taking her eyes from her colouring book.

"What?" Anna, uttered in disbelief, with a mouthful of cheese.

"She said I would turn black if I sit next to them. I fell off my chair yesterday because I leant too far over. Is it true Mamma, will I turn black?" Tina was still engrossed in her colouring.

"This is a lesson in patience for all of us," said Anna, assertively. "I promise you things will change for the better."

Then, when all the children had gone to bed, Anna went downstairs to talk.

CHAPTER 16

1970

"Mum can you hear me?" Ariadne whispered gently into her mother's ear. "Mum… Mum wake up, please!"

Poised and ready for her mother to wake, Ariadne listened for the faint rustle of Anna's starched hospital pillowcase. Perturbed by the meagre shred of information she had, Ariadne retraced each word, each sound and each silence, searching for some secret message tucked between the previous night's events, hoping to make sense of her mother's plight.

Anna lay semi-conscious and bruised between crisp cotton sheets. Utterly exhausted, Ari knew that no matter how many ways she retraced and re-examined the clues, she would always come to the same end. An end that brought her mother into hospital, instilling in her a deep and endless hate for her father. Her pain was indescribable; an isolation no one could understand. Her stomach churned at the sight of her mother's battered face as she slept peacefully like a crushed butterfly. Ariadne clung to her mother's hand, desperate for reassurance she was going to be OK.

"Let her rest now," demanded a passing nurse. Ariadne waited until she left the ward.

"Mum, please!... please wake up!" she begged.

The silence gave way to the sound of heavy footsteps approaching. Ari looked round and saw a tall, grey-haired policeman loom over her.

"Ouch," he said as he squinted at Anna's cut lip and black eye. "Thass a nasty shiner you got there luv!" His laid-back demeanour suggested this was just another mundane routine exercise. "Anyways, I'm ere to take a full statement luv." The thick plumage of his moustache bobbed up and down, masking his lips as he spoke. "I believe yer husband's responsible, is that right luv?" He reached into his top pocket and took out a tiny notebook and pencil.

"Leave her be," demanded a stout nurse in a thick Irish accent, rapidly approaching Anna's bedside. "Away wich yer!" she snapped. "She's no fit te give yer a statement yet officer."

"OK nurse, I might come back la'ers, it's just a barney wiv er ol' man anyways."

He turned and casually walked away in his squeaky giant shoes, whistling the tune of 'Waltzing Matilda'.

Anna had been in and out of consciousness all night with Ariadne by her side. Now, struggling to open her eyes, she began recalling events. She remembered confronting the woman but didn't see Petro's fist. Vaguely remembering the sound of sirens and the smell of iodine, Anna pieced together a collage of events, scrambled together like a grim dream starring someone else. Was she about to join her father? Anna left the answers to her trust in God. His decision was paramount and however brutal and cruel it seemed; he must surely have a plan for her. Tears stung like acid, prompting a swift squeeze of Ari's hand. Anna laboured to open her left eye.

"Where…?" A silent panic ran through her as knowledge of her situation amassed. Groggy and disorientated, she leaned forward.

"Mum don't move…. Don't move, you're in hospital. Do you remember what happened?"

Anna tried to speak but her throat was dry.

"Mum, you have to leave him... He's a monster! He did this to you and it's not the first time, is it? I want to go back to Cyprus, please Mum… Anything's better than this…I miss my friends, please, let's go back!" Ari dipped her head onto her mother's hand and cried.

"Where… where are the children?" she croaked, feebly trying to get out of bed.

"Don't worry, auntie Athena's with them," Ari sniffed. "I phoned her last night after the ambulance." Ari stared at her mother's face and decided it was time to stop pretending that everything was normal. She had to tell someone and do something in case her father went too far next time. She wanted to stop wasting powerful emotions, covering her father's deceit, just because they were dressed up to look like the norm. It was time to wake up, to yell out and to reveal the lie; but she felt powerless.

"Oh my God... Is... is Vasili there?" Anna croaked. "He'll kill your father."

"Well, I hope he does!" blurted Ariadne.

"Ari... I... I have a plan. I've been saving money from the restaurant and from the food allowance. I've done it since the day we arrived." Anna laughed meekly then coughed; Ariadne helped her with a glass of water. But Anna's revelation of her goal to finish her degree and get a job so she could leave Petro wasn't enough to console Ari.

"We have to act now, Mum, surely there's something we can do now." Ari gently helped her mother lie back on her pillow.

"Ari... If you tell the police what really happened, they'll take you and your brother and sisters into care, I'm sure of it. Please, please Ari, promise me you won't tell anyone!" Anna's dehydrated voice was fading. "Anyway, strength doesn't come from winning; your struggles develop and define your strengths, they are the root of your inner power, Ari. We must be patient." She started to cough. "I have to sleep now, I'm very tired."

Anna wavered and unsteadily nestled into her warm bed.

"But we can't wait that long!" shouted Ari, attracting the attention of a nurse whose starched uniform came crinkling towards them.

"Now now, what's all the noise about?"

Ariadne didn't understand her broad accent, but guessed it was time to leave.

Chapter 16 – 1970

"I'll be back later, Mum. I promise," she said sombrely, kissing her mother's cheek.

"Now let's get you comfortable luvvy," the nurse helped Anna lean forward and plumped her pillow. Despite her pain, Anna began to enjoy the pampering. No one had plumped her pillow or asked her if she was warm enough before. The nurse stared at Anna's face.

"Ei, tis a bad soul tha performs such evil acts!" She shook her head in disgust. "Take it from me love, ner man her does this is a worthwhile man," she sighed. She wheeled a squeaky trolley closer and took fresh bandages from a kidney dish. Her fat sausage fingers struggled to refresh Anna's wounds. "Oooooh be jesus, ye may have a scar, so ye may." She cleaned the dried blood from Anna's face.

"Oooch, my shoulder hurts," Anna winced in pain.

"Ohh…don't move tha arm, Yer due fer more pain killers anyhars."

"What's wrong with my arm nurse? I can't move it!" Anna yelped.

The nurse's tone suddenly changed.

"I told yer not to move iy, me darlin. That brute dislocated your shoulder, so he diy. Didn't doctor tell yers?"

Meanwhile, Ari walked the two miles home from hospital, in need of time to reflect. She asked herself the same questions over and over again. Why did her father hate the family so much? What had they done that was so terrible, and so awful that her father wanted to constantly punish them? Dazed and confused, she entered the front door to the sound of her uncle's voice talking to her siblings.

"Aaah, Ari, how is she – how's your mother?" He hugged his niece and tried to remain calm.

"Where is he?" she fumed, looking around for her father.

"Your father's not here, Ari... Look, you're fourteen now and far too clever for your years, God bless you. Now, let's just say your father's been informed and he will never, ever, do anything like this again. You have my word!" Vasili grinned.

"What do you mean? How can you be so sure, I hate him! I don't trust him! I don't trust any of you!" she screamed and ran up to her room on the second floor.

Vasili calmly went after her and found Anastasia huddled next to Athena with Theo clinging to her other side.

In the meantime, Tina's preoccupation with colouring came to a halt. She looked up from the sunsets in her book and noticed she was alone in her mother's bedroom. The warm, comforting sunsets were being replaced with monsters, dragons, ghosts and ghouls, as though they had been hiding but were now ready to pounce on her. With an almighty jolt, she fled up the stairs to be with the others.

"Look at me Ari... in fact, all of you, listen," Vasili ordered with the same authority and calm as their grandfather. "I need you all to be grown up!" His eyes scoured the face of each child. "I'm telling you now, your father will never lay another finger on your mother again. Not while I'm alive. Now... Athena and I have to go and visit your mother."

Chapter 16 – 1970

"I wish you were my dad." Tina buried her face in his warm coat.

Athena looked on with sympathy then left with her husband. Tina stared out the upstairs window, hoping they might change their minds and come back.

"Who's that big man opening uncle Vasili's door?" she asked Theo.

"I don't know, I've never seen him before," Theo was more excited to hear the Jaguar's engine.

"He's huge! And why is he wearing dark glasses?" Anastasia asked.

They watched the car disappear into the distance.

For the next few days, the children didn't know if their father would return. Ari took charge of her siblings. Concentration on her studies verged on the impossible and coupled with relentless teasing at school, Ari was exhausted.

"Ari, thas a boy's name ain it?" The gang of three made a beeline for her again. Recess was the worst.

"Does yer dad fink you're a boy then?" They laughed like robots.

"Does yer mum fink yer a virgin?" They laughed as Ariadne descended towards the gym block.

"Wass a virgin?" whispered the smallest in the group.

"Eeeer, iss someone ooh ain't French kissed a boy before," her friend whispered back.

"Oooh, right!" The gang laughed and made their way to the bike shed with a shared pack of Players No. 6, while

Ari went in the opposite direction and sat in the shade of a broadleaf tree. She'd just started to read when she heard a familiar belly laugh from behind. "I saw wha appened," said a voice. Ari looked up from the last chapter of *Malcolm X* and saw a girl she recognised. "Finks she's ve bees' knees that one. Thick as shit an all!" She laughed. "So, ha' comes you always ere readin on yer own gewl?"

"I prefer books to people. Anyway, I don't have any friends, don't need them."

"We all need friends gewl. Aint ya vat gewl who read vat Shakespeare rubbish in class?"

"Yeah that's me, hate the rubbish actually. Don't know why everyone thinks he's so brilliant!" Ari laughed for the first time in weeks.

"Aint vat the truth gewl!" She shrieked with laughter; thrilled to find common ground with the class brain box.

"Your name's Jennifer isn't it?"

"Yeah, thass me!" she laughed another belly laugh.

Suddenly Jennifer's friends approached. Ari had no idea she was part of the most feared gang of girls in the school.

"Oooo's this?" asked the tallest girl, menacingly looking down at Ari while bouncing a ball in her hand.

"Eer names Ariadne, she's in me English class. A right brainbox she is anall!" Jennifer sat down next to Ari.

"You're Sandra, aren't you? asked Ari, slightly fearful.

"Yeah, everyone knows Sarn," interrupted Jennifer.

"D'ya fancy a game at lunch?" asked Sandra, bouncing the ball hard and fast.

Chapter 16 – 1970

Ari stared incredulously at the formidable group and for the first time, she felt noticed. It felt good.

"Eeer, yeah OK…Yeah I'd like that, I'm not very good, though," she confessed.

"Neither is Jackie!" Jennifer laughed, pointing to another girl in the group.

"Oi… Speak for yourself, bitch!" screamed Jackie as the bell rang. The girls cackled with banter on their way to their respective classes, playfully jousting each other like one big, jubilant family. Ari was thrilled to finally have friends, and not just any friends. These were first rate, frontline warriors she never dreamed would take her into their clan. She strutted across the netball pitch like a model on a catwalk, hoping to be seen by every racist bully in the school.

Eager for the lunch bell to ring, Ari found her new family back on the netball pitch. She played her best game as an inauguration into the family and soon realised how serious and competitive the girls were. Ari felt so comfortable with them that she felt it was OK to express her emotions. She could actually be herself and it didn't matter if she won or lost at the game.

"Oi… Ariadne gewl, yous bin lying!" laughed Jennifer, out of breath and sweaty. "Said you was rubbish but you're good gewl!... You could make the team if you come to practice."

"Thanks, but I have to look after my brother and sisters after school," Ari panted.

"Yeah, me mum works nights. I babysit me little bruver every night… Phew, I'm knackered gewl, gonna eat me lunch now. You eatin now?"

Ari felt awkward. "No... er… I ate before."

"Gewl you gotta eat sumfink if you're gonna make the team. You is skiiiiny!" Jennifer laughed her big belly laugh while Ari went early to her next class with a hole in her stomach. She waited for that feeling every day, it was a comforting friend, something she could rely and depend on daily to feel and control.

Back home, with their father's elusive habits, the children couldn't be sure when he might appear or what mood he would be in. So for the next few days, Tina snuck down to the restaurant fridge and hid food in her pockets. She loved the bitter taste of cold Brussels sprouts and sometimes allowed herself to indulge without hiding it, as though taunting her father to see how rebellious she could be.

"C'mon Anastasia, don't be scared, we'll hear him if he comes," encouraged Tina. "If you hear him coming put the food on this shelf here, next to the tinned peas!" she professed, proud of her resourcefulness. "He won't see it behind the curtain. Then you can sneak back later and get it." Tina smiled at her nervous sister. "It's OK, really," she said proudly, "he won't catch you if you use this trick."

At first the quiet, non-confrontational Anastasia was nervous, but eventually stealing food became a rush of excitement. Hunger meant it was every man for himself if they wanted to eat. Ariadne had no appetite or inclination to feed her siblings anymore.

Eventually, their mother returned from hospital in the Ford Cortina. Petro walked with her up to the flat. "Let me help you with your coat," he fussed. He took her coat then pulled the bed covers down so Anna could get comfortable. Tina and Anastasia hugged their mother's waist.

"Ooooh, uncle Vasili's here too!" Theo got excited at the sight of their uncle's car from the window. "What's he doing? Why isn't he coming in?"

Anastasia rushed to the window.

"That's not uncle Vasili driving, it's that man with the dark glasses," she said as he sped away. Petro's movements became nervous.

"Mamma…I made you a bracelet with red paper." Tina jumped onto her mother's bed and wrapped it carefully around her mother's wrist.

"Where's Ariadne?" asked Anna, manoeuvring carefully with one arm in a sling.

"Oh, she's always in the bedroom reading," Theo complained.

"Mamma, your face is all different colours. Will it go back to normal?" Anastasia stared at her mother's bruises.

"I, er…I've put the flowers in water," Petro interjected. "Now I have to prepare for tonight's menu." He rushed downstairs.

"It will heal soon Anastasia, I promise. Now, please call

Ariadne for me, I want to talk to her." But Ariadne refused to leave her room.

Anna soon fell into a deep sleep but woke a few hours later to the sound of Petro preparing for bed.

"The restaurant was quiet, so I closed early."

Still groggy, Anna wasn't sure if she was dreaming.

"Look, Anna… I'm going to change, I promise you…" He couldn't look her in the eye. "I'll take better care of you and the children… I promise I will!"

"How's the new waiter?" Anna changed the subject, numb to his empty promises.

"Oh, he's good, his name is Angelo. He's Italian." Petro embraced the idea of a conversation with his wife but Anna pulled the covers over her arm and went back to sleep.

The next morning, Tina was surprised to hear her father in the bathroom. She looked at Anastasia.

"Does Dad live here at night now?" she whispered. Her sister shrugged her shoulders and continued to get dressed for school. Both girls avoided the bathroom in case they bumped into their father.

At the end of another school day, Tina heard the bell ring loud and clear. She let crowds of screaming children rush out the gate like a herd of hungry hyenas; she was in no hurry to get home. Her best friend strolled with her.

"I'm having bread and jam again for tea tonight!" Laura was excited. "My grandma makes the best jam in the world." She flicked her dark blonde hair from her face.

Chapter 16 – 1970

The girls walked slowly as the last group of boisterous boys kicked a ball in the air. Tina ducked and the largest boy laughed at her timid reaction.

"I've got tuppence to spend at the sweet shop today." Tina watched as her friend carefully pulled two faded pennies from her pocket. "But we can share them, Tina, it's for both of us. Mr Patel might have Black Jacks today." She put her arm around Tina. Laura had a way of comforting her friend with passionate stories about bread and homemade jam, holidays in Devon and her father's gardening career in the mansions of Dulwich. Tina's favourite were her stories of spring, because her father had more work and that meant they could eat chicken and sometimes ham that came in a big triangular tin. Laura didn't care when children teased her about the random colours on her darned cardigan. Neither did she care when they laughed as she pulled up her small socks that wouldn't stay up because the elastic had over-stretched. Sometimes she even laughed with them. Tina looked on in awe at her strong, brilliant friend. But more important was the life lesson she learnt from observing Laura's response to bullying and teasing.

The girls walked lazily through the school gate and onto the busy road where Tina had once tried to escape. To her astonishment, Tina heard Theo call from her father's Ford Cortina.

"Hurry up Tina, why are you always daydreaming… We're waiting for you!" he yelled, louder than he needed, so everyone could see him in a shiny car.

"Oh, I…"

"It's OK, Tina, I'll see you tomorrow," Laura said and skipped away towards Mr Patel's sweet shop. Annoyed at losing the opportunity to see who had the blackest tongue from Black Jacks, Tina quietly and grumpily got into the car.

"Why's he picking us up?" she whispered to Theo.

"I've got a lovely surprise for you all," shouted Petro from the driver's seat. "We have an appointment somewhere special."

"What does appointment mean?" whispered Tina. Theo shrugged his shoulders and continued to watch passing cars.

"Aren't you excited?" asked Petro, observing his children in the back.

"Is he tricking us?" whispered confused Tina. "Will he get angry if we say something?"

"Oh, be quiet Tina!" whispered Anastasia.

Petro continued to drive towards Herne Hill. A train chugged noisily above the arches as it entered the station, competing with the seasoned roar of the paper man under the bridge. As their car slowed down in traffic, they could hear him bragging about his family history to his customers. "My family's bin ere since 1895!" He smiled confidently. It being a cloudless day in May, he stood in a string vest and faded brown corduroys at the edge of the pavement selling paper after paper to people rushing to and from the station.

Petro drove for a few more minutes then turned onto a sunny street with large Edwardian houses, almost hidden behind cherry, birch and sweet chestnut trees lining the avenue. He pulled up outside number 28 and looked up with a beaming smile.

"This... is ours!" he said proudly. The children's eyes opened wide in amazement. Their mother was at the door, waiting.

"Is this really for us? I won't have to share a room with stupid girls anymore?" Theo raved.

Petro opened the door carefully so the stained-glass panel didn't fall out. The children were so excited they didn't know which room to examine first.

"There are four rooms on the ground floor, four on the first floor with a bathroom and three attic rooms on the second floor..." Peter went to continue but the children had dispersed. He turned to Anna. "We can live on the first and second floors and rent the ground floor." He smiled. Anna was happy for the first time in a very long time. She put her arms around her husband to say thank you and noticed his discomfort. She quickly moved away to examine the house.

Tina and Anastasia rushed to the second floor and found an enormous attic room. "Do we have to have separate rooms, or can we share?" They jumped with joy. Anna rolled her eyes in jest. "I guess it's not worth separating you two is it?"

Ari went to the small room next to her sisters' and looked out of the small dormer window.

"This changes nothing," Anna firmly whispered, then went to find Theo.

Within six weeks, the family moved into their first house and no longer had to share a toilet with tenants and customers or visit public baths.

CHAPTER 17

1971

"We were rushed off our feet again last night," yawned Anna as she examined the menu, looking for further improvements. "I don't know why people love prawn cocktail and steak Diane so much, it's almost all we serve these days."

Seated at the front table of the restaurant next to the glass shopfront, the women drank tea and watched the world go by.

"Sophia, where are your parents? Are they still in Cyprus?" Anna felt guilty about Stella taking care of yiayia Stavrou all these years and wanted to know more about her friends family. Stella was, after all, yiayia Stavrou's great niece and not her granddaughter.

"My father moved to Paphos. Luckily there hasn't been as much turmoil down there and he had distant relatives to go to. They showed him how to fish. He loves it there. He said the day he stops fishing is the day he dies. I'm glad he's happy there and he's finally stopped looking for my mother."

"Do you still think about her?

"As you know, I was only three when she disappeared, I didn't really know her."

"Doesn't anyone know what happened to her?

"No, it used to haunt my father when I was little, but that was a long time ago now. I'm more worried about these so-called peace talks they keep having about the future of Cyprus." Sophia looked away from the window and cast her eyes curiously at the long streak of faded light green carpet. She took a deep breath and flicked her shiny brown curls away from her face.

"How about you Anna, you never talk about Cyprus anymore."

Anna took a long deep breath and looked to her teacup.

"I'm sorry Anna, don't you want to talk about it?

"No, no it's OK, it's probably good to get some of this out in the air." She paused for a moment.

"You know Sophia! What I really miss is my mother. Strange isn't it? I hardly knew the woman, yet I miss her."

"Hmm, are you sure it's not missed opportunities you're yearning for, Anna? Insecurities can have that effect."

Anna was immediately taken back by Sophia's comment. She stared at her friend for a moment.

"You know something! I never thought of it that way. It would make a lot of sense. Well, I'm a grown woman now, I have no time to think about things like that," she said firmly, sounding just like her mother.

Sophia got up and moved her chair out of the sun and looked around the restaurant.

"You're lucky to have space. Michalis and I are still in that pokey flat in Brixton. I hate it. It's so small and dark.

I'm glad you're sticking up for yourself now though, it's about time!" She glared at her friend's scars.

"Well, I've told him I refuse to go to the market every Saturday to buy separate groceries!" Anna raised her eyebrows, displaying a newfound confidence. "Ever since he got that caution from the police, he hasn't touched me!" She sipped her second cup of tea.

"Are you sure the police gave him a caution? I don't know if they do that; it's a domestic issue. Are you sure it wasn't Vasili?" Sophia added. "Anyway, haven't you finished that Open University course yet? Seems like you've been doing it forever."

"I'll be finished in a few months. They've asked if I want to join some kind of graduation party afterwards. Me! A forty-four-year-old mother!" She laughed.

Having decided to skip church in favour of a chat with Sophia, Anna felt self-assured and comfortable. It had taken years to realize her self-worth. But bit by bit she began to live it and apply it to her master plan.

"Ah yes... I want to show you something." Anna flicked through the pages of an old copy of *Time* magazine from 1964. "Take a look at this, someone left it in the cloakroom."

"I, er... I can't read English," Sophia confessed, blushing with embarrassment.

"Oh, don't worry, I'll read it to you." The worn magazine opened easily onto the article. "'Wife beating is good therapy as it balances out each other's mental quirks.'"

Sophia looked at her friend. "What the hell are they talking about?"

"Yep... That's what the American experts think!" exclaimed Anna.

"When is this going to stop...? When will women stop being the property of their husbands to do what they want!" yelled Sophia, "It's so unfair!"

"Well, don't worry about me, I can handle myself these days. You're lucky Michalis is as sweet as honey." Anna tried to make light of the conversation.

With the topic exhausted, the women sat enjoying the view over Brockwell Park. A crisp line of yellow defined the hill brow on such a clear sunny day in May. They watched mothers escorting children, dogs running loose, and people seated on benches enjoying the sunshine. A cloud hid surreptitiously behind a group of trees in the distance, creating ghostly shadows. Immersed in the spring atmosphere, the women were sitting happily behind warm glass when suddenly there was a knock at the door.

"We're closed," shouted Anna, who'd just taken her shoes off. She heard a heavy Irish accent outside. Unable to understand the man, she went to the door.

"Really sorry ta disturb yer ma'm, but we saw yer notice for room ter rent," he pointed to his pregnant wife, twice his size and almost ready to give birth. "I'm Dennis and this ere's me wife Paula." He beamed.

His wife's hair was bleached blond with months of dark roots displaying dandruff and grease. They smelled like they hadn't bathed for weeks. Paula held tight to her green tweed coat that lay lifeless across one arm, nervously twiddling a large button that dangled by a few threads.

"Yers is the first sign we seen that doesna say no Irish and no blacks."

Paula leant against the warm glass, puffing and out of breath from their long walk. Anna could smell her foul clothes. Oh no, not another pregnant woman! She thought.

"Er, yes, I'd forgotten about that sign!" Anna felt sorry for the couple. "Well, I guess, yes, the room is available. I'll show you now if you like?"

"Ei, that'll be grand ma'am." The man breathed with a sigh of relief and followed Anna up the narrow staircase with a small case containing all their possessions.

Anna went upstairs to what was her old bedroom and showed them the bright room facing the park. In the rays of sunshine, Anna ascertained patches of psoriasis on Dennis's neck and chest; he was the whitest man she'd seen in London.

"It's illegal for landlords to discriminate now, but I've seen those signs myself."

"Ei its grand. We'll take it, if that's all right wich yers ma'am!" He gulped and glared at his wife, ecstatic to have found somewhere to live. Anna struggled to understand his broad Irish accent.

"Don't you want to see the bathroom? It's on the landing as we came in. You'll have to share it though."

Paula's lopsided smile unveiled teeth that would scare a small child.

"There's an indoor toilet?"

"Ei its grand ma'am. Can we move in now?" Dennis jumped in.

Anna had taken over the rentals for some time. Leaving everything to her husband meant losing it on poker games and alcohol. His oblivion was her advantage, and she was becoming a master.

Within a few weeks, Paula's baby was born, and Anna was glad to be living elsewhere.

"Are there any jobs yer need doin in the restaurant Anna?" Dennis constantly asked on his days off from driving a bus. "Ei, could use the extra money ter buy a pram ser I can," he mumbled with a grin. "So who's renting that lovely flat on yer ground floor Anna. Yer got four rooms there so yer de," he asked, testing the plug on the Cona Coffee Machine, keen to finish and take on more work. His short-sleeved shirt revealed muscular arms covered in scandalous tattoos of myth and manliness, chronicling his brief naval career.

Anna was uncomfortable and changed the subject. "Oh, err… did you hear Margaret Thatcher's going to stop giving free milk to our children?" Dennis finished his job and went upstairs to his room with a nod, wondering why his landlady felt so awkward. I don't need to tell the world what goes on in my house, she thought, accustomed to her husband's womanizing.

Deciding not to tell anyone about the numerous women that came and went from the flat, especially Vasili, was her best option, for she only had a few months to go until graduation, and nothing could get in the way of that. Anna tingled with excitement at the thought. Her plan was foolproof. Andy had promised to help her find a job, but in the meantime, everything had to be organized with meticulous detail.

Towards the end of May, Anna had her last meeting with Andy before the sit-down exam.

"The *Windrush* has been bringing people from the Caribbean for a few years now, so schools are filling up fast. Some have changed their admissions boundary line." Andy always enlightened Anna with his knowledge.

"Well, that explains why Tina didn't get a place at Dick Sheppard School, despite having two older sisters there," she complained.

"My dear, what I meant was, you're in a good position to get a teaching job!"

"Oh I see! Yes, I'd like that very much," she professed, holding on to hope.

For the next few weeks Anna was swamped with coursework in addition to working at the restaurant and taking care of her house and children. Luckily, Theo hadn't been getting into trouble for fighting or misbehaving at school recently so trips to see the headmaster were less frequent.

"We can't have him selling cakes at school, Mrs Kell... Kellani!" He fumed at their last meeting. "It's against school rules; neither can he set up football membership to a fictitious team!" He protested. "A few weeks ago, he tried selling catapults so the boys can shoot each other in the showers. It's not good enough! This is his last warning from William Penn School, now please sign here!" he said angrily, peering over his thick glasses with a frown that looked like it'd been there since birth.

"Oh, I'm very sorry Mr Squirrel, I'll see it doesn't happen again," she'd said, embarrassed not to have known about her son's antics before.

"And tell him he's got double detention tomorrow for fighting in the toilets!" he'd shouted as Anna got up to leave.

"Ah, Mr Squirrel, he told me all about that. He was being teased again because of his accent..." Anna tried to plead Theo's case.

"Mrs Kellan...Kelleni! I'm not interested in the trivia of childish disputes! I'm a very busy man, now please close the door on your way out!" He continued to look down at his papers with a twitching moustache like a dormouse after a scrape with an eagle.

"And the name's Cyril... Mr Cyril!" he shouted.

"Kallikantzaro" she'd whispered on her way out.

With her thesis finished, Anna started the day on three hours' sleep. She walked to the letter box with Tina to post it that very morning.

"Mum, when can I get my new school uniform?" asked Tina, excited to be going to the same secondary school as Laura.

"We have plenty of time, Tina, you haven't broken up from primary school yet."

Chapter 17 – 1971

"But they might sell out, Mum!" protested Tina as they walked past a large Victorian house displaying the 'No Irish, No Blacks and No Dogs' sign.

Their slow stroll allowed time for Tina to ask questions about the motherland, and anything else that was on her mind.

"But why did she leave without telling anyone?" asked Tina, enjoying the rare one-on-one with her mother.

"It's called shock, Tina. It made her very ill and the only way she could cope was to join the nuns. It was her way of coping with all the terrible things that happened on the island. Cousin Stella sometimes writes to me. She tells me about her yearly visits to see them. She said they're both well, but they don't like talking about their past life. I think it upsets Stella, especially as her father was killed on that terrible day, like bapoo Christopher. Do you remember him?"

"I remember digging trenches in the back field in case of a sudden attack. I also remember the dead birds I had to collect for him. I wanted to say no but I was scared of him." Tina looked at her mother and they both laughed.

"I do miss him sometimes though, Mamma. It was so unfair the way he was killed. Do you know how many people were killed that day?"

"Not really, but it was at least four."

Tina pulled a face and tried to understand the complexity of politics surrounding her homeland.

"Don't you miss your mum?"

"Actually, I do Tina, but the truth is, we were never very close. Not like you and me." Anna put her arm across Tina's shoulders and gazed at the silver birch trees lining her street. How formal and uniform they looked in comparison to her mulberry tree. Tall, thin and elegant against a backdrop of proud terraced houses, they stood to attention with tiny bright green leaves. Flirting with beams of hazy sun; the quintessentially picture of a spring day in England.

Feeling fulfilled at the completion of her course, Anna returned home and immediately started planning the next phase of her strategy. Tina, meanwhile, needed to go with her father to help at the restaurant.

"Don't put your feet on the seat, Tina," Petro groaned.

"I won't, Dad, I like the colour, it's brighter than the other Cortina." She stroked the red vinyl and inhaled the new car smell. She sat upright in the back, staring out of the window.

"When can I get my new school uniform, Dad? When, Dad… when can we go? Can I get a blazer as well… can I get new shoes as well?"

Petro's blood was boiling by the second at his daughter's incessant chatter. Suddenly he slammed the brakes on, bringing the car to an abrupt halt along the curb. In a blind rage, he reached between the front seats and grabbed the hair of an eleven-year-old child who only wanted him to caress and gently hold her and tell her she was loved, then beat her head against the console as if trying to crack a walnut.

Chapter 17 – 1971

"SHUT UP, SHUT UP, SHUT UP…" His hysterical screams were heard by a pedestrian who, having witnessed the incident, dragged Tina's body out of the car and away from her father's fist, still clenching clumps of her hair.

"Call an ambulance," the man shouted to a woman looking out of her bedroom window. Meanwhile, Petro sped away with the back door still open. He was never seen alive again.

Five days later, Vasili and Anna brought Tina home from hospital after a mild concussion. Feeling guilty for taking her eye off Petro, Anna wouldn't leave Tina's bedside. She slept in a chair next to her bed for the first week.

"It's OK, Mum, why don't you sleep in your bed tonight, I'll get up if she wakes," whispered Anastasia. Just then, Tina stirred.

"I'm so sorry… Mum I'm sorry… It's all my fault," she cried. Anna and Anastasia looked at each other in dismay.

"What do you mean. How's it your fault?" asked Anastasia.

"I'm so sorry… I… I made him angry… it's all my fault!" Tina sat up. "I can't say sorry to him, I'm scared… Can you do it Anastasia, please?"

Anna and Anastasia shared a glance. Anna sighed, knowing she had to tell her daughter that her father died in a car accident.

"Look at me!" said Anna sternly. "None of this is your fault, do you hear me? None of it!"

Tina's tear-soaked face nodded; her bloodshot eyes told a different story.

A few days later, after the funeral, Tina couldn't bear to leave her mother's side and even waited for her outside the bathroom.

Ari tried to continue as normal. Every morning she met Jennifer outside Brockwell Park and took the shortcut to school.

"Oh look, there's Blondie over there, smoking wiv er gang," sighed Jennifer.

Ari wasn't interested in anything other than Tina's recovery and her O' Levels. Her father's death was something she didn't want to talk about either; she hadn't processed her own feelings, so how could she talk about them to anyone else? She felt numb, confused and wretched; nothing mattered any more.

"Look Ari, I… I heard about yer Dad, I'm sorry e's dead. Mine ran off wiv some waitress arand Lewisham way when I was seven. Ardly member him. Me little bruva was just a few weeks old at the time."

They walked the rest of the way in silence then were heading to their respective classes when Ari suddenly heard Blondie from behind.

Oh, please God, not today! she thought.

"Not so tough now yer black mates ain't ere are ya? Fink yer better than me downcha." She got into Ari's personal space and glared into her eyes. Valuing her personal space more than most, having spent a lot of time comforting herself there, Ari no longer felt numb.

"Get… the… fuck… outta my face Blondie, or I'm gonna rip your fucking head off." Ari grabbed her by the neck and pushed her against the wall.

The commotion caused a crowd in the corridor and people started chanting, "Fight, fight, fight!" But fighting was the last thing Ari wanted, but for a moment she had no control over her actions. She came to her senses and let go of Blondie's scratched, bleeding neck, while the bully's entourage looked on in amazement.

"Come near me or Anastasia again… and I'll fucking finish the job!" she hissed slowly and clearly. "Oh, and yes… I am better than you!" she shouted, releasing the last drop of frustration from her veins before a deep breath and composure for the morning's exam.

At recess she met Jennifer on the netball pitch.

"Na maaaan!... you smacked that slut good en proper like!" cheered Jennifer, holding out her hand for a high five. Ari didn't laugh. She could see giant Sandra approach with a netball in one arm: her alpha presence still scared Ari. She gave Ari an approving nod and faint smile.

"We goes shoplifting up Oxford street on Fursdys, wanna come wiv us?" she asked Ari, as a concrete sign of inauguration.

CHAPTER 18

July 1971

"We missed you at the graduation ceremony." Andy's limp duffel coat slid effortlessly down his arm. With nonchalant ease he stowed it on the back of a chair, perpetually chatting with his usual burst of nervous laughter. His steadfast grin unfurled to a sigh of relief as he sat back in the chair, stretching his stubby legs. He gazed briefly at the heavy velvet curtains hanging in the restaurant window.

"You can watch the world go by from here." He glared at the windswept, silky clouds outside.

"But I guess you know that; and the reason why I'm here." He turned to his overstuffed briefcase. Anna sat opposite with an empty teacup by her side. Despite her affection for Andy, now was not a good time for a surprise visit.

"Congratulations by the way, you deserve that grade, you've worked very hard over the years."

"Thank you, Mr Andy."

"Anna, how many times have I told you… just call me Andy!" He laughed. "Do you remember that first essay you wrote?" He peered at her bloodshot eyes. "I never told you before, but when I showed it to the head of the course, he laughed and said you'd never pass. The reason why I'm telling you this is because I saw your potential. You soldiered on and… well, look at you now, you passed with distinction!"

"But everything's changed!" she croaked; her hands covered her face. "I can't think straight. I'm scared… I… I can't cope on my own anymore… I… I'm tired all the time! I didn't expect to feel like this!"

Andy wanted to add words of comfort, but he felt awkward, for he'd been a loner for so many years that he was sometimes unsure how to interact with people on a personal level. Especially after the death of his own partner so many years ago. Even the magic of time was unable to heal that wound.

"Look, far be it for me to tell you what to do, but have you thought about selling this place?" He looked at the red flock wallpaper and dark green carpet, inhaling the smell of grilled steak, coffee and lavender polish. "You've been bookkeeping all these years – you told me so yourself. If you sell it as a successful business with rental income, you might make a nice profit. Then you can do what you like."

"I don't know how to sell bricks." Anna pressed her fingers deep into her eye sockets and slowly rubbed them. "In Cyprus you build for life then pass it on to your children. How do I do it?" she asked like a child so incapable of understanding the process that even the question became scrambled.

"You use someone called an estate agent. There's one in Dulwich Village I believe, but I'm sure there are others. By the way, my sister ate here with her husband on Saturday, she said your special is amazing! What's it called, steak Dean?" He sat back in his chair and adjusted his knitted tank top over his big belly.

"It's called steak Diane, it's all the rage in New York but it's named after a Greek goddess." She managed a wry smile.

"Well just think about it, you have my telephone number if you need anything," he said sympathetically, carefully pulling a large brown envelope from his briefcase. "Now...don't consider this the end of your journey, but the beginning of a new era for you." He edged the envelope towards her.

"Promise?" he teased, pulling it back and forth, waiting for a 'yes'.

Anna couldn't play the game. Suddenly it didn't matter anymore. Was this piece of paper really going to make her happy? This piece of paper she'd sacrificed so much for, was it worth it? She took it with trepidation and placed it on the table next to her cup.

"I'm sorry to rush off, my dear, but I have an evening class to teach at Brixton college. Please think about what I said, Anna." Gulping the cold remains of his tea, he picked up his heavy briefcase and coat. "Since they assigned me as head of English for this unit, I've had to take the 'English as a Second Language' classes and I hate it!" he groaned, struggling with the torn lining in his coat, unperturbed by the afternoon sun.

"Phone me if you need anything," he said, playfully saluting her at the door.

Anna sat quietly for a few minutes before making her way to collect Tina from school. It was something she hadn't done for many years but the last month had changed everything. Ashamed of the high price she paid for this piece of paper, she couldn't bear to look at it. Instead, she tried to remember the first foolish moment she decided to pursue her childish fantasy, but it was woven so tight in the fabric of her being that she couldn't unpick it.

Her journey had become more than she expected and less than she expected with a lifetime of selfish pursuit, destroying her family. She felt nauseous. She picked up her keys, tossed the envelope into the bin and rushed out the door, her heavy keys jingling in her hand.

I must ask Dennis to change this lock, she thought, struggling to turn the key. Suddenly, she became aware of a woman staring at the 'Rooms to Rent' sign from across the street. Why would such a well-dressed woman be interested in rooms, she wondered, but had no time to ponder.

She arrived at the school to find Tina and Laura outside their classroom, chatting.

"Ahh, Mrs Kell…Kellyari, I wonder if I can have a word?" asked Miss Martin, who had been a tower of strength for Tina in that last year of primary school.

"Oh, OK. I'll be back in a minute, Tina," said Anna as she followed Miss Martin into the classroom.

The women sat in the old Victorian classroom with a ceiling too high to rid cobwebs. Anna became aware of their voices echoing between vaults and voids above their heads in a chaotic chorus.

"I just want to say how sorry I am for your loss. And you do know that Tina doesn't have to come in during the last week of school, don't you?"

"Yes, thank you Miss Martin but she wants to. She needs her mind occupied. I've been sleeping next to her at night, hoping the nightmares will go away but it's not working, she's very clingy and I want to do everything I can to make her feel secure."

Miss Martin sighed with sympathy. Her tall slender body was wrapped in wool and tweed, in spite of the heat outside. The quintessential teacher of a passing era sat with her legs crossed.

"I allowed her and Laura to sit quietly and do what they want today. Unsurprisingly, Tina took out her book and started drawing." Miss Martin looked up from her pile of books, releasing the stench of stale nicotine. "But I'm sure yesterday's incident with Johnny didn't help!"

"What incident?" Anna glared at the sparse hairs above Miss Martin's lip.

"Oh… I thought she would've told you; it wasn't that bad really. Our classroom bully tried to push in as he always does." Miss Martin rolled her eyes. "But Tina pushed him back. He got very aggressive and punched her hard in the stomach. Luckily, I saw everything and pulled her away. But between you and me…" She looked around to see if anyone was about to enter the room, then leaned forward. "The boy is already a suspected criminal. He's been linked to the recent spate of burglaries on the Peabody estate down the road. I'm telling you this because she doesn't know when to back down…"

"You mean she's brave!"

"Well, er… possibly."

Anna stood up to leave.

"Well thank you for telling me, Miss Martin, but I'll take it from here."

"Also, Mrs Kell…Kelleri, I need to tell you, Tina is behind with her maths. She struggles a lot with numbers. It's worth keeping an eye on that when she goes to secondary school. I've caught her sneakily drawing under the desktop a few times when she should've been listening during maths."

"I know, she's always struggled with numbers, but thank you anyway." Anna rushed out of the sawdust-and-cabbage-smelling classroom to find Tina and Laura waiting for her on the step outside. Maths could wait; her youngest needed her right now and she wasn't going to fail her.

They walked home in the heat, watching burning white limbs attached to sweaty bodies. Everywhere they looked, trendy nylon clothing clung to backs and armpits in a sea of humidity. They ambled lethargically, enjoying the warmth and a show of smiling faces. Voices and birdsongs merged in happy harmony as panting dogs and sun-lovers stole precious, sporadic breezes.

Underneath the railway bridge at Herne Hill station, the boisterous comedic chants from the newspaper man trumpeted. Sweat beads fell from the knotted handkerchief on his head and down his thick neck as he called out, "Read all bout it, Microprocessors taking over. Robots gonna take over, you eard it ere ladies and gentlemen, read all bout it!"

Ten minutes later they dragged themselves through the front door and fell listless on the couch. They shared a gentle silence for a while when Anna got up to open a window. To her amazement, she saw the same well-dressed woman walking past her house. That's strange, she thought, but was distracted by the cool breeze on her face. She looked away and turned to the kitchen for a drink. Tina followed immediately.

"Why didn't you tell me what happened at school?" she asked as she poured a glass of water for Tina.

Tina looked embarrassed. "How did you know about that? It's horrible, anyway I didn't think anyone would believe me." Tina looked away in disgust.

"Why wouldn't anyone believe you?" Anna was puzzled.

"Because he's a teacher."

"What? OK, now you need to explain!"

Tina was reluctant to talk.

"Well… when everyone went on a school journey to the Isle of Wight and Dad said I couldn't go, I had to go into Mr Murray's classroom for a week. I hated it, no one talked to me…except him! He kept asking me to stay behind at playtime."

"What happened?"

"He kept trying to touch me." Tina looked away. She felt disgusted and guilty, as though she'd done something terribly wrong.

Anna felt her blood boil but didn't want to scare her daughter into silence; she composed herself.

"What… what did you do?"

"I ran out into the playground, but I was scared in case he reported me to the headmaster, and I'd get caned."

"Why on earth would you get caned? You didn't do anything wrong!"

"I know, Mum, but he's a teacher, he can do what he likes… can't he?" Tina began to raise her voice.

"Did he actually touch you?" Anna's temper was ready to burst and she found it increasingly difficult to remain calm.

"Only once, he told me to stand in the wastepaper basket in front of the class so I couldn't run away. Then he started to massage my shoulder, it was sooo yucky! He's old, fat and disgusting! After that everyone thought I was teacher's pet. I felt sick, I couldn't explain it to anyone, they wouldn't believe me anyway."

Anna closed her eyes for a few seconds, trying to contain her anger.

"OK, leave this to me," she said, calmly reassuring Tina; but was immediately preoccupied by the thunder of three hungry teenagers rushing up the stairs to the flat.

"We'll talk about this later," she whispered, affectionately brushing Tina's face.

With dinner over, Anna went to close the living room curtains. At first, she thought it was glare from the evening sun playing tricks with shadows, but on further inspection she could see the same woman, only this time she was standing next to Anna's front gate. Anna had had enough; she rushed downstairs to the front door to confront the woman.

Trembling with curiosity and fear, Anna could see the woman through the stained-glass panel on the front door. A mixture of bright colours split and distorted by the low sun, accented the stranger's silhouette. Anna opened the door. The woman at the garden gate was startled.

"Don't I know you?" said Anna curiously. "Weren't you at my husband's funeral? Are you Costa's wife?"

The woman remained silent. Her eyes twitched as they made contact with Anna's. She stood in a green flowery, halter-neck dress with her blond curls holding steadfast in the evening breeze.

"No," she said nervously, adjusting her large white handbag. "Look, my name is Helen, and I think you need to hear what I have to say."

CHAPTER 19

The Assimilation

"Come through, the front bedsit is empty at the moment."

The stranger stepped over the threshold, poised with the elegance and grace of Julie Christie in *Dr Zhivago*, leaving a trail of Chanel no. 5 floating behind her. However, her blue eyes pierced with hostility as she gazed around the entrance hall with trepidation and uncertainty.

Anna closed the front door on the dramatic red and orange sunset, steering the woman into the dimly lit front room. She noticed the stranger peer up the stairs, surveying the house as she walked into the large bedit. Standing side by side, the women drowned in silence for a few seconds.

"Who are you – why are you here?" Asked Anna.

The stranger's news was bound to have something to do with her dead husband. Anna endeavoured to contain her emotions, amassed over years of second-hand tales, misplaced devotion and duty that always left her second best.

"Dear… spoiled… Anna," the woman said as if to herself, quietly scanning the room. "You had him instead of me."

"Excuse me!" Anna's fury came to the fore.

"Don't you know who I am? Golly. Then again, why should you? My name is Helen." She stared daringly at Anna, then sat down without being asked and crossed her legs. "Did you even know my Petey? Or were you just too wrapped up in your own world that you didn't think to ask about his own struggles." Her words were clear, cold and crisp as early morning frost.

"Are you referring to my deceased husband?" Anna stood abruptly, ready to throw the intruder out; but instinct told her otherwise.

The woman, calm and composed, adjusted her cardigan with an air of confidence and superiority.

"Petey and I were married just before you came to live in England. The beast told me he was single. When you came here, he chose you! It was only then I realised he was as a bigamist. What could I do? He left me in a frightful mess. I had twin baby boys to look after and Daddy cut off my allowance when he found out."

Anna tried to process the woman's words, but news just kept coming.

"On that ghastly night he died…" She took her tear-filled eyes away from the window and looked to the floor. "The silly fellow must've taken too many of his pills. Sometimes they made him hallucinate; he'd taken so many towards the end that he became beastly – it's the only explanation. He would never intentionally hurt little Tanya." She stared at the empty fireplace. "It's frightful how much he loved you all; I was always second best. Preposterous isn't it? But you were too wrapped up in yourself to consider my poor Petey's problems, and you know something? I loved him so much I was prepared to stay second best. It was better than losing him altogether." She looked up and down at Anna's worn summer dress, faded from years of washing and a lack of time for ironing.

"Now, you listen to me!... Petro wasn't on any pills; the bastard almost killed my daughter – and her name is Tina, not Tanya. Do you know what that's like – do you? – to have your child's own father beat her head against the car. For all I know she may never recover, and you come here telling me about your fucking Petey. What exactly is it you want from me?"

Anna had never felt so much rage in all her life.

"Steady on darling – you really are frightfully naïve, aren't you? It sounds like my Petey kept everything from you. I guess it's about time you found out the truth. Why should I be the only one to carry it around?" She looked at Anna with contempt then reached into her bag for a cigarette. She offered one to Anna as a potential peace offering. Anna shook her head, scrutinizing the stranger as she tapped her long cigarette holder onto the pack.

"Well get on with it then!" Anna demanded.

Helen reached into her bag for a lighter, and with a swoosh of her thumb, the barrel ignited with familiar action. Anna was dumbstruck.

"I... I gave Petro that lighter for his birthday a few years ago!"

"I know he told me," she gloated, taking a large drag from the cigarette, leaving an excess of pink lipstick on the holder.

"When he was twelve, my Petey witnessed a dreadful murder in his village. It was horrendous. Three British soldiers brutally attacked and tortured a helpless little chap – about seven years old apparently. He said the beasts seemed to be enjoying the boy's cries. The soldiers heard Petey nearby and realised they'd been seen, so they chased after him. Blighters even took a shot at him. Jolly good luck he knew the area better than them! He ran up a large olive tree and hid there for almost two days."

She paused to take another drag of her cigarette. Anna watched her uncross her legs and resume her graceful poise.

"But with it being such a small village, they knew exactly where to find him, so the poor chap ran away in fear of his life. He went to Kyrenia; scared and at death's door from near starvation. He told me he was so hungry that one day he stole a fish and ate it raw on the beach. After that, he lived on oranges, tomatoes and those funny little syrupy fruits you people eat. The poor fellow stayed in hiding for almost six months. But as the weather got colder, he became desperate. Then one day he was passing a coffee shop in town and saw a couple sitting outside." She looked around for an ashtray, caught sight of one on the coffee table and leant over to tip her ash.

"They were so frightfully wrapped up in each other that he thought she wouldn't notice him sneaking her leftover cake as she got up to leave. Spiffing opportunity that went wrong. Had he waited until she left, we wouldn't be having this conversation now." She turned to a bewildered Anna. "Golly, don't you know the story? The woman was Katerina, and the man was Pavlo! Apparently, they were having a seedy love affair and planning to elope!" She sat back and made herself comfortable. "Do I really need to join the dots for you?" She gloated with superiority.

It wasn't the first time Anna had been made to feel a fool of; but this was horrible. Distraught and empty, she stared at her hands and remained quiet. She was tired of fighting. Tired of her life being dominated by Petro's influence; tired of consequences that never ended. Her eyes softened and, without warning, she looked at Helen with sympathy. Her arch nemesis was feeling the same pain, the same confusion and the same torment as her. Helen continued her story.

"They took him in as their own, moved to a village just outside Kyrenia and no one suspected anything for a while. Superb plan – they even found a doctor that could treat him for trauma. Little fellow was prescribed barbiturates, and everything was fine for a few years. He told me that was the happiest time of his life, but it wasn't long before your interfering people became suspicious – golly, how you people gossip!" She rolled her eyes away from Anna. "Anyway, poor Petey reacted badly to the rumours. Even with medication, he became delusional. Began to suspect the buggers were waiting for him outside the house – got into lots of ghastly fights, so they had to move again. Ended up in your village; it was meant to be a fresh start for them." She laughed sarcastically.

"What about his real parents? What happened to them?"

"He was an orphan, Anna, didn't you know that? His real mother abandoned him, he thought she must've had a lover – he didn't know what happened to her but to save their family name, his grandparents wouldn't take him in either. They handed him over to an institution where he was raised like a child slave until… well, you know the rest. Crumbs, didn't he tell you anything? When they moved to your village, the new doctor knew nothing about barbiturates and refused to help him. Beastly chap told him to take cod liver oil."

"Oh, I know that doctor!" Anna interrupted. There was silence for a few minutes. Anna tried to process everything while Helen continued to take long drags from her cigarette, elegantly blowing smoke towards the window.

"I can't believe… All those years… Why didn't he tell me anything?" Anna murmured.

"They couldn't tell anyone the truth, it was such a frightful mess!" Helen leant over and stubbed her cigarette in the ashtray. "His ego wouldn't allow him to tell anyone he was suffering. The fool thought it would make him look weak and unmanly."

Anna's eyes moistened. Yet more tears spilled on a man she barely knew. The two women sat in silence for a while. Seconds felt like hours as hostility melted into empathy, soothing and binding the women together without their consent.

"I can't believe I knew nothing about this. They told my father they moved there to be near his boarding school. He was just using me, wasn't he? They all used me, even my father!"

"It pains me to say this Anna, but he thought you were the most beautiful woman he'd ever met, inside and out. He was afraid your family would reject him if they knew the truth. Poor blighter, he just... well, he just struggled all his life."

Acknowledging their shared plight as victims of Petro's startling and tragic saga, Anna and Helen began to relax.

"He told me he was a driver at a British base. He became chums with a frightfully good soldier who gave him lots of cigarettes. He's the one who got the fake passport and birth certificate so Petey could leave the island. I wish I could say that he wanted to leave you because he was unhappy, but... but that would be a lie, and it's time to be truthful now. He came here to get real medical help, not because he didn't want to be with you. It drove him to drink, and that's when I first met him. I was working as a barmaid in a wretched little bar in Tower Hill while I was a student. I should've walked away there and then." Helen took the cigarette butt out of the holder and placed the holder back in her bag.

"Can, er... Would you like some tea?" Anna asked tentatively.

"Golly… That's very decent of you, yes please."

Anna went upstairs to the theme tune from *Bonanza* blasting through the living room. Curious to get to the bottom of Helen's story, she gently pushed the door ajar to check on Tina. Both Tina and Anastasia were serenely curled up and snoozing on the sofa in harmony.

A few minutes later, she went back downstairs with a tray of tea and found Helen admiring the Edwardian fireplace. Anna carefully placed the serving tray next to the ashtray.

"Thank you, I really wasn't expecting this." Helen took the cup with her left hand and sat back on the sofa. A huge diamond engagement ring flashed next to a wedding band.

"Petey never bought me gifts, it was Mummy's," she insisted, noticing Anna's eyes on the rock.

"I have more to tell you, old er… Anna. When Petey went back to Cyprus and got a job at the army offices, he said something about a new sergeant, I can't remember his name now… anyway, Petey recognised him from the scene of the wretched torture. Said they came face to face in his office but he didn't recognise Petey. Petey thought it was just a matter of time, so he walked away, but…" Helen put her cup and saucer on the floor and opened her large white designer handbag. "On his way out, he took this from a drawer that only he and a few other chaps in the office had access to."

She pulled a large folder from her handbag and handed it to Anna. "I flicked through it the day after the funeral, saw lots of Greek then put it back. I don't want to know what's in it anyway," she conveyed with a sigh of relief. "I've had enough of all this, it's time you took possession."

"Didn't he tell you anything about it?" Anna enquired, staring at the ragged cover.

"Petey kept it hidden, and I never asked him about it, but what I do know is that this file *must* contain some classified information. I'm just not interested anymore!"

It was getting late and Anna could hear her once serenely snoozing daughters arguing upstairs but felt compelled to stay downstairs with Helen. She was determined to glean as much information as possible. Suddenly, Anastasia burst into song, and the two women smiled.

"Is that Tina?"

"No, it's Anastasia, my thirteen-year-old. Those two are as close as twins."

The thorny atmosphere and frenzy of emotions settled into a new calm as the women realized they were caught in the same web. Helen took another sip of tea.

"Look, for what it's worth Anna, I really am sorry for what happened to Tina, and the times he attacked you. But I had a beastly time too you know! I felt like the mistress! Waiting for him to come to me whenever he had a moment."

"Helen…you *were* the mistress, your marriage wasn't legal!"

"And how do I know yours is legal here in old Blighty? Have you ever checked?"

"Of course it's legal, we were forced to do everything the British way on the island. But you know something? I don't care anymore!"

"All these years I wanted to meet you Anna. To hit you and to curse you for making my life so difficult." She paused for a second "But none of that matters anymore. My Petey's gone."

"Did he ever hurt you?" enquired Anna, hoping she'd say yes.

"He tried a few times; we did have frightful arguments! But I was ghastly to him. I threatened to come here and tell you. That worked every time."

"So, I'm the bigger fool… yet again!"

"No, no, you're really not." Helen looked thoughtfully at Anna. "Look, this is a little sensitive old chum, and I don't know if you already know, but did he say anything about the... um, money laundering business?"

"Dear God… Will this man ever stop tormenting me?" Anna looked up to the ceiling, made the sign of the cross on her chest and tried her best to contain the Greek drama.

"Calm down… He told me about some beastly Middle Eastern gang that were operating in South London. Blighters were laundering money through food parcels from the wholesalers. Got to a stage where he didn't know which box, sack or bag the money was coming from. Did he try and prevent you from going into the kitchen or opening the fridge?"

Anna's eyes opened wide as she plucked the memory from a foggy blur.

The sun began to set, leaving a chill in its place, as she recalled the times Petro willingly let them go hungry.

"These people were… are… dangerous, Anna. They often ate in the restaurant, that's how they checked up on him apparently. Their go-between was a dumb bleach blonde who went by the name of Pamela. She would collect the money and leave Petey his share. Did you ever meet her?"

Anna choked and coughed but didn't divulge Pamela's role in her life. It was a place she never wanted to re-visit.

"Didn't you ever wonder how the restaurant could make so much money, Anna?

"Well… no, not really. It never seemed excessive to me. The restaurant was often full."

"Anna, all South London immigrants were in on it! How else could they feed their families? How do you think Petey got the deposit for this massive place?" Helen looked around the charming room. She took a deep breath, gathered her bag and cardigan, and stood up with a sigh. One final adjustment to her tights and she was ready to depart. They stood at the front door and briefly looked at each other with an altered perspective.

"Oh… and by the way, I'm sorry but your brother was in on the money laundering too."

"What, Vasili? No… You must be mistaken, he'd never do that!"

"Poppycock! Ask yourself this – how did he get the money to set up the restaurant when he came here with nothing? How was he able to afford a brand-new Jaguar, furs for his wife… what's her name, Anthea? And what about all the houses he had? Petey told me everything. Golly, now I think of it…" She looked down at her shoes, trying to find the memory. "I… I think it was Vasili who introduced him to this wretched racket." Helen rolled her eyes in an attempt to recall her conversation with Petro. "Well anyway… When he noticed how unstable Petey was getting, he or one of his henchmen would follow him. Of course, that set off the paranoia, so the who thing spiralled out of control again. Look, I know it's a lot to take in, but I am telling you the truth." She reached into her big bag again.

"Well…as we're on the phone now, I'll give you my number in case you need to talk. It might be something important, old chum."

"How do you pay your bills, Helen?" Anna blurted. "Is it from this so-called money laundering racket? How do I know you're not the mastermind, come here to spy on me?"

"I'm a lawyer – ironic, isn't it? I should know better, but I have my limits. I stayed out of that as much as I could. Daddy would disown me completely and cut me out of his will if he found out. So, you see I've come to you baring all. I've been waiting so long to do this Anna, but it's not as satisfying as I imagined it would be. I'm doing my best to move on and I think you should too. And Anna – I'm serious about those wretched men. They're dangerous, be careful."

She buttoned up her cardigan in the evening breeze then left. Anna watched her strappy heels bob up and down as she carried herself down the garden path like a vogue model.

Shocked by the impromptu meeting, Anna took the file and ran upstairs to check on Tina. She went to bed that night wondering which was worse; the pain of what she discovered, or the ache that would stay with her from that day on. But for now, all she had to do was hide her eyes and heal, until one day she could be so far removed from the situation that she could become someone else.

CHAPTER 20

The Three-Day Week

"Oh, I put dis ere coupla years ago." Angelo cried from the restaurant kitchen, precariously balancing on stacked chairs. "Found it in de bin – thought it was an accidente."

"What is it?" Anna yelled, competing above the din of an antiquated vacuum cleaner.

"I dunno, got your name on it though, Hanna."

A sudden chill ran through her. Fearing the worst, she dropped the nozzle and darted swiftly to the kitchen. Despite two years of looking over her shoulder and searching both the house and the restaurant, she'd found no evidence of money laundering that could possibly incriminate her.

"Where is it?" she croaked.

Angelo carefully slid the brown envelope from between old volumes of Yellow Pages and the accounts folder. Anna immediately recognised the embossed logo. It was the envelope Andy gave her shortly after Petro's fatal accident.

"Oh, I thought I threw that away! I'm so glad you retrieved it, Angelo. Wow, I thought I'd lost it forever." She pulled the certificate from the envelope, caressing her name with her rough dry hands, evoking a flurry of negative thoughts and feelings she once associated with it. Her spirits rose as fresh potential washed the misguided thoughts away, leaving just a morsel of pride she once felt.

She watched for a moment as her long-standing friend and employee continued with the clean-up. Having been in her employ for many years, Angelo had become one of the family. Now in his late forties, he was still content to work in a small restaurant with a family atmosphere in order to escape the violence and poverty of Naples; a subject Anna learned to avoid. Having helped keep her business together for so many years, Anna – along with most of the country – was now falling on hard times.

"I worry, Hanna. This inflation thing, gonna leave you with no restaurante and me wid no job. Whad appen if we ave dis three-day week they talkin about?"

"I know, it's a scary prospect, that's why I need to sell up as soon as possible. Takings have been down a lot the last six months." Anna also knew that Petro's unorthodox finances were having an impact on her family.

"Why dis appening anyway? Why de Arabs hold all the oil and no sell."

"They're treating us like hostages. They think we're supporting Israel, so they've put up the price of oil, and if the miners go on strike, we'll definitely have the three-day week. People have no money so the last thing they're going to do is go out to restaurants."

"I dunno whad you wanna keep and whad to trow away," Angelo asked, seizing handfuls of papers from the shelf.

Intently focused on the clean-up operation, his chubby fingers disturbed a scrawny piece of paper that twirled to the ground like a feather.

"Ah, that's my mother's recipe for spanakopita. Thought I'd lost that too!" Anna reached for the scrap of paper, faded and limp from the ravages of time and fetid air from the musty kitchen. She recalled the day her mother struggled to write it down for her, determined to pass down the recipe. "Don't tell the Turkish girls in the village," she demanded vehemently, handing over the paper from the cheese man's wrapping. "They'll change it and pretend it's Turkish. Then generations of Greek girls will lose it forever."

Anna laughed as her mother made her swear to it with the sign of the cross on her chest.

"I promise, Mother," she'd said, taking the cheesy smelling paper from her hand.

Her spirits rose as she tenderly held the scrap of paper to her nose, hoping to smell the old man, his donkey, and happier times.

"Do you remember when we tried it as a special with Greek salad a few years ago? Only one person ordered it! I spent far too much time explaining it to grimacing faces, so I took it off the menu."

"I guess it too foreign; no meat in it eiver!" Angelo laughed.

"Anyway, I want the place looking immaculate, Angelo – I really need to sell as soon as possible but I have to go to Brixton and pay the electricity bill before they cut us off.

Won't be long, just carry on without me, the viewing's not till this evening." She placed the envelope and her mother's recipe carefully in the accounts folder for safekeeping.

Eager to get the place looking its best, Anna collected the mail from the porch on her way out. As it was Thursday, a free edition of the local paper got shoved through the letter box by an impatient paperboy. But on that day, the headlines caught her eye.

'Police arrest three Syrian men on suspicion of demanding protection money, money laundering and fraud.'

Her heart jumped into her mouth. She immediately recognised the men in the picture; they'd been regulars at the restaurant.

How could that be? They were so pleasant and friendly. They even made an effort to speak to her in Greek! On days when she was rushed off her feet, they told her to take her time. They always complimented the food and service. Over the years, she'd told them personal things about her life – something she rarely did, even to friends – and they theirs. The daunting prospect of what this could mean frightened her. Could she be roped into a courtroom somehow? She rushed out the door, trying to recall exactly what she'd told them over the years.

But I haven't found anything, and I know nothing! she thought. Whatever Petro did, he left no clues; even her accounts showed nothing untoward.

With the newspaper under her arm, she sprinted across the street under a light shower to catch the 1.35 to Brixton.

Two stops further down Dulwich Road, Anna spotted her best friend in her familiar tweed coat and blue nylon headscarf. She waved frantically.

"Ahh, so glad you made it, Anna, I haven't seen you for ages!" Sophia got on the bus bringing a trail of crisp air, just before a pungent waft of her signature hairspray. Chirpy and full of news, she quickly took off her headscarf and plumped her hair back to shape. They sat together for three more stops, chatting more than breathing.

"So, how's the new flat?" inquired Anna.

Sophia was dying to tell her all about it. "Oh Anna, you won't believe how beautiful it is." She pointed proudly at the new tower block facing Brockwell Park. "It's taken us years to get re-housed, but it was worth the wait. We have fantastic views, and there's so much glass to enjoy them from. You must come over after church on Sunday, I won't take no for an answer."

Anna laughed. "OK, I promise."

"Bring the family too; by the way, how's Tina these days?"

"Oh, she's a lot better, I think. Tough little cookie, the nightmares are decreasing thank goodness, but I'm more concerned with Ari, she's getting desperately thin. She doesn't talk to me like she used. She spends all her time revising for her A Levels, locked away in her room, listening to Carole King."

"Do you think it's serious?" asked Sophia, still plumping her hair.

"I don't know, but I've seen her get up in the middle of the night and do something very strange."

"What? What is it?" Sophia stopped preening herself.

Anna looked out of the window, too embarrassed to face her friend.

"Well… she makes herself sick!"

"What do you mean, is she eating bad food? I don't understand."

"No, I mean she does it on purpose. She puts her fingers down her throat and makes herself sick. Have you ever known someone to do this?"

"Good heavens no! Why?"

"I really don't know, but I have to do something because she's wasting away."

"Why don't you speak to her doctor, see if he can help."

"He'll probably laugh and humiliate her; she's too sensitive, he might make it worse. I really don't know what to do with her. She keeps saying she's not good enough, but I don't know what she's talking about."

"You should try seeing him on your own, Anna, before it gets worse! Doctors here are more advanced than they are in Cyprus and he probably won't prescribe cod liver oil."

Outside, the wind unleashed its blustery fury, howling like a starving hyena, relentlessly blowing everything in its path. Stepping on to the platform, they held tightly onto the pole with one hand and adjusted their headscarves with the other in synchrony. The bus screeched to a halt outside the Town Hall, jerking passengers into one another. Anna and

Sophia wrangled past a wind-beaten queue of embarking passengers trying escape gale-force winds, now with the added misery of horizontal rain.

Their conversation switched to Greek as they rushed across the busy street to the electricity board and Anna told Sophia about the Syrians in the newspaper.

"Are you sure it's them? They might be dangerous."

"I'm not scared anymore." Anna put on a brave face. "I've spent the last two years looking over my shoulder in case someone thought I had their money, but nothing happened. If they are involved, I don't think they'll do anything to me. They can't – I know their families, the schools their children go to – even where they work!"

"Anna, you're being really naïve! They could've been lying to you, they're criminals and they're dangerous!" Sophia became agitated.

"Oh, Sophia I just don't care anymore! That chapter in my life has to close. I have no time to be worrying about possibilities. Anyway, they've been arrested. If they really are guilty, they'll go to prison. That's that as far as I'm concerned!"

Just as her amazingly confident rant ended, Anna became speechless. A man wearing a mauve velvet jacket, lilac corduroys and a yellow shirt opened the door for her. Stumbling almost into his face, Anna recognized him immediately. It was her old friend and tutor, Andy.

"Oh…er…" Andy was lost for words. Ashamed and embarrassed, he went to button his jacket, endeavouring to hide his flamboyant scarlet cravat, paralleling the glow from his flushed cheeks. But before he could speak, his partner walked over and slid his arm around Andy's waist.

"Who's this, darling?" The ostentatious partner inquired.

"Hello, my name is Anna," she interjected, trying to spare Andy's feelings. "I was one of Andy's students a few years ago, and this is my friend Sophia." Anna held out her hand and Andy started to breathe again.

"Yes… er, Anna was one of my best students."

But the partner was staring at the latest eclectic cooker on display and couldn't take his eyes off it.

"I… er… I didn't know myself," Andy said.

"You don't need to explain anything to me." She smiled warmly, moving away from the busy entrance.

Just as he went to speak, a group of young skinheads walked past outside, laughing at Andy's colourful attire. "Oi… you bloody poofter!"

Andy's scarlet face couldn't increase in intensity. Their mocking wolf whistles turned to homophobic gestures for amusement.

Anna looked back at Andy.

"You know, Andy, I've been spat at, discriminated against, and Tina often gets called a fucking Paki because she's the darkest in the family. I didn't even know what a Paki was until last week! So, I understand how you feel. I try and focus on bigger problems when it happens, not irrelevant, meaningless nonsense!"

Andy tried to be comforted, but it was difficult. "It's OK," he said with a childish grin, trying his best to mean it. "I've been actively fighting for gay rights. We just came back from an important conference in Morecombe, Johnny thinks it's just a matter of time before we get more recognition." He glared lovingly at his partner who, having twiddled with the knobs on the stylish cooker, couldn't work out how to open the oven door.

"Well, it was lovely to see you Andy, I never did tell you how much I appreciate your help and support. I was in a bad place the last time we met."

"Oh, hey, don't even mention it! You were going through a tough time."

Anna looked at his grey lacquered hair and sincere eyes and was reminded why she'd warmed to him in the first place. Unable to contain her affection for him, she leant over and hugged him while a young mother ushered her child away in disgust, driving Anna to hug him tighter. A resounding kiss on the cheek sealed her affection. Andy was her friend; she could do that!

"Ah, I just remembered," he suddenly said. "I don't know if you're interested, but I'm hosting a cultural evening at the Town Hall in a few weeks. Would you be interested in reading some of the poems you used to send to the magazine from Cyprus? It's a celebration of diversity in Brixton. Please say yes! To be honest, I haven't managed to fill all the slots yet."

"Oh! I don't know if I still have them… I…"

"Please say yes, they were so inspiring and fertile. It could help to put this community on the map – much like David Bowie!" He giggled, trying his best to entice her.

"I don't like speaking in front of crowds, I'll freeze and humiliate myself."

"Please think about it, Anna. We have African dancers, Jamaican calypso, Jewish readings and even Olive Morris will be there talking about the 'Black Panther' movement. I'm trying to convince Desmond from the record shop to get his mother to write a piece on the Windrush group. A lot of them settled here, so I'm fairly optimistic it will be a triumph.... a cultural smorgasbord if you like! And who knows, maybe David Jones...I mean David Bowie might be in the audience. I still have the same phone number, call me tomorrow and we can talk more. Please... please say yes, Anna!"

"Well... I'll think about it," she said quickly, noticing Sophia's impatience.

After paying their bills, the women left the electricity board and set off towards their favourite café by the arcade where they used to meet on Saturdays. Surrounded by graffiti, boarded windows and rubbish strewn across pavements, Coldharbour Lane looked pretty much the same as it always did. Sophia looked for the frosted glass door with net curtains in the window, decorated with streams of greasy plastic flowers between each panel. An elderly man in a donkey jacket was leaving the premises, coughing and spluttering, a roll-up cigarette stuck fast to the corner of his mouth.

"Ere yer go luv." He wolf-whistled at Sophia, holding the door open with dirty, stained hands.

Inside the busy cafe, the familiar sound of a hissing tea urn, mumbled voices and high-pitched clinking and clattering from crockery filled the room. As always, the waitress tried to keep up with demands for hot tea while taking orders through a haze of chip fat. Anna and Sophia rushed to the only free table in the café. They fit snugly between Lambeth council workers, local shop assistants, artists and a homeless man stooping over a cup of tea he'd nursed for an age.

"Phew! Glad to get out of this horrible weather," sighed Sophia, pushing dirty plates to one side for the waitress. Anna put her bag down and took out the slightly soggy newspaper, inhaling the smell of fried eggs and bacon, intermingled with cigarettes and sweat from the two workmen next to her. The ambience sparked reminders of a phase in her life when she was feverishly planning a brighter future; a future she was convinced she could build without complications.

"Have you had any interest in the restaurant yet?" Sophia enquired, interrupting Anna's thoughts.

"Only one, this evening so I can't stay long. I'm getting a bit desperate now to be honest. The bills are mounting up and I'm worried."

Sophia beckoned the waitress over to take their order. It was always the same for her, a cheese and tomato sandwich with a large mug of tea.

"I'll have the same." Anna shook the last of the rain droplets from her hair.

The waitress limped back behind the counter in her slippers and reached for a burning cigarette, as if she'd forgotten how to breathe without it. She took a deep drag and blew thick smoke down the middle aisle. It floated away like a ghost in a child's drawing, immersing customers in its path. Instantly relieved, she yelled the order to her husband in the kitchen.

"What about your rental income?" enquired Sophia.

"What rental income? Everything's ground to a halt, no one's got any money. Angelo can barely scrape by and the other tenant has just lost his job in the theatre – the building kept getting vandalized and the producer was receiving death threats."

"What! Why?"

"Not really sure, to be honest. According to Louis, the show had men dressed up as women. I don't know exactly what happened, something to do with trans pheasants... trans pher...they had to cancel it."

"Are you going to let him stay?"

"What else can I do? Poor man's been disowned by his family. Got a great selection of dresses though!" She grinned. "Louis – or Lucy as he likes to be called – showed me his wigs last week, they're amazing Sophia, we should go out one day, I'm sure he wouldn't mind us borrowing them." They laughed just as the waitress bought their food.

"Eaaarr me darlins, nice cuppa ter warm yer cockles,"

she chirped, placing mismatched china and cutlery on the table.

"Urry up Doris, table free's bin waitin!" yelled her husband.

The waitress suddenly became possessed.

"Shurrup en fuckin wait old man!" she yelled back in a husky voice, followed by a hacking cough. "Finks e ken boss me abaat!" She looked to Sophia with a 'girl power' look, then walked back to the counter, intentionally slower, just to irritate her husband.

"Don't you love this place!" giggled Anna, tucking into the thick white bread with a thin slither of cheddar and tomato in between.

"You should do that poetry reading Anna, it could be good for you, get your mind off everything for a while."

"Hmm, I'll think about it. Feels a bit indulgent at the moment, what with Ariadne's problem."

"Ask her to go with you, what's the worst that can happen?" she chewed hungrily.

By now, Doris and her husband were in the swing of a full-blown war. Unperturbed regulars, used to their drama, continued with their lunch.

"Ere we goes agen!" the young bus boy rolled his eyes, left the kitchen and started to clear tables.

"Time to leave, I think." Anna left money on the table and stood up.

"Awww, it's just getting interesting. Do you remember the time she threw a teapot at him from the kitchen when she thought he was having an affair with the girl in the record shop?"

"Not really, but if you're so keen on shows, why don't you come to see me if I do this poetry reading?"

"Of course, I'll come with Michali and cheer you on. Wow, I have a brilliant, famous friend!"

CHAPTER 21

1973

"I'm so sorry, Angelo, I can't afford to pay you anymore. The takings have been down for months now; I've got no choice. You can keep your room in the house, until you find something else. I'm so sorry." Anna delivered the bad news she'd been dreading.

"Ooo Hannah, I dunno what I ken do. My English, shesa not so good."

"Come and sit here, let's talk about it." She took a bottle of wine from the rack, and like a well-orchestrated performance, Angelo synchronised with an effortless grasp of two glasses. They sat at their favourite table next to the window, watching wet pedestrians trying to take cover from yet another barrage of rain as it made its way between work boots and platform shoes.

Angelo stretched his short legs with a huge sigh, followed by a brisk rub of his knee.

"Aaah, my knees, shesa no good. I ave, ow you say… arthrite." Not wanting to discuss it any further, he quickly changed the subject. "So, you still wan me to go on Sunday?" He asked, pouring the wine.

"Of course, I do… Actually, I really don't want to do it, but I promised Andy now. Hope I don't mess up, I can't really focus on such frivolity these days."

"Oh, you be very goo Hannah. You always liv scribbles around. You talke some funny thinks sometime too."

"Do I?" she asked, savouring her first sip. "Mmm! this wine's really good."

She sat back in her chair and watched Angelo swirl the wine a few times before taking a big gulp, followed by a mouthful of black olives, contemplating how he would manage.

"You're a great chef, Angelo you might find something with better pay. I'll give you a very good reference… I'll tell them they're stupid if they don't take you on!" They laughed and took another sip of their wine.

"White men employs only white men," he muttered.

"Surely not in an Italian restaurant?"

"I don know, but my frien, shes been look for long time. She say they call im a greasy daigo. What this mean?"

Anna rolled her eyes. "I don't know, but it can't be good!" She placed her glass on the table. "Seriously though, have you ever thought about going back to Naples?"

Angelo's eyes widened above the rim of his wine glass.

"C'mon Angelo. You're like a brother to me. What could you possible say after all these years to make me think anything different about you?" The absence of a definitive explanation had bothered her for years, maybe now was a good time.

He looked outside at a man struggling to light a cigarette in the rain, then rubbed his chin. He was finally ready to talk, when a ringing phone broke their silence, blanketing any hope of an explanation for now.

"Less hope isa bookin." Angelo called, relieved to escape his interrogation.

Anna could hear murmurs of a panicking female on the other end; Angelo's gaze turned to confusion.

"What is it?" she asked, grabbing the phone from his hand.

Within fifteen minutes, they'd raced up Herne Hill on Angelo's Ducati and reached King's College Hospital before the ambulance arrived. Anna jumped off the bike leaving Angelo to park.

"Where's my daughter?" she asked frantically "Why isn't the ambulance here yet?"

"Calm down madam, we're doing everything we can… Can you just..." Before the receptionist finished talking, Anna heard the scraping of a gurney rushing through the emergency doors down the corridor.

"Madam, you can't go down there, it's restricted!" Her words faded into the background as Anna approached the medics.

"Is she going to be OK? What happened? I'm her mother!" Anna's heart pounded in her ears like the sound of the ocean.

"How did you get here so quick?" asked the medic. "She collapsed at school, she's malnourished, when did she last eat?"

Chapter 21 – 1973

"What do you mean? She eats breakfast, lunch and dinner… I..."

"Don't worry, we have her on a drip, her blood sugar levels are improving, as is her hydration level. But we need to know when she last ate."

"I… I work nights… I leave my children to get their own breakfast and get to school…I don't know!" she sobbed.

"Wait here, madam," he demanded.

"No, I need to be with her…"

"Ma'am wait here, or we'll ask you to leave the hospital," demanded a staff nurse just approaching the scene.

Anna sat outside the room, just as a flustered Angelo sprinted towards her. An hour later she was called into the doctor's office. Afraid and shaking, Anna was ashamed she had allowed her daughter to starve almost to death and done nothing about it. She sat opposite a young doctor, ready to take her punishment.

"First of all, I just want to tell you she'll be fine," he said, looking at her puffy eyes. "So, don't worry. You haven't done anything wrong."

"Can I see her?" she asked, bolting upright from her chair.

"Actually, I'd like to discuss her condition first. We believe she has a newly recognised condition called bulimia. Have you heard about this before?"

"No, what is it? Did she catch it at school?"

"No… It's not something you can catch; it's an eating disorder. Fortunately, you're in the right place. We want to move her to Maudsley Hospital across the street. There's a professor there who published a book on this very condition, we're very lucky to have him."

"Maudsley! No thank you, it's a mental institution, she's not going there!"

"No… no it's not, that's a common misconception. You really should consider it."

"Do you mean you want to lock her up?" Anna couldn't believe what she was hearing.

"No, not at all. She would come here for consultations, say, once a week. We weigh our patients, discuss their eating habits and try to get to the bottom of what's making them feel depressed."

"Depressed? What do you mean? It's nothing like that, she just doesn't want to eat."

"Mrs Kell…Kelly, your daughter needs help. Please let us help her."

"Well…" Anna hesitated as she thought for a moment. "Are you sure you can help her?"

"The only promise I can give you is that we will do our best."

"Er…I'll talk to her about it first. Can I see her now? Please… I need to see my daughter!"

The young doctor took her to Ari's bedside. Lying listless in a ward full of geriatric patients, Ari was fixated on the ceiling.

"Get… away… from... me!" she growled slowly. "I have nothing to say to you. Leave me alone!"

Chapter 21 – 1973

"Ari, what are you talking about? It's me!"

"Well, there had to be a 'me' in the very first thing you said, didn't there, mother?"

The same staff nurse who had assisted Ariadne from the ambulance heard the conversation. Wry faced and imposing, she edged closer.

"You're distressing the patient, please leave my ward!" she demanded.

Anna looked at Angelo, barely able to speak.

"Is OK Hannah, I stay wiv er, you get bus ome, I see you later."

Half an hour later Anna approached her house to the sound of Dave and Ansell Collins' 'Double Barrel' on repeat, spelling Theo was home from school. Now sixteen, Theo was no longer the angry, brash little boy he used to be. Unlike his peers, he wasn't interested in smoking and going to pubs. His love of reggae urged him to wrap himself in music and practice his guitar that he learned to play from books and by listening to Jimi Hendrix, Buddy Holly and John Lee Hooker.

When he heard the front door close, he came running out of his room. He watched his mother come up the stairs to the flat and hang her wet raincoat.

"Mum, I…" he hesitated.

"What is it… Tell me Theo, is it about your sister? Do you know something important?" she implored, looking at him in case he had information.

"Do I have twin half-brothers?" he asked, blushing and unable to look at her.

"Aaaah… I've been waiting for the right time to tell you all," she said, nervously, waiting for his response. "How did you find out anyway?"

"Two boys with the same surname just started at our school. No one has the same surname as us! I told Ari about it this morning, she was very upset. What's happened to her? Why is she in hospital?"

Anastasia and Tina were listening at the bottom of the stairs. Anna took a deep breath.

"Come upstairs girls, it's time we all had a long talk." She sighed, dreading the conversation that had the potential to alter her family's view of their identity; wishing for once that someone would wrap her in a blanket and tell her everything would be alright.

Anna spent hours explaining everything to her three children. She did her best not to leave out anything so they could understand the magnitude of the situation. She was thoroughly exhausted and wished she didn't have to dig up everything again. But she ploughed through, hoping this was the last time she would have to face Petro's bygone days.

"So… we have twin half-brothers?" Anastasia and Theo looked at each other in disbelief, wondering if this was a good or bad thing.

"So…so… he was ill when he did that to me?" Tina asked, trying to make sense of her trauma. At thirteen, life couldn't be more challenging for Tina, and now this.

"I really can't say for sure, but it's possible."

Chapter 21 – 1973

"But…but Mum, it's been almost two years, why didn't you tell me before?"

They all stared at their mother, waiting for an explanation.

"I… I don't know, I thought it was best if you tried to… to forget the whole thing, I didn't know if it would make things worse... I just wanted what's best for you, Tina." "My father almost killed me! And you thought it was best if you didn't tell me it wasn't his fault? This is on top of uncle Vasili promising me he would never allow Dad to hurt any of us, and you telling me you would take care of that disgusting pervert teacher at school?" She flew into a rage Anna had never seen before.

"I hate you! I bet you drove him to it! I'll never forgive you for this. Why can't you be like Laura's mum… You're evil!" she screamed, running upstairs to bed.

Theo barely noticed her tantrum; he was still processing other pieces of the puzzle.

"So, what was in that folder the woman left for you?

"What folder?"

"The one you said she couldn't read because it was all in Greek?"

"Oh, I don't even know, I put it away and haven't looked at it since."

"Don't you think you should go through it?

"Well… yes... I will when I get time, now we all need to go to bed. Let's talk about this tomorrow." She yawned again and headed straight for her room.

Never before had her bed felt so inviting. Drunk with fatigue, she collapsed into bed and buried her face in her pillow. But inconsistent with her weary body, her mind oscillated between the realm of what could have been and what was. Now her eldest and her youngest daughters hated her with a passion, and she had no idea how to make things right.

She lay cocooned under her candlewick bedspread, wishing she was immune from her current state of mind. A reminder of what it's like to be lost in darkness reared its ugly head again and brought with it the craving of a fleeting memory of an English soldier she barely knew. How could she think of him at such a crucial time? And where was she going to find the strength and wisdom to fix this?

CHAPTER 22
Easter 1974

Thrusting his way through legions of people dressed in dark clothing to commemorate the crucifixion, Vasili waved frantically above the congregation then lunged towards his sister.

"Aaah, there you are! Every Good Friday this place gets more and more packed!" he shouted, agitated by the volume of people in his path. The siblings made their way towards the quaint stone courtyard, notorious for teenagers brazenly looking for love.

"This is the only reason they come to church with me," laughed Anna, as she watched teens trying to hide behind the pillars, deep in conversation. She loosened her head-scarf and shooed pigeons from a rice feast left by wedding parties. Vasili motioned Anna to perch on the fountain wall in the middle of the courtyard.

On Saturday mornings, the griping sound of Greek children struggling to keep up with their native language echoed along the courtyard corridors. But today was the most important day in the Orthodox calendar, still it was incapable of restraining ambitions to find love amongst the younger generation. Anna felt very uncomfortable.

She buttoned up her coat to keep warm from the howling wind.

"How are the children?" Vasili turned down the collar of his sheepskin jacket, revealing an exemplary Savile Row suit in the finest wool, then rubbed his hands together.

"I think I'm finally making progress with Tina; she started talking to me because I said she could skip Greek school for a while."

"Ouch, that must've hurt, sis," he jested.

"Well, it was the only thing that worked. I guess everyone's had their fill of entertainment at my expense by now!" She looked sheepishly at the crowds.

"Oh, who cares sis? Do you think this lot here is squeaky clean?" He laughed, sizing up the crowd. "Look over there." He nudged her. "See that tall fat man in the brown suit? He comes to my restaurant almost every Friday night with a different woman. That pretty young thing next to him is his wife!" Vasili looked around for more evidence of imperfection. "Ooh, look to your left. Do you see the skinny old man in a Crombie? They say he's the heaviest gambler in London. I met him a few times, he gambles with wads of fifty-pound notes! You gotta ask yourself, sis, where would a simple market-stall greengrocer get that kind of money? Look, I… I'm sorry I didn't tell you about that business with the… you know, the money and Petro, but I knew you wouldn't approve. You've always been so prim and proper, sis. Besides, the less people knew about it the better. These people are… well… let's just say you need to play by their rules. And sis, I swear in the house of God! I knew nothing about the bar…bar…barians he was taking. I'm so sorry sis, I really am. I had no idea he would hurt Tina the way he did, especially after I promised he wasn't going to hurt her, or anyone else."

He leaned over and hugged her, enveloping her in an aroma of sweet spices. "I'm still angry with you for not telling me the restaurant was in trouble though!" He squeezed her a little tighter.

"We would be homeless by now if it wasn't for your help," said Anna. "I didn't want any more from you Vasili, I'm a grown woman."

"Look! Athena and I weren't blessed with children like you and Kate. Who do you think is going to inherit everything when we're gone? Between your four and Kate's five kids, there's enough to… well, let's just say they'll be well looked after." He noticed the ruddiness of his sister's face; worn and scarred from domestic violence, earnestness and moral obligations.

"No one cares about anyone in this world, sis! Don't you know that by now? You gotta look after your own!"

"I… I know. It's just been a bit painful lately. I see the foreclosure notice on the restaurant every day from the bus. I feel like a fool! Everyone knows I'm a failure. I put my heart and soul into that business."

"You're not a failure! The banks don't care about people, Anna. You're a woman raising four teenagers on your own;

there was nothing you could do!"

A sudden clearing in the courtyard exposed Ari in conversation with a boy about her own age. Anna's mood suddenly changed.

"She's smiling! Look, Vasili." She nudged her brother discreetly. "I can't remember the last time I saw her smile."

"Wow... she's still very thin, sis, didn't the bulova... er, bolina treatment work?" Vasili frowned. Anna heard him but was fixated on her daughter's smile.

"Didn't the antibiotics work? Have you tried cod liver oil?"

"They told me it could take years," she said, unable to stop herself beaming. "Has to do with therapy, rather than pills."

Ari sensed someone watching and turned to see her mother and uncle frantically pointing at pigeons splashing in the fountain.

"How's the job going anyway?" asked Vasili loudly, hoping Ari would be convinced they were just talking about work.

"Broken Peek Freans biscuits for dinner is better than no dinner at all!" Anna laughed.

Vasili realised he could stop pointing at pigeons and looked at his sister.

"Is it?" He asked, desperately trying not to laugh with her.

"No! I can't stand the bloody things. You should see the rubbish they put in them at the factory."

As Anna and Vasili waited for the procession, they

resorted to their childish memories for reprieve.

"Do you remember the pole in yiayia Stavrou's house?" He asked, wickedly brushing his hand across his mouth. Memories of an old lady chasing them round and round a large pole in the middle of her hut came rushing back. The pair came close to falling in the fountain, surrendering to their heinous sense of humour.

"Aaahhh, there you are!" Athena approached her husband in time to witness his juvenile behaviour. "What are you doing?"

"We're watching doves!" he squealed, pointing to Theo who just happened to be within sight. Theo could hear his uncle's familiar laugh above the din of bragging boys.

"Mother you're embarrassing me!" He fumed under his breath.

Then, as if on cue, a wave of bodies pushed their way towards the family, making a path for the Procession of the Epitaph, a symbol of the tomb where Christ was buried.

"Stop laughing! We're supposed to be in mourning!" Said Athena. "Here, take your candle and keep it alight, we're following the procession this year."

"Did you avoid housework today like a good Orthodox woman?" Vasili whispered to his sister, still giggling like a schoolboy.

"Yes, I packed biscuits at the Peek Freans factory in Bermondsey instead!" Anna giggled quietly.

The family watched the priest button his red and gold vestments, ready to lead the procession onto the street.

Waving the censer back and forth, he fired puffs of incense to the sound of jingling bells, representing prayers rising to heaven. Anna stood on tiptoes for a glimpse of the flower-covered Epitaph, extravagantly covered in luscious spring flowers. The enchanting scent of narcissi was reminiscent of her childhood fantasies on Koukles. Its mesmerizing aroma filled the air with a lingering garland of hopes and possibilities, infiltrating her senses with a memory of a simpler time.

Before long they were in the street, trying to keep their candles alight in the cold spring evening. Hundreds of people followed the perfumed, flower-filled frame, while the priest chanted the gospel of events leading to the crucifixion of Christ. A formidable character, unapproachable and revered by his congregation, the priest was constantly agitated by candles getting close to his long, flowing grey beard.

"I see our priest's making a fashion statement again," Ari giggled with her sisters, trying hopelessly to keep her candle alight. The boy she had spoken to earlier suddenly appeared with a lighter.

"He braids it so it doesn't catch fire from the candles," he grinned, sprinting periodically to keep up with Ari. "So… er, what are you studying?" asked the stocky boy, sweating profusely while others around him shivered in the cold.

"I'm in my first year studying English literature," she said, proudly. "How about you?"

Before he could answer, there was a commotion from the waiting crowd behind barriers on Camberwell Road.

"Fucking foreigners! Comin ere wiv yer weird shit!" fumed a driver from behind a barrier of temporary traffic lights. He revved his engine to show his anger.

"Won't be long now sir," a policeman said, and pointed out the temporary road diversion.

No one in the procession was surprised by the familiar racist comments they'd been hearing for years. Some felt like it was their calling. For surely, they must be second class citizens? They'd been told so all their lives.

"Go back ter yer own country!" yelled a woman pushing a pram. "Fink they own the place," she growled at a scrawny man holding a pint of beer outside the pub.

"I naaar," he spluttered slowly, between gulps of beer and an indescribable dance. The woman frowned at him, wishing she hadn't said anything, then wheeled her pram towards the Peabody Estate.

The boy continued. "I help my dad run his chain of dry cleaners and travel agencies," he said, nervously looking into the dancing flame in Ari's eyes and trying to ignore his surroundings.

The procession walked around the block as crowds of onlookers either smiled in awe at the beautiful flower-covered Epitaph or pulled confused faces.

About twenty minutes later they ended up back at the church with a majority socializing outside the gates, and a large group of teens resuming their conversation in the courtyard. Chaos was re-instated as people searched for family members, while others audaciously snuck phone numbers in pockets.

"I told them all to meet me out here!" Anna was beginning to shiver uncontrollably. Vasili took his white silk scarf and carefully wrapped it round her neck.

"Ahhh, you know what it's like at that age, sis, let them have some fun! Anyway, have you looked through that folder you told me about?"

"No, I still haven't done it. Why don't you stay for a while when you drop us off? We can go through it together."

"Well OK, but my Greek's is not as good as yours."

Anna curiously turned to her brother.

"But you went to school until you were fourteen!"

"Yeah, I know, sis." He lit another Rothmans. "But I'm not a poet like you." Smoke quickly left his mouth and danced around his face with the breeze. "Why did you take that horrible job anyway? You can do so much better. You're the only one from our generation to go to college, you're wasting all that brain power, sis."

A sudden gust of wind brought the smoke back to her, but she didn't mind. Her father relished Rothmans when he could get them, George smoked them even when he was gutting fish back in the village – while Kate looked on in awe – and Petro always had one in an ashtray, or between his stained fingers. Vasili flicked his ash to the ground.

"When the bank pounced I had to get something quickly... and… I don't know how to look for anything better. The factory job was easy to find," she confessed.

"Sis, you gotta get tough! And you should demand rent from those two deadbeat lodgers downstairs!"

"Angelo and Louis are unemployed, they're my friends, I can't throw them out. Besides, I'm the one who made Angelo unemployed. I feel responsible for him."

"Well why don't you ask that tutor friend, what's his name?"

"His name is Andy, and she did a great job reciting those funny poems at the town hall, didn't she tell you?" Sophia suddenly appeared with a beaming smile.

"Oooh there you are!" Anna embraced her best friend.

"Sis, you gotta learn how to take advantage of these opportunities, it's been three years since he died."

"Oh, you're both being silly. I'm almost forty-seven, who's going to hire a dried-up foreign woman with four needy teens to look after? No, the factory suits me well for now! Anyway, Tina's started talking to me after all these months, I don't want to disturb our progress."

At last, they were all piled into Vasili's brand new Jaguar, fighting their way through crowded Camberwell, on route to Herne Hill.

"Love the new car, uncle!" Theo scrutinized the interior, inhaling the new car smell. "I'd love a car like this one day."

"Nothing to stop you, Theo," Vasili said, candidly.

They cruised to the hum of the Jaguar, as masses of people lined the pavements in the cold. Ferocious winds blew heavy on red cheeks, tossing hats, hair and scarves in swells while floundering birds flew back to their nests in the chaos.

Stuck in traffic, Theo noticed a pretty girl from

Greek school waiting at the bus stop. He took the perfect opportunity for a gentle wave and distant smile, like a movie star on his way to the Oscars. He felt good.

Despite enjoyment being contraband in the church, everyone was happy. Even Anna's girls were partaking, talking and absorbing the atmosphere.

"Can you put the radio on please, Auntie?" Tina asked, hoping to hear Olivia Newton-John's 'I Honestly Love You'. The radio hissed and beeped like Morse Code as Athena twiddled with the dial. The BBC news at ten had just started; Athena stopped to listen. First there were reports of trouble in Northern Ireland, then news of a final settlement for the thalidomide families, followed an international report from Cyprus.

'Fighting between Greek and Turkish Cypriots resumed, after talks between ministers failed to find a solution. Britain fears if the escalations continue, the two sides may go to war…'

Anna caught sight of Vasili's reaction in the rear-view mirror. She manoeuvred closer to the driver's seat from the back. "Did you hear that?" she asked. "Oh God, not again!" The adults talked about recent news on a peaceful settlement, then remained silent for the rest of the journey.

Back at Anna's house, the children dispersed while a sombre mood lingered among the adults.

"Wait here, I'll get the file." Anna went straight to her wardrobe and reached under neatly starched linens. Yiayia Stavrou's impeccable flowery needlework sat in its rightful place, peeking between layers of crisp cotton sheets, folded to perfection. She spotted the cream folder and carefully extracted it, taking care not to allow dried, cracked edges to break away. No title or 'Top Secret' words were written on the cover, just three faded initials in the top right-hand corner: C.I.A.

Anna took it into the living room and placed it carefully next to the fresh coffee Athena brought in from the kitchen.

"And you knew nothing until this Helen knocked on your door?"

"Nothing… nothing at all. Did you?" Anna turned to her brother, hoping to extract a meagre slice of information from his involvement.

"Of course not! Do you think I'd let him get away with that? ...Wait a minute! From what you've told me, do we know… I mean, was that even his real name?"

"I have no idea… I… I have no idea who I was married to, what his real name was, who his family is or if he has any siblings. I was married to an imposter!" Anna's gaze became glassy.

"Dear God, sis, we should've gone through this before."

"What's the point? No one can turn back the hands of time. Besides, I didn't want to humiliate our family any further. The less people knew, the better!" She was adamant.

Athena slid along the sofa and put her arm around Anna, yawning with her eyes half closed.

"I don't know how you did it, Anna. You're the bravest

and strongest woman I know!"

"No...no, I'm the fool. The idiot who couldn't see what was right under her nose. Look...it's late, let's do this another time."

"No!" demanded Vasili. "We get to the bottom of this tonight." He sat forward, lit another cigarette and carefully picked up the mysterious folder. "Wow, it's very thick!" he noted, turning the front cover. Still in chronological order, he meticulously lined up letters, memos, reports, notes, and maps, side by side.

They sat through the night, pumped with adrenaline and caffeine, shocked at what they unearthed. Contrary to Helen's flippant observations, the majority was written in English.

"There are notes here about people's whereabouts. Some of it has a C.I.A stamp. What does the C.I.A have to do with anything?" asked Anna.

"I don't know, but there are some minutes here from the 1960s." Vasili flicked the papers back and forth, trying to make sense of them. "They're stamped and embossed, they look legitimate but I'm not sure what they mean. I think this one is in Turkish." He carefully placed it to one side.

Anna picked up a sub-folder. She read down a little way then saw a list of names. "Vasili, do you recognise any of these names?" She handed him the limp folder.

Vasili looked closely. "They're all English names, I don't know what it means, Anna."

She picked up a paper with Turkish names written

with the English alphabet. "Oh…" She pointed to a name that seemed a little familiar. "Yilmaz…wasn't that Azra's surname?"

"Was it? I never asked." Vasili looked at her. "Didn't you say you saw her son running on the day father was killed?"

Anna slowly nodded. She put the papers back in the folder with graphs, maps and reports.

"What should I do with it, Vasili?" I don't want it in the house anymore."

"So this lawyer woman said she never looked at it? Said it was all in Greek?"

"Well, yes, that's what she said."

"D'ya think perhaps the only reason she came to see you was to give you this burden because she knew exactly what it was?"

She looked up into her brother's eyes.

"I love you sis, but you can be so naïve at times!"

"I…I don't know. Vasili… Do you think he could've been…involved? Why did he take the folder in the first place? How did he even know about it?" Vasili shrugged.

They sat in silence listening to foxes ravage bins from the terraces across the street for a few minutes, both recalling their mother's words: *That woman is a spy! Mark my words. She'll not buy my loyalty with her second-rate honey!*

"I don't know where we go from here, sis, but what I do know is that if Petro was involved… it would make a lot of sense. I know for a fact your deceased husband wouldn't do anything unless someone paid him! Did he ever splash out on something extravagant?"

Anna's jaw dropped.

"Do you remember that car he bought? He never did explain where the money came from. He was the only one in the village with a car, even the Antonios didn't own a car."

The siblings looked at each other in disbelief, trying to process the outlandish situation they found themselves in.

By 4 a.m., the finches started to sing the morning chorus. They sat silent for a few moments, wondering what to do next.

"I think I need to take this to the police. I can't have it in the house," Anna whispered.

"You'll do nothing of the sort! Just think what they'll do to you, especially after this Profumo scandal. We know you did nothing wrong, but do you think they'll believe you? Think, sis… think!"

"Then I'll burn it! No one will know if I make it disappear!" she proclaimed, her eyes welling up with tears.

"No… no don't do that. Hold on to it for a while longer, let's think about it before we act. Now, I need to take this sleeping beauty home." He got up from the copper-coloured vinyl couch, groaned from his aching back and tapped his sleeping wife on the shoulder. She sat up, shivering from the early morning frost and took her husband's arm.

"There is one thing we can do," he tried his luck just as

he was leaving. "We could find a reporter and see if we can sell…"

"Oh no! Don't even think of that!" she said vehemently, shivering in the cold hallway. "Let's talk later, we all need to sleep now."

The door opened onto a lustrous glow of moonlight, accentuating a translucent layer of crystalline frost on the ground. Anna shivered then quietly closed the door behind them.

She went up the stairs to her flat, avoiding the creaks and moans from old floorboards, and now alone, she ventured back to the living room and stared at the puzzle. Every effort to understand the enigma made it more obscure. As if addicted, she couldn't stop delving into the conundrum, hoping to find something that would make sense of her past, but all her exploring led her back to where she started. Petro had to be involved somehow! Why would he feel the need to take the file in the first place? That had now become her responsibility, and her liability.

CHAPTER 23

Sat 20th July 1974

Early morning brought the sound of wood pigeons cooing and blackbirds singing in the distance. Wayward and carefree, they opened their throats to sing, argue, and articulate as if they were the only living creatures in a slumbering street, abandoned by unconscious bodies tucked between brushed cotton and candlewick.

For Anna, it was a time for restful contemplation before another day of monotonous servility at the factory. She sat at the kitchen table, going over the conversation she had with Helen on that shocking day that disconnected everything she thought she knew.

The gentle swoosh of Ari turning pages from her bed reassured her that all was well in her household.

"Here you go!" she handed Ari a cup of tea and a plate of toast, trying to entice her to eat.

"Oh, thanks Mum... Wait, it's Saturday! Are you going to work?"

"Yes, seems like the whole country's going mad for biscuits. They offered us time and a half for today so I'm going in. Can you look af..."

Chapter 23 – Sat 20th July 1974

"Yes mother! I know the routine by now. They only have a week of school left before the holidays, and already they're behaving like brats!"

Anna smiled, knowing full well that if Ari promised, she would deliver. She went downstairs toying with the idea of calling Helen, but a hundred reasons not to, flashed before her. She sipped her second cup of tea and ate toast, staring through the kitchen window at the brilliant pink magnolias, accentuated by an early morning shower. Gazing into the yawning of another morning, she watched the raindrops race silently from the sky, landing with a blot on the window and leaving liniments of lace.

Anna packed a lunch of leftover cheese, salad and some bread, then sat to finish her tea. She looked at her watch; it was seven thirty. With raincoat and bag in hand, she crept down the stairs trying not to wake her tenants. Could a single leap of courage to call Helen end the curiosity? The thought had been eating away at her strength. But false lies come from false liars! How could she trust a woman who, having slept with her husband, had her own agenda, rationale and the power of entitlement on her side?

Anna strolled along the wet pavement with its blurry, formless, silvery reflections. Sometimes the intoxicating smell of damp trees made thoughts become clearer; but not today.

She looked ahead to the bus stop and saw the familiar figure of her colleague Rose, who caught the same bus every morning.

"Hello Rose, beautiful morning isn't it?"

"Aahh, too damp for me Hannah, days like dis I miss Jamaiyca!" Her body rippled with a hearty laugh. "Dis weather make me air arl frizzy," she complained, adjusting her PVC rain bonnet over a perfect afro. Right from the start of their employment, Anna and Rose bonded. Their affinity helped them get through long tedious days at the factory. Both had fled from violence; both suffered a similar aftermath.

"Did Winston come home last night?" Anna enquired as the bus screeched to a halt.

"Unfortunately, yes!"

They took a seat at the front.

"Him tol me iz girlfriend about to ave a baby, but er landlady trowing er out. He want er to move in wit us!" She laughed sarcastically.

"Wow! What did you say?"

"I cyana repeat it me darlen. Im tell me I should beave like a Jamaiycan wife. Im tink e can still play aroun like e did in Jamaiyca when we got two kids to feed!" Rose was getting agitated and turned to look out the window.

The two women got off the bus at Clements Road and walked to the factory gates just as workers began to gather. They clocked in, took off their coats and put on their white hats and aprons, ready for a day of rolling sweet biscuit dough. A bustle of activity, clunky machines and boisterous noise were all part of a typical working day, but after a while the commotion went unnoticed. Anna's thoughts and daydreams drowned the unbroken rhythm pounding in the background.

Chapter 23 – Sat 20th July 1974

"I'll see you later, in the canteen, Rose."

"Sure, me darlin. Lookin forward to Glady's slop." Rose put two fingers towards her mouth and mimicked a retch.

"Morning Anna, I want yous on New Berry Fruit Jewels today," her supervisor demanded with his hair in a net and a clipboard the size of his entire chest. "Demand is growing, people can't get enough o' the bleedin fings, and we need someone reliable so vere's no mistakes."

"Oh, OK!" Anna walked over to the jelly fruit floor and was hit by a torrent of artificial fruit smells, all fighting for air space. Any break from her usual routine was welcome, but this meant she could take home discarded jelly fruits. Tina would be delighted, and maybe she could get another step closer to the bond they had before.

"Don't tell no one, but boss is finkin o' makin yous a supervisor like me!" he whispered, then surreptitiously touched his nose as a sign of classified information.

Anna was delighted at the news, but soon her thoughts came back to the same topic. What was she going to do with the folder? Trying to identify if Petro was involved – if indeed that was his real name – was a double-edged mystery. Were Azra's husband and son being paid to spy on the village? Was her husband hiding somewhere all along and being rewarded with payment in Turkey?

But that just left her with more questions. What reason did her mother have to suspect Azra's family were spies and why didn't anyone listen to her?

All morning, Anna packed sweet jellied fruits into

boxes, ready for shipment to supermarkets and newsagents, isolating herself from co-worker conversations.

"Dreaming again? Girl, you ave a big imagination!" Rose was suddenly standing next to her.

"Oh, my goodness, is it lunchtime already?"

"I ope so, me belly rumblin like a volcyano." Rose laughed.

The pair took their lunch boxes and hurried across the flour-drenched corridor towards the feted smell of Glady's stewed cabbage. However wretched the smell, a break from standing up all morning was always welcome. Besides, no one cared about the foul odours, inedible food or grease-coated floor in the works canteen. Anna shut the door behind them with a sigh of relief from the cacophony of stainless-steel tanks and conveyor belts in motion.

"Eeeere, Anna, what ya got for lunch today? D'ya bring more o' vat mouse caca?" taunted Ethel, waiting in line.

"You're such a cow, Ethel, leave er alone."

"All right Gladys love? What lovely grub ya got for us today?" Ethel chuckled, taking lunch coupons from her purse.

"I gotta lovely bit a sausage n mash, or there's egg n chips, Ethel love," hissed seventy-year-old Gladys, struggling to breathe after smoking forty Players cigarettes a day for more than half a century.

Ethel and Jean sat at a table next to Anna and Rose, with platefuls of mashed potato and two anaemic sausages drowned in gravy. Ethel stretched her arms and yawned.

Chapter 23 – Sat 20th July 1974

"Nice night out then, Ethel?" laughed Jean.

"Yeah, went te the pub wiv me bruver in law. He's got imself a big house over the river. He's rentin rooms, says he's gonna retire. Don't want no foreigners mind!"

Anna and Rose ignored her and continued with their own conversation.

"Your Winston sounds like my late husband. Do a lot of Jamaican men behave like that?"

"Dem all do! Tink it make dem a man. Them cyan ave as many women as dey like in Jamaica, and me still got wish im dirte underwear!" Rose sighed heavily.

As usual, they finished their lunch discussing things they had in common, a cathartic experience for both women. Eventually, Anna picked up her lunch container and stood upright in front of the packed canteen. Even though she usually shied away from attention because of the scar on her face from Petro's beatings, she was seething from yet another racist remark from Ethel.

Anna and Rose were walking between the crowded tables towards the door when the BBC news theme tune began to blare on the canteen radio.

"Heavily armed Turkish troops landed on the northern coast of Cyprus, meeting resistance from Greek and Greek Cypriot forces. Ankara said that it was invoking its right under the Treaty of Guarantee to protect the Turkish Cypriots and guarantee the independence of Cyprus…"

Anna stood frozen for a moment. Her village was on the northern coast: her family, friends and roots were there.

What was she to do? With little control over her reaction, she found herself heading to the manager's office.

"Ahh, Anna. Come in, I was going to…"

"I have to go home Mr Fatter, my village is being invaded." Anna's voice trembled.

The manager slammed the filing cabinet drawer and sat down.

"What the hell are you on about? I was thinking of calling you in, to see if you want a promotion! Now I'm not so sure!" He scowled, his eyebrows sliding forward, chasing his sweaty, bulbous nose.

She stood staring at him, but all she saw was her father's face covered in blood, the last real memory of him, while her boss continued to rant about orders to fill.

"I have to go home Mr Fatter!" she repeated with glassy eyes.

"Then don't come back!" He yelled furiously. "And the name's Hatter… why you foreigners can't pronounce your aitches is beyond me!"

"I think I was right the first time!" Anna whispered under her breath and quickly left.

Forty-five minutes later she was struggling to get her key in the front door. Angelo heard the clunking from inside and went to open the front door from his downstairs bedsit, dressed in his waiter's suit.

"Ahh, Hannah, I been for hinterview, I gotta job, now I…"

"That's very nice, Angelo!" she said, storming up the

stairs to her flat. Ari heard her mother's voice and came down from her bedroom, still in her dressing gown. She saw her mother frantically tuning the television into the BBC.

"Mum, what's wrong? Why are…"

Before Anna could answer, a report from the BBC came in loud and clear.

"Oh my God, Mum, are they talking about our village? Did they land right in our village?"

The two sat in front of the television all afternoon, flipping between all three channels, trying to glean as much information as possible. As the hours went by, eventually the whole family were at the mercy of BBC news. Some footage of Turkish trucks with soldiers waving their arms in victory was shown, as well as groups of Greek Cypriots holding on to a few belongings, being ushered out of their homes at gunpoint.

"Mum, where are they taking them?" Aris's voice trembled.

"I don't know... I know as much as you!" Anna snapped.

The phone rang many times as family and friends shared snippets of information. Anna eventually got through to Vasili.

"Why are you surprised, sis? We've known for years this day would come," he said calmly. "The worst thing we ever did was get rid of the British!"

CHAPTER 24

1975

"Let sleeping dogs lie," Andy reiterated, carefully placing a Moroccan copper serving tray on the coffee table.

With a weary sigh, he sank into the perfect confines of his grandmother's weathered chesterfield chair, flawed to perfection and fitting him like a glove.

"What does that mean?" asked Anna.

"It means, my love, that some things are best left as they are." He handed Anna a cup of frothy coffee.

"What's all this fluff?" Anna blew at the froth to discover what delight lay beneath.

"It's called a cappuccino; the froth is milk. Taste it! It's all the rage in Italy. Johnny and I drink it all the time since our trip."

"Oh, how is he by the way?"

"They don't know. Something's attacking his immune system and he just doesn't get better."

He stared at the sheepskin rug beneath the coffee table, trying to quash his despair. His empty expression was devoid of his usual optimism. Eyes normally filled with a thirst for life and all its glories began to fill with tears. It was a glimpse into his troubled soul and it made Anna slightly uncomfortable. Nevertheless, the critic inside reminded her that to be human is to be imperfect. She inched closer; took the cup from his hand and kissed his cheek, accidently printing a milk moustache on his grey beard.

"Oh, listen to me, blubbering like a baby. I must accept the situation for what it is, not as I wish it to be!"

"Blubber all you want; I just wish there was something I could do to help. Would you like me to come with you to the hospital with you?"

"Oh good heavens no, he wouldn't want anyone else there. Anyway, enough about my problems. How's Ariadne doing these days?" He brightened like a sun peeking behind a pesky cloud.

"I wish I could say she's put on weight. It's been years now and she still won't sit and eat with us. I hear her purging in the middle of the night sometimes. She thinks no one can hear her, I'm worried she may have to go into hospital again."

"Aaah." Andy's thirst for conversation, like a lover's kiss where one might forget to breathe, resumed its natural course. "I read up on this just recently." He leaned over and picked up his coffee from the stylish teak coffee table. "Apparently, it's a form of depression. It stems from them not having control of their lives! Don't be hard on her, Anna, she and Tina have had a lot of trauma thrown at them. Is Tina displaying any signs of bulimia or anorexia?"

"God no! She eats like a horse, but she's still small

and thin for her age. My worry with her is how sensitive and introvert she's become. I know she's lonely, and she still has nightmares. She's angry at all of us. I don't think she'll ever trust anyone again. To make matters worse, she's still being called a fucking Paki! At school.... and... am I missing something here, why is it terrible to come from Pakistan?"

"Oh that!" He took a big gulp of coffee then put his cup down next to a copy of *The Seven Minutes* by Irving Wallace, gathering his thoughts. "Have you ever looked at the work of one of your own genius philosophers? By that I mean Socrates."

Anna shook her head.

"Strong minds discuss ideas, average minds discuss events, weak minds discuss people."

"Well, that does seem to sum it up." She laughed. "Although I still don't understand why specifically the Pakistani community gets picked on so much?"

"Who knows, my friend! You, on the other hand, are a peaceful warrior because the battles you fight are from within! Another quote from your genius philosopher. Now, I hate to say this, but I'm glad you got fired from that awful job. Have you found anything else? Because I have a proposition for you."

"Well, no, I've been scraping by on Angelo's rent – and the occasional rent Louis gives me."

"Is that old drag queen still with you? I hadn't realized!" He laughed.

"Ha ha…yes." Anna took another sip of her now cooled coffee. "Mmmm… I think I can get used to this coffee; I can't imagine the cafes in Brixton selling it though. Anyway, I kind of feel life is defined not by what we let go, but what we let in. Poor thing has nowhere else to go. He's been with us so long he's part of the family now. He studied law apparently, but never practiced. He has an incredible insight for diplomacy that I've never come across before. Besides, the girls love having make-up sessions with him, he's also got an amazing wardrobe."

"Well that just confirms what I called you here for." He struggled to slide forward from the confines of his chair and took a prospectus from the coffee table. "Your beautiful mind was wasted in that factory. Now… I've been swamped with admin at work and I want you to take over the role as Administration Manager at the college. There's also a good opportunity for you to cover for me during sickness and leave, which is increasing every term. I'm approaching sixty and want to reduce my hours. I need someone reliable, intelligent and with good old-fashioned common sense to help me. I won't take no this time, Anna!"

At times like this, Anna was reminded of how her friendship with Andy was one of the most valuable things she possessed.

"But I… It's been years since…"

Andy put his hands in his ears and closed his eyes.

"I'm not listening," he said firmly.

They spent an afternoon discussing personal and political issues, which Anna was convinced she would go mad if she couldn't air and share. They ability to offload heavy burdens without walls, reservations and judgment had become a lifeline.

"Now, I want you to come to my office on Monday and I'll introduce you to the secretarial team who'll show you the ropes. It's so easy you can do it with your eyes closed… but I wouldn't recommend it!"

"Oh... Are you sure, Andy?"

He gave her the 'Don't you dare doubt yourself again' glare.

"Well, OK… Thank you, thank you very much. You're such a good friend. Now, it's getting late, I'd better get going." She stood up, checking out the African-inspired décor influenced by his extensive travels.

"Is it true they're tearing down this entire estate? I wouldn't be surprised. It's so dark and cramped! What were they thinking when they built it?"

"You say dark, I say private! But you're right, it's very grim. The council don't repair anything anymore. Mrs Patel next door hasn't had hot water for three months. Though Johnny thinks one day Brixton will become one of the trendiest places to live in London!" They laughed out loud, unable to entertain the preposterous notion of Brixton becoming a trendy place to live.

"Don't forget: Monday, nine sharp, I'll be waiting!"

Anna saluted with her head tilted in jest but terrified

at the thought of a new job with people she didn't know; people who were bound to ask about the scar on her face and why she spoke with a strange accent.

For her safety, Andy waited until she reached the ground floor before closing the only scarlet front door on the estate.

Relieved to escape the stench of stale urine from the stairwell, Anna entered the courtyard, surrounded by brick, concrete and a lack of sunlight. Two drunken Irishmen were arguing on a bench nearby, hurling a torrent of slurred abuse and empty threats, surrounded by empty cans.

Another man lay on the ground next to overflowing bins, with urine stains around his crotch, staring blankly at the sky.

"Eeaarrr, ave a drag o this," said a dishevelled woman who staggered around him, offering a discarded cigarette she'd found in the bins.

Anna quickly walked past the only tree in the courtyard. Its roots lay so deep under concrete that it struggled and pulled, trying to free itself from incarceration. Carved names of old loves scarred its chest in an attempt to immortalize their devotion. Spills of methylated spirit and beer dampened its ability to grow healthily, inflicting a lonely silence, occasionally comforted by grasping birds staring at listless leaves on the ground.

Anna stepped out of the courtyard, leaving the smell of exotic spices, marijuana and poverty rising to the heavens between the three large blocks of flats. She stepped out onto a crowded Coldharbour Lane, and through the crowds saw

Tina testing lightbulbs in Woolworths across the street. She waved frantically, proud of her for finding a Saturday job and gaining some independence. Anna walked into the shop and squinted at the bright light fittings on display.

"Hi Mum, did you go to see Andy or are you here to check up on me?"

"I'm not checking up on you, darling, I just had something to discuss with Andy."

"I finish in an hour if you want to wait. We can get the bus home together… Actually, Bon Marche have a sale on. Why don't you see if they've got those nice army shirts all the girls are wearing? You know my size." She laughed.

Anna rolled her eyes and left just as Tina's supervisor caught sight of them talking.

An hour later, outside Woolworths main entrance at 5.45 p.m. on a Saturday, was a scene of mass evacuation. Hundreds of people, originating from all over the world, waited for buses to go home. Even though the Tube station had opened a few years previously, it didn't alleviate the congestion. In fact, it made it worse as more people were attracted to Brixton's selection of cosmopolitan food, incredible markets and independent shops.

"Hold tight to your bag," Anna whispered as the crowd swarmed towards a bus.

"I know, Mum, I do this every Saturday!"

They found seats upstairs with the smokers, delighted to be out of the cold and away from pushing and shoving. Anna looked down at turbans, dhukus, hijabs and brightly coloured mohawks. Brixton become trendy, indeed! Besides, where would all these people go? she thought.

CHAPTER 25
2003

Anna worked as an admin manager for twenty-eight years. She continued well past retirement age and barely missed a day's work. Her faith, friends and family kept her happy. Her thirteen grandchildren became a new source of inspiration for little scribbles and stories she wrote in private; never having the confidence to compete with the educated elite.

At the age of seventy-six, she questioned whether it was time to stop trying; stop creating; and stop dreaming. For she'd encountered a new path in life that allowed her to forget the negative side of her past. Once she felt her world was nothing but endings that wither or linger like leeches, devouring, outside of her control. Now she was content, confident and happy, even in the most adverse situations.

The file was tucked away in a draw she never opened. Even memories of the English soldier faded. As the years passed, so did her addiction to that tiny brush with the essence of perfect love that made her forget to eat, sleep and drink, tormenting and enslaving her against her will. Potential suitors never came close to the passion she knew she was capable of. For that reason, she never re-married and never had a gentlemen friend. Once she believed she was an independent entity, not understanding the countless cause and effect of her actions. But now she knew better. Now she stopped trying to find answers in the pit of the night, for the night casts shadows.

"Damn eyes! Why don't they work properly anymore?" she fumed, forgetting where she'd put her reading glasses.

Listening to the whirring oven and the gentle sizzle of roasting lamb, Anna sat in wait for her eldest granddaughter. It must be almost midday, she thought; eager to perfect Sunday lunch and prove she could still live independently. As April showers gently ambushed the first daffodils of the season, Anna watched flashes of citrus yellow quivering courteously to the rhythm of the rain. The satisfying aroma of roast meat restored a delicious smell to every corner of her kitchen.

"I'm coming!" she called down the stairs to the piercing buzz of her doorbell. Clutching her walking stick in one hand and grasping tight to the handrail with the other, she made it down the stairs, masking the pain from her arthritic hands and knees.

"Yiayia!" yelled a wet Alexia, hugging and squeezing her grandmother as the door flung open.

"This is Graham!" She looked towards her prize, her eyes brimming with affection for a tall thin man with wet blond curls stretching down his forehead, partially covering his steamed glasses. He smiled anxiously, revealing a perfect set of teeth, then held out his hand for a well-rehearsed greeting.

"Yassou Yiayia," he said, with a thick middle-class accent. Anna stared for a moment.

"Is he Turkish?"

"No, yiayia, his family are from Surrey!" Alexia rolled her eyes and blushed with embarrassment.

"Then he's welcome!" She shook his hand then headed back upstairs to the flat.

"Mmmm, that smells lovely, Yiayia… Oh, I forgot to tell you! Graham is a vegetarian."

"A what?"

"A vegetarian… You know, he doesn't eat meat!"

"Ah! that's because he's never had slow roast Greek lamb."

"No, Yiayia, he doesn't eat any meat at all, he hasn't since he was sixteen years old."

Anna looked Graham up and down.

"Is that why he's so skinny?"

Alexia was getting irritated with her grandmother and quickly changed the subject.

"So, erm, what happened to that tenant who lived downstairs? Mum told me you found him dead in his bed or something?" she asked, helping her grandmother to a chair.

"Ah yes, poor Louis!" Anna waved her hands, expressing her deep disgust. "His relatives refused to claim the body and wouldn't come to the funeral… It's a terrible thing to abandon one's own family!"

Chapter 25 – 2003

"Poor man, he must've been very lonely. Did you find out anything else when you cleared his belongings?"

"I found some worn photos of him as a child, with what I assume are family members, but he never talked to me about them. I remember… a dreadful smell coming from his room, and I hadn't seen him for a while… I just knew something wasn't right, so I had Angelo force the lock. Poor Louis… He had a kind of foam mixed with blood leaking from his mouth. He must've been dead for about a week when we found him."

"Ew, must've been awful! Do you know why he took his own life?" Alexia stirred the French green beans in tomato and garlic her grandmother cooked to perfection, while Graham helped to set the table.

"It was no secret; he'd always been a troubled soul. I found a lovely portrait with a note clipped to it from the artist. Seems like they were friends. Someone by the name of David, there's no surname on the note but the sketch is signed, something ending in 'ney'! I can't figure out the first part. I had it framed because it reminds me of our friendship. It's hanging over the settee in the living room if you want to see."

Alexia and Graham's eyes met. They rushed to examine the signature.

"Oh, my goodness, we should take it to Sotheby's, Yiayia, I think it's a genuine David Hockney!"

"Who's David Hockney? Is he famous, dear?"

Alexia touched the frame and gasped.

"It's not moving from there, dear, now come and eat."

They sat at the table, quietly listening to raindrops turn to hailstones. The little white crystals rapped against the window in the blinding white of wind and mist, while they savoured the delights of a Sunday roast.

"So, Graham, how will you take care of my granddaughter when you marry her?"

"Oh my God… How… what? That's what we came to tell you!" Alexia blushed like a ripe tomato.

"It's written all over his face, dear!" said Anna, nonchalantly adding slices of roast lamb onto Graham's plate.

"Anyway, as you're the most sensible of all my grandchildren, I wanted to talk to you about this proposition from your great uncle. Did you speak to him?

"Yes, it sounds wonderful, I think it's a great idea. But can he really afford to pay for so many people to visit the village?"

Anna laughed.

"I don't think you realise how wealthy your great uncle is, dear. He sold five successful restaurants and three houses in Clapham; he can afford it! Besides, he's seventy-eight, how many more years does he…or even I…have left?" She laughed again.

"Yiayia, don't say that! You're as strong as an ox, you'll live to be over a hundred, like yiayia Christina and yiayia Stavrou. Didn't yiayia Stavrou live with Stella until she was a hundred and three?"

Chapter 25 – 2003

"Good heavens, how could anyone possibly know exactly how old she was. Before the British forced us to register births, no one bothered with birth certificates."

"Mum worked it out one day and told me. Anyway, are we allowed to visit yiayia Christina when we go? It would be amazing to see the insides of an Orthodox convent in the mountains."

"I don't think so dear, the last letter I got from Stella was years ago, she couldn't manage the walk up the mountain from the bus anymore. She said her mother and yiayia Christina were still alive but didn't want any contact at all from the outside world anymore. Anyway, I'm more concerned about those nasty Turks at the border. I bet they'll find a reason to detain our men at the crossing,"

"Don't worry, Yiayia, they can't do that! They need to be seen to comply because they want to join the E.U."

"You trust too easily, dear! That's the problem with your generation." She stared at Graham to see if he was eating meat. The afternoon continued wet and windy, giving no time for a frustrated sun to make its appearance.

"So is the flat downstairs empty now?"

"No, Angelo still lives in the big front room, although you'd never know it. He's like a mouse."

"Wow, I had no idea he was still around." "He doesn't have much choice dear. If he goes back, a feuding family will have him killed apparently. His father took on huge debt from a notorious family in Naples back in the fifties. He couldn't pay it back so now they're looking for revenge. They'll never give up; poor man can never return. Anyway, it's too late now, I've got him addicted to English tea!" She chuckled.

Graham listened quietly, getting attuned to the charisma of a feisty little old lady with unrefined, unpretentious and unfiltered chronicles of a robust life.

Every shove of his glasses to the bridge of his nose brought a new expression of perplexity to his big blue eyes. He listened to his exuberant fiancée discuss wedding plans with her grandmother, who tried hard to keep up with phrases like 'ping it', 'on the same page', and 'at the end of the day'.

"I love listening to your stories about the village, Yiayia, but you never told us why your mother went to join the convent in the first place."

Anna was uncomfortable and slightly agitated.

"Please, Yiayia! I know you don't like talking about it, but I'd really like to know."

Anna sighed and took a deep breath.

"The only thing I know is that she joined a convent when your grandfather died and spent the rest of her life taking care of displaced children from all over the island. She occasionally wrote to Stella; never to me! Stella used to send me her letters when she'd read them. It seems she blamed me for your grandfather's death – claimed that if it wasn't for me, he wouldn't have been in the coffee shop that day. He was waiting for me to tell him if your auntie Tina would be forced to use her right hand to write with. It was her first day of school you see, and we had a bet. He wanted to know if I'd challenge the teacher. How foolish we were! If it wasn't for that stupid bet, he could've been spared."

"Well that's not fair, is it? From what you tell us, he spent a lot of time there."

"Since when has life been fair, dear?" Anna stared at the lamb platter and helped herself to more meat. They talked for hours; an experience Alexia relished. She loved listening to her grandmother's stories from the island. Taking note of her heritage had become key to understanding herself and where she fit in as a second-generation migrant.

A few hours later, the teasing sun unexpectedly made a brief appearance then vanished almost instantaneously.

"That was delicious as usual, Yiayia, but I think we have to go now!" Alexia announced sleepily.

"I'll tell Mum to call you so you can arrange travel plans between you." She took her damp raincoat from the coatrack and together the lovers disappeared into the soothing chaos of bouncing hail.

CHAPTER 26

The Last Mulberry Tree

Summer rushed on the heels of spring and four months later, twelve members of the family landed in Larnaca and made their way to a large villa on the outskirts of the city. Almost forty years had passed since Anna left the island and even though it was just a visit, never did she imagine this day would come. How would she feel, seeing someone else living in her house? The amazing, modern house envied by all the young women in the village. The only house in the village with running water, a gas cooker with the luxury of temperature control and flyscreens at the windows. How proud she had been to show off her indoor toilet and cool, marble floors.

The night before the crossing, she lay in bed thinking about the mulberry tree. Unable to picture it without her father's smiling face, Anna's anxiety level rose to a state of rawness.

"Are you awake?" she heard Kate whisper.

"Yes," whispered Anna. "Let's go out onto the veranda, it's too hot to sleep anyway!"

The grey-haired sisters struggled out of their beds and hobbled to the veranda, impervious to the grating sound of cicadas and distant echo of barking dogs. The air was cool and pleasing.

"Do you still have that photo we had in our bedroom?" asked Anna, suddenly remembering it for the first time in years.

"Oh yes! I remember that picture. I took it with me when I left, didn't I? No, I threw it out a few years ago. It faded so much it wasn't worth keeping anymore."

"Hmmm... No one tells you pictures fade!" Anna mumbled, suspended momentarily in a timeless breeze whilst watching moths flicker towards the light, mistaking it for the moon.

A few hours passed and the sisters were still awake; reflecting, reminiscing and laughing. So much time had passed, yet Anna's heart remained inexhaustible.

"Do you remember that soldier you had a crush on?" Kate asked, giggling like a little girl.

"What! How...?" Anna couldn't find the words.

"I saw you, Anna! I saw you talking to him during that terrible storm. Do you remember?"

Anna was furious! After all these years, it was as if Kate had been spying on her thoughts, looking into her private psyche and mocking her ridiculous fantasies.

"Don't worry, I never told anyone! But I did see you looking for him when they marched through the village." Kate grinned. "He asked me where you were once. He reached into his pocket to give me a note, but I wouldn't take it."

"What!...How could you wait till now to tell me!" Anna was livid.

"Don't look at me like that, Anna! He was an English soldier! What good could have come of it? I was doing you a favour!"

Anna was speechless. Temporarily lost between what had been and what could have been, she took a long deep breath and felt herself drifting back into his spell. Floating back to reality, she tried to convince herself that it was just a foolish illusion of her youth; a dream where she thought life could stretch just as far as you were willing to dream. But what did it matter now anyway? Sparks had dwindled and old age left her with the wrath of unsent letters, unspent passion and unfulfilled dreams.

"I don't want to let go of the old, Kate!" She sighed. "What's wrong with me?

After a moment's reflection, Kate nodded in acknowledgment, with her own memories of George and how she wished he were still alive to share these moments with her. They sat outside until the rising sun moved closer to day. Then before long, one by one, the family began to wake.

"What've you got in that big bag, Mum? It's not lunch is it? Remember we're stopping off at a hotel near Kyrenia castle to eat?" Theo remarked.

"Yes son, I remember," she mumbled, discreetly feeling inside her bag.

As they drove towards the border Anna looked out the window and couldn't help feeling perplexed.

"What's the matter, Mum?" Tina asked. "Are you nervous?"

"No, I just wasn't expecting to see it look so normal, so built up – like nothing ever happened here." She looked out the car window at crowded streets with people sitting outside cafés, tourist shops and chain stores she had become familiar with in London. She saw a large number of people with white skin, burning in the sun.

"The tourists returned, and they've become a huge help to the economy," Theo called from the driver's seat.

The family took their place in line to have their papers checked. They sat in the car for almost an hour in the soaring heat.

"Oh my God, he has a gun," Anna whispered, trembling with fear.

"Stop worrying, Yiayia, he's a soldier, of course he has a gun. Nothing's going to happen to us," Alexia whispered back, holding her grandmother's hand. The soldiers spoke Turkish. Anna felt her heart thump hard against her chest as the tallest peered through their open window and stared at the passengers, one by one. Satisfied with their papers, he beckoned them to go forth.

They drove north in what felt like an unnatural, surreal stillness. They were mesmerised at the contrast between north and south of the border. The north was devoid of life in all its harmony: devoid of conversation outside coffee shops, devoid of street vendors selling watermelons and souvlaki off the back of trucks, filling warm air with the mesmerizing smell of oregano, sage and roasted coffee.

They drove for an hour and a half along dusty roads, scattered with dry Permian limestone rocks. Wild gladioli, asphodels and giant fennel fought the heat, making their mark, boasting their ability to survive in such high temperatures. Close to the dusty roadside, dry bracken covered in fine dust like talc, disguised as colourless ghostly sculpture, waited for rain to wash them clean and give them a welcome drink in the wilderness.

Anna looked around for more signs of life, but she was consumed by the lack of care. Graffiti-covered buildings had been left to deteriorate; litter was strewn in the streets like it was a rightful home, sporadically trying to fly on the back of a rare breeze. She closed her eyes and took a deep breath in search of a sensuous beauty to lift her spirits, then opened the window to be closer.

"Oh Mum, please close the window, it's too hot out there!" Theo complained.

"In a moment, dear!" She leaned out the window; wanting, needing to feel the bombardment of eucalyptus, sycamore, junipers and pines as they released their floating scent in the midmorning heat. She wanted to lose herself in their vigour as it paraded past her, thinking what amazing luck she had to see them again: absorb them and wrap them around her wounds to make peace with herself. She took an overdue breath and for a moment, it felt like nothing in the past really mattered anymore.

"Are you alright, Mother?" Tina asked, fanning herself with a map.

"Very much so," Anna exclaimed, with her eyes shut.

They drove along the familiar ridge above the village; a formidable mountain road, where treetops burst into view and where Anna once thought she might touch the sky. Moments later, their cars pulled into a layby. Choking members of the family took their first breath, their first smell and their first taste of their heritage in a heat so thirsty it tried to consume every drop of moisture from within them.

"So, this is it?" said Tina thoughtfully, standing next to her mother.

Tina looked down from the ridge to the quiet village. She wanted to feel the attachment her mother felt but couldn't find it within her. She understood and sympathised with her mother, but she couldn't muster the same deep-rooted feelings of belonging her mother felt. She felt like she was two people. One who originally came from this beautiful island, full of history, trauma and poverty, and the other who was now caught up in the sophisticated lifestyle of a British citizen.

The village was so quiet it looked empty, but the mosque in the middle of the village was a reminder the village was no longer Christian Orthodox.

"You were born here; don't you remember it?" Anna asked her daughter.

"A little," she said, pointing to the mosque. "Wasn't that where…?"

"...Your great grandmother's house used to be? Yes!"

A thin Ari approached them from behind, her body never fully recovered from the effects of her eating disorder.

"But that's our land!" She pointed to the mosque. "I don't know if we would ever get that back. Isn't there something in the Koran that makes the house of Allah permanent?" Anna's heart sank.

Ari looked on in bewilderment, silently comparing the then to now. Being ten years old when she left the island, she had more memories of the village than her younger siblings. She looked at the mosque and pictured her great grandmother's hut in her mind. She remembered running around the central pole, teasing her with playful youth and stealth, just like her mother and uncle before her. She remembered how velvety her naked toes felt afterwards, from the dry muddy sediment. It was the first time she'd thought of it. If only she could say sorry! Sorry, Yiayia, for teasing you! Sorry for the anger and upset I caused you! Guilt painted a picture with colours more intense and more vibrant than exactitude and for a moment, it gnawed at her.

"Uncle Vasili, you should get back in the car, you'll be more comfortable there," Ari suggested, trying to prove her compassionate side.

Vasili struggled into the car, puffing and panting from years of smoking that left him with emphysema. In the cool of air-conditioning, he looked out of the window for a moment then dozed off.

Meanwhile, Anna and Kate held hands as if they were still eight and ten years old and gingerly crept towards the only footpath linking the mountain road to the village. Theo tried to stop them in fear of a fall.

"No." Tina grabbed Theo's arm. "Let them go."

With hearts pounding in the quiet of a parched thicket, they surveyed the formidable prickly pear cacti that once tore their tights and scratched their arms. Feeling they were disturbing the quiet, sleepy village, they slowly made their way down the path; Tina followed.

The village was barren, yet the curious familiarity of a distant dream came to the fore. Anna mourned its moods, its laughter and its fury. She understood its emotions by day, by night, in winter and in the intensity of summer, therefore why did she feel like a shadow? From some nocturnal bloom that unfolded in her memory, she closed her eyes and became submerged involuntarily into the sweet smell of mint and aniseed tea she shared with her father every morning.

Anna walked warily to the house where she grew up, and although she barely recognized it, the courtyard that was once filled with fruit trees now housed goats, cows and sheep, surrounded by ruins. The spot where she was formally introduced to Petro was now a pile of rocks with grass and moss growing randomly between gaps.

She recalled the heavenly shade the courtyard provided at the end of the day, when she chased her disobliging shadow, scaring her five-year-old sister into believing a beastly heat inferno would swallow her up into a world of gypsies, Kallikantzaros and slavery if she didn't find shade. Now, it was disfigured by war, with missing doors and walls, framing views of a sapphire sea in the distance like a Salvador Dali painting.

"Do you remember Dad's wine?" she asked Kate, staring at a lizard, bobbing its head on a hot rock.

"Yes, I tried it when I came over for your wedding. It was awful, wasn't it?" Kate tried to lighten the mood and looked around for signs of life.

"Was it?" Anna stared at the broken glass, drifting plastic and animal faeces amidst the thick roots of the fig tree where she hid from the English soldier. She'd watched that tree grow from a young sapling. Now, it stood tall and healthy with its fruit almost ripe. Its thick branches reached in all directions, allowing birds to sing and swoop down for a fig feast at any time.

Across the street the antiquated arch, where the three soldiers took refuge from the storm that day, lay in the same state of abandonment. The forty years since her departure was but a moment in its history.

"Look!" Kate suddenly pointed to the trio of rocks with excitement. "Do you remember the dolls we used to make up there?"

Anna looked up. She remembered almost every moment she'd spent there; stretching her arms during strong autumn winds, occasionally wondering if she jumped, would she fly back down to her house or be taken away to dream for all eternity?

They walked for a few hundred yards, conscious of the sound of a man throwing food out for noisy, hungry chicken. They felt nervous and out of place.

Then, the glimmer of a distant memory triggered Tina's thoughts.

"Is that our old house?" She pointed to a small, dilapidated house with broken windows covered with torn bed sheets. Broken fly screens stitched together replaced the front door that was blown away by gunfire. Large chunks of concrete had been ripped from the path, the exterior walls and the small veranda, resembling the scene of a recent battle.

"I don't understand." Tina was puzzled by the devastation. "Why hasn't anything been done in all this time?"

Anna couldn't answer.

"Is this what they wanted all along, just to make a point?"

They stared at the dilapidated roof that was caved in on one side. Anna was flabbergasted that the house was still standing. Then she cast her eyes at the curved fence surrounding the yard – and there it was! The last mulberry tree in the village, still towering above the buildings and enjoying the best views out to sea. Amongst the poverty of a new dynasty, this fortress, this monolith, and this intrinsic part of her heritage remained ready to welcome her home. Anna stared at it for a moment, remembering the last time she set eyes on it when she slipped the front door key into her pocket. The only mulberry tree in the village, was still the only mulberry tree in the village. She smiled at the happiness and meagre wealth it provided for her father. They were the best memories of all.

At that moment, a dishevelled young woman wearing a shalwar and layers of worn cotton rags for a blouse opened the gate in front of Anna. Her hair was wrapped in muslin and her skin looked older than her eyes. Her bronzed face shone like polished leather in the bright sun. Anna guessed she was no more than sixteen years old. Their eyes met, and Anna felt uneasy. The young woman looked frightened and tried to go back behind the gate but struggled to move her wheelbarrow in the grooves of dried mud.

"It's OK…," said Theo. "We…" He used his hands as language. "We lived here once. We… friends." He pointed to his mother who was in tears.

The young Turkish woman's expression suddenly changed in acknowledgement of who they were. A man, clearly her father, came out and stood in front of her, wary of rare visitors, then communicated basic English. Within a few minutes he cast aside his suspicions.

"You... come… inzide… tea?" he asked the family.

Anna was flabbergasted. Vasili made it down the path to witness an epic moment in their family history.

They entered through the front door via a collapsed porch, where Anna stood arguing with Petro on many occasions after his disappearing acts.

Once inside, Anna's senses were heightened. She tried not to listen to her heart pound and clench, preferring to investigate what she felt was still a part of her. She saw goats, chicken and a young donkey roaming freely in the house as if they were members of the family. Anna didn't know what she was expecting to see, but it wasn't her uncle Yanni's electric cables used as a clothesline to divide rooms with sheets, or holes in the ceiling revealing birds' nests, or door frames propped up with large tree branches. She tried not to frown at the piles of straw in every corner, some covered with blankets.

"We... slip," said the man, putting both hands next to his cheek. Then he opened his emaciated palms and fingers, revealing callouses that prevented them from stretching all the way, evidence of a lifetime of providing for his family.

They walked across the subsiding floor to what was once Anna's fashionable kitchen. There was a smell of animal faeces, but respectfully they sat on mats on the floor, witnessing poverty more acute than they had ever known or experienced in their own lives. Torn from their village in the south, these people, along with many other Turkish Cypriots, had been forced to move north, then abandoned by their government. It's what Anna had been reading in the newspapers, but now she saw it first-hand. There was no denying their plight was just as bad as hers.

Thirty years on and no assistance or plans to restore basic infrastructure had been communicated to remote villages that once lived in harmony. Now she understood her father's tolerance towards both cultures living in the same village. Did he foresee this possible outcome?

The two families tried hard to exchange stories of events. Then suddenly, the father took out an old copper chess set from the heavy wardrobe that Anna's mother handed down to her. She'd forgotten how ornately carved the door was. Still in pristine condition, it gleamed amidst the grotesque squalor. Anna remembered the lipstick and perfume her mother kept hidden in it, only to hand them to her on her wedding day.

"From my fader…I…save." He took a pawn from the shabby chess box and waved it around, pointing between both families. Theo nodded, understanding the man's message.

"My mater…she kill wid baby broter…" The man kept waving his arms around to suggest it was done in front of him. His daughter got up from the floor and put her arm around her father.

"We habby…" he pointed south, suggesting they were happy with their lives before the war.

At that point Tina felt a cockroach run up her leg and yelped suddenly, knocking over the glasses still full of sweet hot tea. The man's wife laughed and gestured her not to worry, but it was time to leave.

Years of bitter thoughts and hate suddenly melted into a new awakening for Anna as she began to understand there are no winners in war. It became clear that if she was to survive the pain of war and all the wounds it leaves, she had to show compassion for all. The end had to bring a new way forward for future generations.

They left the house, thanking the family for their hospitality. Now it was time to show her family where her father was killed. The square and the café were still there, only the men were smoking shisha and wore tarboosh hats, and the new proprietor played Turkish music in the background. Anna couldn't bear to look; the sacred spot where her father was shot now housed a small rack of Turkish souvenirs for the occasional tourist that stopped by. After a tearful moment, they heard the call for prayers from the mosque; it was time to walk away. To walk away from the politics that tore them from their heritage; their past; and their legacy. Anna realised that if she was to make peace with herself before she passed away, she had to let go of the what ifs, the whys, and the if onlys. It was as if Anna experienced the place for the first time; through the eyes of someone new, yet she was home.

As they drove away, she watched the mulberry tree fade behind her in a floating horizontal haze. Heat beams rippled, framing it like a Japanese watercolour as moisture rose from the dry clay earth, leaving it in sober silence outside, while inside, her heart screamed. The family drove to Kyrenia in silence.

When they stopped in town, Theo sat his mother and aunt in the shade by a rooftop restaurant, with views over Kyrenia castle.

"I've ordered six large bottles of water." He sighed from the heat, wiping the sweat from his forehead. Anna sat with her bag on her lap, drank voraciously and scanned holidaymakers from Israel, Bulgaria, Russia, Hungary and Turkey.

"Hardly anyone here speaks Greek or English," Tina observed.

At that moment Anna heard an elderly man, sitting in a corner going through receipts and quietly sighing. He called his waiter with passive aggression.

"Abeer!" The young Indian waiter understood and nervously headed towards the three tables occupied by the family.

"Sorry sir," he whispered nervously, bowing to his boss. The young waiter hurried to their table and tried desperately to understand the large order, aware he was being watched.

After a delicious lunch, Anna went to the bar to order more water and took a long, deep breath as a cool breeze swirled and embraced her, leaving a feeling of indescribable exhilaration. She turned her head to the alcove where the owner sat, working. His eyebrows were bushy and grey, spiking in all directions, one even flickered in and out of his left eye.

"Abeer!" he whispered aggressively. "I didn't get where I am by shying away from situations – now go and ask if they need anything else!" As his voice grew louder, it revealed a perfect English accent.

"Yes sir, Mr Ed sir!" The young boy rushed to Anna's family, offering a delicious array of Middle Eastern desserts.

Feeling someone staring, he looked up and smiled curtly at Anna.

She looked at what was left of his thinning grey hair, then noticed his eyes were different colours. She watched him wipe the sweat from his brow with the back of his hand in the same way he wiped the rain on the day she first set eyes on him. She watched him frown, trying to tally his bills, and after almost sixty years, she recognized him as the man who tried to claim her. They were the same eyes she got lost in and never found her way out.

She'd met people who were safer to love in her life, but he was the distant and the dangerous, the arcadia with all the answers to a young girl's fantasies. Once she was close enough to hear his heartbeat, now it was just beyond reach. They were breathing the same air again, with the same echo of silence throbbing in her ears trying to consume her; but this time, it didn't.

She watched the ice melt in her glass as her heart jumped through hoops. Her heart was still capable and willing to recognise the most intense emotion she'd felt in her whole life. She gasped for a moment, wondering if she should say something.

She continued to stare for a few moments while the family unwound and enjoyed their desserts, then she went back to her table.

"Mum, are you OK?" Anastasia asked. "You don't look well all of a sudden, drink some water, you're probably dehydrated."

Anna took a big gulp of water then reached into her big bag. She felt the old butter tin, now a rusty curio, with her first poems and stories still rolled up inside. She had brought it with her with the intention of reading them the night before they visited the village, but instead she'd sat up talking to Kate.

How could it be that the source of those poems, written so long ago, was sitting within ten feet of her? Written at a time when all she knew was unhindered infatuation, or even love – she never could tell the difference.

"I think we should go now!" Alexia silently nudged her mother and pointed to a snoring Vasili.

"Yes, it's been a long day for him." Ari yawned. "We need to get him, Mum and aunt Kate back to the villa as soon as possible."

Once the bill was paid, the family bundled into the lobby to wait for the lift, hankering to get into air-conditioned cars.

"I… I'll be down in a moment, I'm just going to the toilets." Anna's voice quivered.

She watched as they poured into the lift, leaving her alone; then she panicked. She was unsure of what to do, but she felt compelled to go back. She stood in the empty lobby and peeked into the restaurant, watching him for a moment with her whole body trembling. Just then, he got up and went into the kitchen. Anna reached into her bag, walked quickly to his table, and emptied the contents of the tin on his ledger. Her heart pounded like Morse Code, tapping and pumping, wondering whether to wait for his return or bolt to the lift. She'd gone past the point of a rendezvous; the point where unspoken words could become secret stares and nothing left unsaid. In that fleeting moment where dreams were born and fears subside, where distance and time have no relevance. Sometimes, when she slept, she whispered to him in in her dreams, but now it didn't feel the way she once hoped it would.

She rushed to the open lift, just in time to see him pick up the rolls of papers with a mystified expression and caught sight of the undeniable energy that once existed between then.

Did he suddenly remember her? She didn't want to know; for it was too late for anything and everything, but as the last pitch of light closed between them, he opened his mouth to speak.

He watched her disappear through the lift door, with the roll of papers in his hand. Fearful of what he might think, she continued down into the car park with a new awakening.

Her head was in the clouds and her heart danced. She hadn't known anything about him before, and she didn't know anything now, but what she did know was that she felt liberated.

"There you are!" Theo frowned. "We were about to send a search party for you."

"Oh, you youngsters know nothing!" she declared, smiling assertively on her way to the car.

The journey back to Larnaca was long, but the sun was becoming softer. How quickly it changed, and how seductively it danced, setting against the slow chase of light, lulling Anna into a peaceful sleep, while it cleansed and purifying old shadows.

Three months later in London, the four siblings stood at the altar in the Greek Orthodox church in Camberwell. It was one of a few places that lifted Anna's spirits. Now her soul was laid to rest with her family and friends around her. It seems Anna's pains of old age had been far more serious than she anticipated. Vasili, in a wheelchair, held on to Kate's hand and wept. Anna's thirteen grandchildren stood in the pews behind him with lit candles signifying her presence was still with them.

"I will never understand how colon cancer can kill so quickly," whispered Tina to Anastasia as a tear fell on to her candle. Anastasia held her hand tight and tried to stay strong.

A week after the wake, her family sorted through her belongings. They found the C.I.A. file, a selection of David Hockney sketches, and piles of journals with stories and sketches wrapped in a piece of her wedding dress, cut around the green rhinestones so they appeared large and essential to everything they shrouded.

"Who are these letters from?" asked Anastasia, handing them to Ari whose Greek was perfect. Ariadne read through more than a dozen letters from a doctor in Greece, from the late 1960s, begging Anna to join him. It seemed he wrote to her for three years, pleading with her and assuring her of his devotion.

"I… I've no idea, said Ari, slowly re-reading. "But if no one wants them, I'd like to keep them."

The following year, Theo and Tina took Anna's ashes back to the island. Having parked in the same place as before, they walked down from the ridge road and came to the house where they were born. As on their previous visit, the village was quiet with the sound of an occasional cock crowing, sheep bleating and bird singing.

"This is it," Tina said softly. They looked at the tree, now a giant with rich, dark mulberries growing like caterpillars on its branches. Tina reached up with her right hand and picked a few to eat. She watched the juice run between her fingers and down the scarred channels, left by the broken glass all those years ago.

"This is the best place." Theo sighed. They scattered her ashes in the direction of the tree, then watched as a gentle breeze carried them across the branches and berries then into the sky like a veil, lifting on the wings of a bird.

Theo sighed then spoke softly. "Don't ever believe there is anyone braver, kinder or gentler than you were. Now you can sleep peacefully and stop trying to convince people you were worth loving."

Printed in Great Britain
by Amazon

65251208R00183